Dangerous Ties

Dangerous Ties

Devyn Quinn
Jodi Lynn Copeland
Anya Howard

APHRODISIA

KENSINGTON BOOKS
http://www.kensingtonbooks.com

Contents

Personal Possessions

Devyn Quinn

Prologue

Bisti Wilderness Area
New Mexico

Nikki Malone expected to start the new year off with a bang. Kicking it off with a shootout over stolen drug money—not. But that was what had happened.

Nikki glanced at the backpack in the passenger seat. Even in the dim interior of the car she could make out the dark patches of blood staining the faded blue denim.

Sammy's blood.

A shiver shimmied down Nikki's spine as her gaze cut back to the long stretch of unpaved road in front of her. Remembering how Sammy had died, she felt fear drench her in her own cold perspiration. As far as she knew, his corpse was still sprawled where she'd dumped it—somewhere in the desert. Only God knew exactly where.

Nikki hadn't done the killing, though. No, far from it. Sammy had gotten his own self killed.

"Holy shit," she muttered. A nightmare come to life, noth-

ing she'd encountered in her twenty-three years had ever prepared her for this. She'd just witnessed an act of shocking bru-
tality, seeing her boyfriend shot down like a rabid dog.

The sound of shots ringing out still echoed in her ears, kick-
starting her breathing with an involuntary burst of adrenaline.
Complete, paralyzing shock. That pretty well described it. She
tightened her grip on the steering wheel as if expecting to hear
the sounds all over again.

Her vision momentarily blurred. Fear blossomed inside her
heart all over again. She hastily blinked away the tears. Lose it
now and she'd go to pieces.

Nikki gave her cheek a slap, relishing the brief sting of her
palm against her skin. Sometimes pain could be a good thing.
This was no time to cry, or time to mourn. She had to be hard,
cold, and emotionless. Get the job done by getting her ass down
the road, far away from the danger Sammy had plunged her into.

She pressed her lips together until her jaws began to ache
from clenching. Her whole body felt hot, sticky. Fueled by disbelief, shadowy thoughts swirled in her mind. *Don't look back.
You can never look back.*

The last thing she needed was to think. But her brain betrayed her, rewinding and replaying the same bloody footage
until she thought she'd scream.

"We were stupid," she muttered bitterly. The memory sent a
hot tremor through her. Their lives had been less than stellar,
but at least they'd been alive. With one stupid act of greed, they'd
erased their chances of a clean start like chalk washed off a side-
walk by a furious rainstorm. Stealing from drug dealers was a
bad idea.

Initially, the setup had seemed foolproof. Too easy to go
wrong. Throughout the lonely desert hinterlands bordering the
Navajo Indian Reservation, the illegal drug trade flourished. A
lot of narcotics—and cash—passed through the rarely visited
and largely unknown area, most of it trafficked from Mexico.

With a little patience and a pair of binoculars, it wasn't hard to chart the comings and goings of light aircraft making regular drops in the inhospitable region, part of the pipeline bringing Mexican contraband into the country. The plan to catch a drop and heist some cash should have gone off without a hitch.

It didn't.

The Mexicans had shown up, armed to the teeth and ready to fight for what belonged to them. Not only were they illegals and drug dealers, these fugitives were also cold-blooded killers. No one cared who died in the desert except the vultures.

Caught in the crossfire, the only thing Nikki thought about was saving her ass come hell or high water. She damn sure didn't intend to die because she'd gotten tangled up with a con man like Sammy Blair. This time her attraction to bad boys had gotten her in deep shit, to the hip and sinking in more ways than one. The allure of walking on the wild side had definitely lost its appeal.

Nikki drew a deep breath, forcibly calming herself. This mess hadn't been her doing, but she'd willingly gone along for the ride. Now that she was in trouble, the only thing she could do was pull a Houdini and make herself disappear.

Fugitive. The idea made her shudder. Whether with horror or fascination, she didn't know. It should be the former. Save for a few petty misdemeanors, she'd never been in a lot of trouble with the law. Now she was a bad girl, wanted by pissed-off Mexican drug dealers. If they caught up with her, no doubt they'd put a bullet right between her eyes. She'd seen what they looked like, knew what they'd do. No question, no doubt.

Going to the cops was definitely out. Especially since she'd already disposed of Sammy's body. Hell, he was dead. Certainly not any help now, and traveling with a corpse in the back seat creeped her out. It made sense to get rid of his remains—one less impediment between her and a clean getaway. She might have felt sorry for Sammy, but she wasn't stupid. The felonies she'd racked up in fleeing the scene of a brutal murder weren't exactly going to be brownie points to the judge or jury. Time was already against her. She had to get out of New Mexico as soon as possible.

She scowled. That is, if she could ever find a way out of this goddamned desert. She'd torn out to the sound of gunfire, not knowing where she was going or even what direction would take her to safety.

Even if she had a map, Nikki had no idea where to begin looking. There were no signposts. The wide, open stretch of desolate high desert enveloped the land like a disease. As dusk descended and the night deepened, it had become abundantly clear she was going nowhere fast. All she could do was drive and hope for a sign that would point her back toward the highway.

No such luck.

Tightening her grip on the steering wheel, Nikki lowered her gaze to the dashboard. The fuel gauge registered a quarter of a tank. Muscles bunching in her shoulders, an alarm sounded in the back of her skull.

She gulped, licking dry lips. Her mouth and throat felt dry as the sand covering mile after mile. She would give anything for a drink of water, or a shot of Jose Cuervo. "Shit." The day she'd thought couldn't get any worse had done just that. Running out of gas in the middle of nowhere definitely wasn't the way she wanted to end up. All sorts of bad thoughts unspooled through her cranium, all ending with hungry coyotes running off with pieces of her body to gnaw on.

To distract herself, Nikki flicked on the radio. Static crunched in her ears. Breathing hard, she viciously twisted the dial, hoping for the sound of a human voice. Nothing.

She snapped off the radio. The rumbling of the car over unpaved road was giving her a headache. She started to open her mouth to curse, scream, shout. Anything to break the intense sense of isolation washing over her. No words would form in her throat.

Her gaze darted in all directions, desperately searching the murk. The desert was a veritable ocean of nowhere. She racked her brains for a better way to go. It seemed like she'd been driving through this godforsaken place all night, even though the dashboard clock testified that barely an hour had passed.

And then she saw them.

Lights.

Sprinkling the far horizon like stars come to earth.

A quick smile flashed across Nikki's face. Her mind quickly processed that maybe her luck was about to change. Almost simultaneously an image floated up by the side of the road, a green signpost framed and painted with white. Most of the letters had faded away, erased by time and the elements.

HELLE–12

"Hallelujah," she breathed out in relief. Thank heavens. Oh, for some good food to fill her gnawing stomach, a hot shower to wash away the grime, and a bed with clean sheets. A bag full of money would buy a lot of luxury. No more trailer-trash chic for her. She could afford nice things now, forget secondhand. As for work, well, she'd definitely served her last fucking beer.

Paradise definitely lay ahead.

Nikki's foot pressed harder on the accelerator, urging Sammy's seventeen-year-old Oldsmobile down the craggy road. Urgency rode her hard. The transmission was already grinding in the worst of ways. She needed to ditch it as soon as possible.

She eyed the backpack again. What it held inside was something so precious that men would lie, cheat, and steal to have it. Kill to have it. Cold, hard fucking cash.

Enough to start over. New town. New life.

Shit. Face it, getting himself shot and killed was the best

thing Sammy had done for her lately. He was scum. No one would miss him. Not the law or the family who had written him off as a liability years ago.

Nikki bolstered her resolve. She wasn't going to fold like a wet paper sack just because Sammy had to be cut loose and left behind. So he could slap her around and fuck her like a stallion afterward. That didn't make him good for her. It just made him an abuser, something she seemed to have no trouble picking out time and time again.

Rubbing a hand across her burning eyes, Nikki nodded to herself. Maybe this time she'd learned. Mess around with ex-convicts and you got screwed right back, however twisted your own intentions to enjoy the fucking. Definitely karma . . . but maybe good karma this time. By dying in such a convenient way, Sammy had set her free. Handed her the ticket to ride.

That's all she had to do now.

Ride.

With salvation drawing her forward, Nikki lost touch with her own sordid reality. She focused on the lights ahead, not the slow blossom of blood staining the front of her shirt. Concentrating on the mechanics of driving, she ignored the pain. It didn't exist, not now, not when salvation was so close. It was nothing. A dull ache in her gut, not the reality of a mortal wound torn through flesh and muscle, leaking a steady flow of blood. It was nothing. Nothing at all.

Nikki shivered and groaned under her breath, ignoring the uncomfortable sensation. Suddenly, she felt so tired, drained, as if a heavy weight had attached itself to her thoughts, dragging them down into a spectral abyss. Go there and she wouldn't be able to climb out of the everlasting darkness. Bowels clenching, the insidious grip of fear grappled with mind-numbing exhaustion. Worry started low in her belly, oozing upward until she could taste the bile burning the back of her throat.

She focused on the lights ahead, growing brighter and more

welcoming with every mile the car ate up. Ample evidence of the truth crowded into her skull from all sides, but her mind refused to accept it. Heart fluttering, her pulse began to falter. Sweat drenched her even as a cold chill settled inside her core. A sense of déjà vu flashed in the forefront of her brain, the horrific images of Sammy's shot-up body. She'd never seen a man die before. The panic she'd held at bay tightened into a death grip around her senses. Eternity had just come knocking.

"I want another chance," she choked out, dismayed that freedom appeared to be slipping through her fingers like so many grains of sand. The chances of getting out of the desert were slim to none. It wasn't going to happen.

Nikki's heart thumped harder. Creeping panic wrapped itself slowly around her lungs and began to squeeze. The air she breathed seemed to hang like cobwebs in her lungs, heavy and sticky, slowly smothering her. An involuntary shiver raced across skin already goose bumped with chills. Her head spun and her eyes didn't seem to be focusing properly anymore. A thousand impressions tumbled end to end, colliding and clashing. All came to the same inevitable conclusion that took only seconds to compute. Her body already understood what her mind refused to process.

Nikki cursed viciously through numb lips. Fury obliterated all other emotions. It wasn't supposed to end like this. "Fuck . . . I'm going to die. . . ." The idea almost made her laugh. Almost.

The shock and adrenaline pushing her abruptly ran out. Her world reeled, then slowly tilted over. The last of her energy drained away. In that same instant, a ferocious shudder consumed her entire body. She drew a breath to scream, but darkness slammed through the fading wisps of final, grasping consciousness.

Before a sound passed her lips, everything went black.

1

Nikki drifted back to consciousness.

She kept her eyes closed as familiar sensations seeped into her fuzzy brain. An ocean of cool softness cocooned her, the luxurious slide of silk on bare flesh. The support beneath her body bespoke of a mattress cradling her outstretched limbs. The soft pillow beneath her head invited her to slip back into the embrace of gentle slumber.

Close to wandering back into peaceful darkness, Nikki felt a hard male body settle next to hers. Without thinking, she stretched languorously against the solid mass of what felt like pure muscle. A firm hand settled on her breast, teasing fingers slowly circling the hard bud of her nipple. Warm lips descended to explore the soft hollow between her neck and shoulder. The nuzzling felt wickedly good. Her heart skipped a beat inside her chest; a warm ribbon of need coiled around her. A low moan slipped from her throat.

Smiling, Nikki rolled into her lover's embrace. Half on top of him, her breasts lightly brushed his chest, her legs tangling through the sheets with his. Big hands cupped her ass, settling her comfortably against narrow hips wielding a nice, hard cock.

She didn't open her eyes, wanting to enjoy the sensations just a minute longer. Mmm. What a way to wake up. How great was that sensation?

"God, Sammy," she breathed, "you wouldn't believe the dream I had." Her skin was already sweaty. The kind of sweat generated from having a naked man cuddling you after sweaty sex.

Strong fingers skimmed through her long hair, twisting, holding, tightening. Teeth nipped at her neck, pinching the soft skin of her throat. "Oh, but I do know," a softly accented voice replied. "I know everything about you, darling Nikki."

The voice was male, definitely.

But not Sammy's.

Eyes opening, a series of strange impressions assailed Nikki's senses. Dismay flooded through her. The man lying beneath her was a stranger. He wasn't naked either, though he was held fast under her in the most intimate of ways.

Nikki recoiled violently. One hand fumbling toward her face, she closed her eyes and rubbed them hard. "This isn't real," she gasped. What she was seeing couldn't have any basis in reality. She'd never seen this man before and certainly hadn't ever been in bed with him. It had to be a dream.

A really, really far-out dream.

The male voice under her said, "But it is real, Nikki."

She ignored him. "No, it's not."

A warm hand slid over her hip, traveling up her side to find her breast. "I'm definitely not your imagination either." Thumb and forefinger rolled her nipple in a most enticing way. "You have the most amazing breasts, my dear. Firm and round like peaches. I really must get my lips on them soon."

A blatantly sexual shock tore right through her gut. Nikki definitely couldn't ignore *that*. Her breath hissed past her lips in a short burst as her body responded with a powerful surge of red-hot lust. Memory of the cock she'd felt pressing against her came right back into her mind. A small trickle of moisture seeped between her thighs. Her body unquestionably had ideas of its own.

She looked down at the stranger. A thick mane of messy black hair haloed his head, curling just enough to give the unkempt mass charm. Arched brows ruled over a gaze of unusual intensity. His eyes were a coppery green shade, like brand-new pennies surrounded by freshly cut summer grass. The mix was so unusual that his eye color just had to be fake.

Two words instantly came to mind: breathtaking and gorgeous.

Nikki blinked in disbelief. Being in bed with the best looking man she'd ever seen in her entire life wasn't a bad way to wake up, especially when he'd been in the process of making sensual love to her.

There was just one problem: She didn't know him, and she didn't know where she was. A search of her mind revealed a big black hole in the center, as if every memory of the recent past had been vacuumed up.

For the first time, she realized she was naked save for the white sheet tangled around her hips. Though a little belated in coming, she demurely crossed her hands over her bare breasts. The feeling that he knew everything about her and that she knew nothing about him was more than a bit frightening. He seemed perfectly comfortable to have her in his bed, and perfectly willing to take advantage of the fact.

"Who are you?" she asked, very confused. She recognized nothing around her. It all felt so alien, as though she'd been shot into outer space and landed on another planet. Trouble was, she didn't recall signing up for the trip and couldn't quite remember what had happened before liftoff. Some mind-bendingly radical thing had occurred, something she really needed to remember.

Her seducer's enchanting gaze skimmed her face. "Ah, a lady who wants a proper introduction, I see."

His mouth wasn't more than a foot away from hers. A thrill of anticipation raced up Nikki's spine. His lips were so sensuously enticing that he had to be a terrific kisser. Somehow she just knew it.

She drew back from the temptation. Moving off him, she tucked the sheet around her body. "It would help knowing who's pawing all over me."

The flash of white teeth revealed a charming dimple on one side of his mouth. "I wasn't pawing you, my dear. I was merely attempting to make you more comfortable."

Nikki narrowed her eyes. "Comfortable, my ass," she snorted. "You were taking advantage of a naked, sleeping woman." Lust surged through her again. Somehow the idea wasn't enough to douse the sparks of sexual appetite he'd ignited. In fact, it did just the opposite. Waitressing in bars inevitably led to a few one-night stands. This wasn't exactly the first time she'd awakened beside a nameless stranger.

An unblinking kaleidoscope gaze met hers. "So I was." He hesitated a beat. "If you wanted to whip me for it, I would let you." His deep voice vibrated with innuendo.

Handsome and *kinky. Hmm. Not a bad combination at all.*

Arousal shimmied through her body all over again. Nikki glanced at him warily, tempted to play. First, she'd like to know who the hell he was. Knowing where she was might help too.

"Let's take things one at a time," she said. "I like to know who I'm abusing."

A scowl crossed his face. "If you insist."

Nikki smiled right back, refusing to be put off or intimidated. She'd played the games before, knew the rules well. If he expected to hit any more bases with her, he'd better start clarifying a few things. Identity, location, and an explanation of how she ended up naked in his bed would help a lot. If she liked the explanation, she might consider climbing back into that bed. If not, she wouldn't let the door hit her on the ass on the way out.

Assuming any of this was real to begin with.

"I do," she hammered in sweetly.

He hoisted himself into a sitting position and settled back against a pile of pillows. An immaculate white shirt hugged his shoulders and impossibly broad chest. Unbuttoned halfway, it revealed a nice slice of his chest. Perfectly creased slacks were well tailored to fit his narrow hips and long legs, and black leather boots covered his feet. He was the picture of casual elegance.

"Jackson." A curt nod followed. "Jackson Sullivan at your service, darling Nikki."

She frowned. "I guess I don't need to introduce myself since you already know my name."

Jackson's gaze raked over her like a laser beam, seeing all and missing nothing. Primal heat simmered behind his gaze. "I know all about you, Nikki Malone."

His blatant visual appraisal and statement sent an involuntary shiver racing across her bare skin. The delight burning in his eyes said he already knew her in the most intimate of ways. The way a man knew a woman he'd made love to.

Familiar warmth prickled the fine hairs at the back of Nikki's neck. In her fantasies, Jackson was the kind of man she'd always dreamed of having. No doubt about it. He was a gorgeous hunk of man. If she'd met him under any other circumstances, she'd be fantasizing how he would look naked. . . .

Attempting to quell desire, she clenched her fists until her fingernails dug into the sheet, already too sheer for her comfort. "That's impossible," she said. "I've never met you before in my life."

He chuckled. "Well, you couldn't have met me before," he countered in a slow, exaggerated drawl. "Because only the dead can enter the seventh circle."

His words caught her like a dash of icy water to the face. She stared at him, startled by his statement. It took only seconds for the meaning of his words to sink in. For the first time she noticed that his skin was unusually pale, as if he'd never been exposed to a single ray of the glaring sun. Strangely, it did nothing to detract from his attractiveness. He possessed the kind of electrifying beauty and masculinity only a generous god could impart, an otherworldly quality that set him well above the plane of ordinary men.

A chill prickled the fine hairs at the back of Nikki's neck. Fear knotted her bowels, the knots growing painfully tighter. Jackson, as easy on the eyes as he was, must be crazy. There was no other believable explanation. Somehow she'd stumbled into the keep of a madman.

Nikki eased off the bed, moving slowly so as not to let on that he was scaring her shitless. "I think I need to get going."

Leaving definitely seemed to be a good idea. Go where, though? Save for the sheet, she didn't have on a single stitch of clothing. Still, she supposed she could make do given the emergency. Time to hotfoot it out of this bizarre place while the getting was good.

She glanced around, looking for the way out. The room with its huge four-poster bed, thick carpets, and elaborately masculine furnishings was swathed in the shadows cast by an illumination of no discernable or readily apparent source. Nevertheless, there was a door. And a door usually meant a way out.

Easily discerning her intent, Jackson's smile widened. "You can't."

She stilled. "Why not?"

He waved a casual hand. "Don't you still feel that bullet tearing up your guts?"

Wait a minute. That sounded eerily . . . familiar.

A frightening and familiar panic filled her. For a moment, she just stared at him, legs threatening to collapse under her. Her mind warred with his words.

A bullet? In my guts?

Soupy images from the recent past swam in front of Nikki's wavering vision. She lowered her head, staring at her abdomen. There was no blood on the sheet, no wound that she could feel. Why would there be? How could there be?

And then it hit her.

Images of the Mexicans blasting Sammy to pieces suddenly flashed across her mind's screen. Two and two were coming together awfully fast, and she didn't like the equation. Strange as things were, they were beginning to make sense.

In a twisted and bizarre sort of way.

Her hand traveled to her mouth as she looked at the man who seemed to have hijacked all sense of reality and hidden it away from her. She choked down the rise of bile at the back of her throat. "Oh, God, no . . ."

Jackson scowled under scrutiny. "God has nothing to do with this place." As he spoke, he reached over to the bedside table. Flicking open the lid of a silver box, he extracted a cigarette. The tip burst into flame seconds before it reached his lips. He took a quick drag, exhaling a white rush of smoke through flaring nostrils. "I quite assure you."

His tone wasn't reassuring. Neither was the fact that his cigarette was self-combustible.

Dumbfounded, Nikki stared at him. She desperately dug through the dark recesses of her mind. More had to be there. Any memory, however vague, would help. Then she saw her clothes draped across a chair. Something else too.

Sammy's bloodstained backpack.

Two words escaped her numb lips. "The money—"

Focusing on the object of her damnation, more ghostly images unspooled, playing across her skull like a film badly mauled by the projector. But there was enough left to tell the story. The plan gone so terribly awry. Tearing through the desert. The car, low on gas. The lights in the distance offering the hope she'd find help.

No. She shook her head against the thought. *I'm not . . . I can't be.* Her brain refused to process the reality that loomed like a vulture perched on a rock searching the desert sands for carrion. Human flesh. Rotting human flesh.

"You're wrong," she said slowly. "Sammy died. Not me."

Jackson Sullivan slid off the bed. The man was a tower, all rippling muscle and sinew. Predatory heat driven by a visible edge of strength radiated off him in waves.

Nikki had to tip her head back to look into his eyes. Nearly six feet herself, she wasn't what anyone would consider fragile. She could knock back a drink or send a fist flying with the best of them. Jackson Sullivan not only made her look small, he made her *feel* small. The top of her head barely came to the level of his shoulder.

Nostrils flaring with annoyance, he flicked the ashes off his cigarette. They vanished before hitting the floor. "No, I'm quite sure it was you. You've kicked it. Bit the dust. Taken a dirt nap. Pushed up daisies. The list goes on endlessly."

Uh-huh. Nikki didn't think he was being very damn funny at all. She frowned fiercely. "No need to be an asshole about it, Jack."

He shrugged. "I'm not being an asshole, as you so crudely put it. I am just telling you the facts as they are. You're dead, babe. Get over it."

Nikki drew a deep breath and forcibly stopped herself from rolling her eyes at his elaborate theatrics. "Seems to me that crack you're smoking has gone to your head. I've heard of date-rape drugs. You might be a hallucination for all I know."

He stared at her, absorbing her declaration. The brutal knowledge of the insider permeated his gaze. "Hallucinations don't make you cream and moan like a bitch in heat. Wet dreams, yes. But this isn't a dream—and you know it."

A subtle tremor buzzed through Nikki and her body trembled visibly in reaction. She clearly remembered her desire for him, evidenced by the insistent throb between her thighs. *Better not think of that.*

Her grip on the sheet clutched around her breasts tightened. "But I don't feel dead," she pointed out reasonably. "In fact, I feel perfectly fine."

Jackson cocked a knowing brow. "That is one of the best benefits of death. All the sensations of living, and none of its nasty inconveniences." He spread his hands expansively. "What's not to like about the afterlife?"

Weird as the logic was, it made sense. However she'd made the change of location—whether by choice or not—she was here.

Nikki's tongue immediately lodged in her cheek. "So who are you?" She eyed him suggestively from head to foot, repeating the once-over he'd given her. Turnabout was fair play. "My reward for being a good girl?"

Jackson shook his head, sending a tumble of sexy dark curls into his eyes. "I'm your punishment for being a bad girl." Planting his cigarette in the corner of his mouth, he ticked off his fingers. "Let me think. Of the capital vices that will get you sent here, you've already fallen to greed, envy"—with a knowing little grin, he wriggled all his fingers—"and lust. Well, I haven't got enough fingers to count the times you've spread your legs for a man." A knowing gleam lit his eyes. "Or should I make that last plural?"

Confronted with her sins, an uncomfortable sense of dismay filled her. True. True. And very, very true again.

Heat rose to her cheeks. "Like you weren't trying to cop a feel, you letch," she mumbled under her breath.

Jackson's hand flew to his heart. "Ah, you wound me. That viper's mouth of yours is very much alive, darling Nikki."

Patience snapped. "I'm not your 'darling.'" She drew a breath to steady herself. "So who do I have to screw to get out of this place?" She sniffed with disdain, adding in as a barbed aside, "You, I suppose."

Taking one final draw off his cigarette, he flicked it toward the fireplace dominating one wall. Cracking flames burst to life, devouring the butt. They vanished as quickly as they'd arrived, without a trace. "Nobody leaves hell, Nikki. Ever. Once you arrive, there is no going back."

Nikki blinked, startled by the supernatural display. The second one she'd witnessed but hadn't yet computed. Now she did and her chest tightened painfully. *Hell?* Oh, Lord. She'd apparently jumped out of the frying pan and into the fire. Literally. Panic clutched in the most unpleasant of ways.

Without her being quite aware of his movement, Jackson glided closer. Looming over her, he reached out and caught her chin. Tilting her head back, he looked deeply into her eyes. His eyes, now the color of blazing hot copper, narrowed with nefarious intent. With a subtle flex, his strong hand threatened more pain.

An unbidden image of their bodies locked together in an intimate embrace washed through Nikki's mind. He handled her like he owned her. Her heart tripped at the idea of being pinned beneath his massive body, his hips descending between her parted thighs, cock sliding into her sex with the purpose not only to claim, but to consume.

She shuddered under the onslaught of pure gut-twisting fear. No. God, this couldn't be real. This crazy place had to be a figment of her fevered imagination.

But it wasn't. Some terrible thing had just come knocking at the door of her eternity.

Jackson lifted her until only the tips of her toes touched the floor. One more inch and she'd be dangling. Fresh sparks of electricity sizzled through his touch. The hedonistic beast in him seeped into her blood, then penetrated to the marrow of her bones.

Nikki's stomach fluttered and her knees went weak beneath her trembling weight. She couldn't make a move even if she wanted to. His essence overpowered. Raw desire warred with terror, threatening to pull the air from her lungs.

Bending closer, his lips brushed her mouth. His breath mingled with hers, the moist heat caressing. She ached for his kiss, would welcome the taste of him. But why? She had no doubt that he'd abuse her, and in the worst of ways. It also didn't take a lot of imagination to figure out that he knew how to use that cock of his like a weapon.

Jackson's voice, smooth as crushed gravel wrapped in velvet, broke into her turbulent thoughts. "Welcome to hell, Nikki Malone." His fine mouth turned up in a lethally sensual smile as his grip tightened, ever so subtly. Tension throbbed between them.

A rush of adrenaline quickened her heartbeat. Judgment day had just arrived. No doubt that she definitely wouldn't like the outcome. Her bowels knotted. She doubted praying for salvation would help. It appeared the devil himself had gotten his hands on her first.

And his threat was crystal clear: She'd pay dearly for her sins.

Over and over again.

2

Hovering on the edge, Nikki looked Jackson straight in the eye. Her eternal soul hung by a thread over the chasm of eternal damnation, and the fall seemed imminent.

"What are you going to do?" she breathed, voice thin and high.

Jackson chuckled. "Everything that is unspeakable." His grip unexpectedly fell away.

Balanced so precariously, Nikki felt herself falling. Knees collapsing, she hit the floor in a heap. She struggled to sit up, fighting the sheet tangled around her body. More naked than covered, the thought to cover herself wasn't a top priority on her list.

Jackson knelt. "You might as well know you belong to me now." He snagged the sheet, tugging it slowly away from her. Each tug revealed another inch of vulnerable skin. "Any way I want to torment you—" More sheet vanished. "Well, that's best left unsaid."

The cover slipping away, Nikki felt goose bumps invade her

exposed skin. Nausea welled up in the back of her throat. She felt a little disoriented, woozy. The idea of being some demon's sex toy didn't exactly make her day.

"I don't deserve this," she blurted. "Robbing those Mexicans wasn't my idea."

Jackson's gaze skimmed the length of her body, following the lines of her long legs and slender torso, her breasts, then finally her face. His expression was one of utmost appreciation.

"Ah, the innocent doth protest. But you forget, darling Nikki, that the road to hell is paved with sinners on their knees begging for another chance. Greed, hand in hand with envy, is what cost you your soul." He reached out, stroking her cheek. "But it isn't as bad as it seems."

She recoiled from his touch. Her vision blurred, and her throat throbbed painfully. *No,* she warned herself. *No crying.* Crumble now and she'd be lost. Instinct warned her that she must hang on to her strength. "Seems pretty bad to me," she grated out.

"Not every soul on the way to hell passes through my care and keep." He grinned. "Only the special ones."

His words did nothing to ease the burden of a heart already heavy with remorse and regret. "How am I special?" The question threatened to hang on the lump clogging her throat. She almost didn't ask. Maybe it would be better not knowing. Who wanted to know they'd earned enough brownie points to enter the infernal region of the damned?

Jackson tweaked the tip of her left breast, giving it a little tug. "If I told you, it would be no fun to find out."

Nikki's traitorous body reacted instantly. Her nipples tightened into hard little peaks. A sharp breath sent a tremble down her spine. Her cheeks warmed with acute humiliation as pleasure curled through her clit.

Oh, God. How humiliating to think that in the darkest recesses of her mind she might be looking forward to what Jackson threatened.

Their gazes connected. His burned hot, a knowing gleam lingering in the depths of his eyes. Oh, he knew exactly what he was going to do to her.

"That you intend to rape me repeatedly?" she hissed back.

He pretended to mull her words a moment. "I like to think of it more as forced seduction."

Nikki looked at him incredulously. "You have to be kidding me," she guffawed. Only the male sex could delude themselves into thinking that most women secretly desired to be handled the way a chimp handled a banana. Typical.

Jackson's gaze drifted away from her face, traveling suggestively, uncomfortably, lower. "Not at all," he said, perfectly serious. He reached out and cupped her breasts, squeezing their generous weight.

A soft gasp escaped her when erotic delight blazed straight down to her core. Her head dipped back as she subconsciously grappled with the enticing sensations. The bastard just knew how to excite her. Whether she wanted to admit it or not, his touch delivered several hard jabs to her libido. Muscles deep inside her vagina rippled with fierce appetite.

His thumbs circled her erect nipples, lightly flicking the tender nubs. "Besides, you can't rape the willing." He winked. "At least try to pretend you don't like it, Nikki. Makes it more interesting for me."

Swallowing back a moan, anger suddenly welled up inside her. Like hell she would! The arrogant asshole had no right to assume that a few well-placed caresses would send her willingly swooning into his arms.

"Interesting, my ass!" she spat. "I'll just lay there and spread my legs." Her grin was little more than a gritting of her teeth. "Should be like fucking a dead woman."

Jackson grinned back. He glanced down toward his crotch. Those fitted slacks he wore hardly concealed the fact that he was impressively endowed, even when flaccid. "I guarantee that you won't be still very long. I happen to know for a fact that you have a very virgin asshole and I have a very large cock. Going to be a tight fit, but I believe I can manage every last inch."

Nikki gulped. "I won't enjoy it." The idea of anal sex definitely didn't turn her on. She'd rather die a thousand more times with a thousand more bullets in her guts than have a dick shoved up her ass.

"This is hell. You're not supposed to." He smirked. His burning gaze slid over her like a caress. "But I will enjoy it. Thoroughly and completely."

Nikki clenched her jaw and wrestled fury down. Right now she'd like to wipe that smirk off his face with a Louisville slugger. She forced herself to stop trembling, to remain focused. Letting him intimidate her wasn't going to work. Catching a breath, her pulse sped up a notch. She made a decision right then and there. He wasn't fucking around with her as long as she had two arms and two legs to fight with. The one thing she hated most was being controlled—by anyone or anything. She might have fallen, but that didn't mean she couldn't still land on her feet. The number one rule in her life was to look out for herself first.

No one else ever had.

When you have everything to lose, doing nothing wasn't an option. She'd never really believed in fate, that doing good deeds would, in turn, beget any blessings. Living on the streets of Vegas since the tender age of fifteen, she'd learned early that her life wasn't going to be an easy one. She'd also learned the only person she could lean on for sure was herself. Life hadn't given her a free ride or an easy pass.

She'd gotten herself into this jam. Somehow, she'd get herself out. Mental gears shifted, going into overdrive. Waiting for a break to escape would be the wrong thing to do.

She was going to have to make one.

Jackson Sullivan was a big man. No doubt about that. On any given day he could probably overpower her and twist her into a fucking pretzel. She'd only have one chance to get away.

Hand sinking behind one leg, Nikki slowly clenched her fingers into a tight fist. Focusing every ounce of pent-up fury into her hand, she cocked back her arm and let her fist fly. She caught him square in the face with a roundhouse blow, knocking him right back on his ass.

Righting himself with a hand against the floor, Jackson shook his head. Blood dripped from his mouth, courtesy of a nice fat split lip. He pressed curious fingers to the flow, then visually explored the damage. His tongue flicked a fingertip, tasting. He tilted his head and smiled. "Not bad at all."

Without warning he moved into a feral crouch, then gracefully rose to his full height. With a slow and deliberate move, he swiped his hand over his mouth. The damage she'd inflicted melted away.

"Oh shit." Nikki scrambled back on all fours, somehow making it to her feet just as he lunged for her and missed. She'd damn near cracked her knuckles on his face and it didn't seem to have affected him in the slightest. She'd taken her best shot and blown it. Fighting her way out of this mess clearly wasn't going to do one bit of good. He'd shooed away the damage the way one would a pesky fly—with no trouble at all.

She skittered around the bed, putting as much distance between them as physically possible. There wasn't a lot of room to run.

Hooking his hand around one of the tall bedposts, Jackson eased himself around the bed. "I take it this means we're doing things the hard way."

No shit, Jack. But not if Nikki could do anything about it.

Feet don't fail me now.

Never minding that she was buck-ass bare, Nikki bolted toward the door. Fuck her clothes. Fuck the money. She was leaving. Right now.

Jackson sped after her, closing the distance between them with shocking speed. He slammed the door shut before she could open it wide enough to slip through. "Plans haven't changed, my dear. You aren't going anywhere."

Nikki tried to slip though his grabbing hands. Swinging around, she tossed off another roundhouse blow.

Jackson neatly sidestepped her flying fist. His hand shot up, fingers closing around her wrist like an iron band. "Once was fun. Twice is tedious."

Nikki swore viciously and twisted out of his grasp. She barreled into him full speed, trying to knock him down again.

Again, no dice.

Jackson ducked and came up under her flying limbs. Huge hands cinched her waist. He lifted her off the floor with no effort whatsoever. "You are a handful, darling," he commented, not a bit out of breath.

Hefted like a doll weighing just ounces, Nikki couldn't get her feet under her to gain any sort of leverage to kick the living shit out of him. Just let her get one foot near those balls of his, and she'd punt them like a Sunday kicker going for the extra points.

She wiggled and squirmed, but she simply couldn't break away. Jackson was a solidly built man, all muscle under warm flesh. She couldn't inflict any damage.

He hauled her, kicking and screaming, toward the bed. Tossing her naked body onto the mattress, the full impact of his weight came down on top of her. Nikki made a final valiant effort to scratch out his eyes. He easily captured her wrists, pinning them down above her head.

Stretched out under him, Nikki felt every sinewy inch of his body overpowering hers. She gasped, shocked that the fight was over so quickly. What had seemed to take hours had lasted mere seconds. Skin hot and flushed, her breath came in ragged bursts as she twisted helplessly under him.

Armored like the warrior in the prize of conquest, Jackson smiled down at her. "Let's play."

3

Nikki wouldn't admit it out loud, but she liked the feel of Jackson on top of her. Sleek. Powerful. Every contour of his male body molded against her softer, more pliant frame. His chest felt like a brick wall, her breasts flattened against him save for the two hard nubs that insisted on betraying her arousal.

Thoroughly restrained, she felt deliciously vulnerable. Curiously, she liked the feeling being captured entailed. That thought alone had her moist and slick between the legs. Not that she could help it. The solid ridge of his penis pressed against her flat belly. Her fingers ached to feel the ripple of his muscles.

Moving on instinct alone, Nikki attempted to align her body with his. Maybe she could turn this thing to her advantage. It wouldn't be the first time she'd used her body to cut a deal or get herself out of hot water.

Catching her not-so-subtle move, Jackson eased his weight off her hips. "Not so fast, my dear," he warned. "I'm the one who's in control here."

Nikki bit down on her lower lip. Men were usually willing to take advantage of what she offered. Remembering his threat to ream her tender rear, she winced. *Guess there's no chance he'll skip that part.* "What are you going to do?"

Jackson gave a piranha's smile. "I'm going to do the best that I can." His grip on her wrists tightened. He gyrated his hips into her, giving her a little taste of what was to come. "To fuck you thoroughly and completely in every position I can think of."

Senses heating with desire, Nikki moaned as carnal hunger roared. She twisted her wrists against his tight grip. "You don't have to force me," she breathed. "I'm willing. . . ."

"Willing isn't enough," he murmured. "Part of submission is pain, the penance you must pay for sinning. Embrace it and it will cleanse you. Reject it and it will damn you."

"I-I don't understand."

"Our time together will determine how you spend eternity, Nikki. But only you can decide if you will be damned to eternal pleasure"—his fingers dug deeper into soft skin—"or writhe in the grip of perpetual agony."

His words offered no reassurance, nor, she realized, were they meant to. If there'd been a time to get scared, really scared, that time had clearly arrived.

She winced. "Does it have to hurt a lot?" she asked softly.

He winked. "Only if you want it to."

She cleared her throat. "Listen, Jack, I don't want it to hurt at all, if you don't mind."

He chuckled. "I do mind, and it will hurt." His voice darkened with emphasis, almost dripping with menace.

Anger simmered anew. "You son-of-a-bitch." Her voice was shaky but venomous. She started to struggle again, bucking under him in an attempt to break free.

He easily kept his grip. "You are a feisty one, Nikki. I knew you would be."

Nikki bared her teeth. "Fuck what you think you know about me." She wiggled harder, succeeding in squirming halfway out from under his weight.

Jackson easily recaptured her. "I'm so glad you've got a bit of spirit to you, my dear. So many souls come through here weeping and gnashing their teeth. It's quite refreshing to have a woman who really enjoys fighting damnation."

She glared at him through slitted eyes. "Oh, I'll fight you, all right. I'll scream all the way through it."

"That sounds about right," he returned cheerily. "Shall we get started?"

"Fuck off and die!"

He grinned. "The dying is already done and the fucking is about to begin. We just need a few things to get us started properly."

That didn't sound promising at all.

"Whatever you've got in mind—" She started to backpedal, "Let's not and say we did."

His grip tightened. "How could we not when we're so close." He ground his hips in another nice, slow circle. Trapped in the confines of his tight slacks, his cock strained for release. "First I've got to do something about those hands of yours. I prefer to give rather than receive."

Nikki shivered. Damn, if he kept that up much longer she'd go right over the edge, whether she wanted to or not. "How generous," she groused tightly.

"Thank you." Using one arm to keep her wrists pinioned down, Jackson rummaged around the headboard with his other hand. He pawed a length of rope out. "Ah, there it is."

Trying to crane her head up to see what he had, Nikki felt herself go stone-cold inside. "Oh, you're not—" she started to say.

Jackson interrupted, "Oh, I am." He fingered his treasure. "And this is going to help me." He let it go. Wriggling with an unholy animation, the rope slithered toward her left wrist.

Her eyes widened in disbelief. Now she understood.

Nikki started to flail frantically. "No, no, no, I don't think so," she cried.

Jackson lifted her arm off the bed. "The lady doth protest too much," he countered dryly.

She tried to evade the unholy thing. "No, don't!"

No luck. Jackson held on.

Caught in the grip of disbelief, Nikki watched the rope circle her wrist. One, two, three times, before knotting itself securely. Its coarse weave chafed, tightening uncomfortably against her tender skin. The other end of the rope curled out, securing itself around the bedpost.

"Oh, that's just the way I wanted you," Jackson noted, pleased. "Good and tight too. Don't want you getting loose in the middle of something important."

Nikki was far from pleased. "This isn't submission," she babbled, "it's rape." She kept struggling, but to no avail. As the first rope tightened to a barely tolerable degree, Jackson produced a second length out of nowhere. Within seconds both wrists were securely bound.

She twisted against the ropes keeping her arms so cruelly locked above her head. It felt as steely as barbed wire. No bonds of silk for her. He had complete access to every part of her body and would clearly take advantage of every exposed inch.

Jackson rolled off her, stretching out his long, lean body. Propping himself up on one elbow, he traced a slow circle around her left nipple. Studying her naked form, a smile twitched at the corner of his mouth. "If I wanted to rape you, I'd have been finished and smoking a cigarette twenty minutes ago."

Nikki's back arched reflexively. Against her will, desire warmed her blood. Damn it! She didn't want to respond to his touch in any way.

She clenched her eyes shut. *I won't,* she silently vowed. *Let's see how much he likes a dead woman playing dead.*

It took barely one beat of her heart to find out.

A warm palm settled on her breast. A thumb brushed back and forth over her hard nipple with an arousing pressure. "Feel anything?" The weight of his hand was strong and sure.

Shaking her head, Nikki stubbornly kept her eyes closed. "No," she lied, "nothing."

She heard him say, "Then I am doing something wrong. Let's see . . ." She felt him lean forward, capture the pulsing bud in his mouth to suckle the hard nubbin.

The warmth of his mouth immediately penetrated to the blood in her veins, sending shivers up her spine. The sensations traveled through her, sending carnal signals all the way to her clit. She groaned out her frustration.

Jackson nipped each quivering peak in its turn, his tongue making warm, wet tracks around each pink aureole. "I feel a thaw coming on." He rolled her sensitive skin between his fingers, all the while suckling, then pinching her pencil-hard nubs.

A tiny moan worked it way up her throat, slipping past her lips before she thought to stop it. *Oh God!* What he was doing to her felt *so* good. Pleasure surged up inside of her, the erotic sensations streaming through her body without abandon.

A disturbing turn of events. How the hell was she supposed to resist him if her body kept responding to his touch?

Gulping down a breath of air, Nikki opened her eyes. Their gazes met, and locked. "Damn you," she choked out in a strangled voice.

"Yes, I am." Jackson lazily stroked his palm down the flat plane of her belly. "And so are you." Moving lower, his hand brushed through the curls of her Venus mound, then back up to her navel. He drilled a finger into its shallow depth, a hint of what he intended to do to her sex.

Her stomach fluttered when his hand skimmed back down for further exploration. "Why are you doing this?" She clenched her hands, fighting to keep control. Giving up her body willingly was one thing, having it taken was another.

"Because I enjoy it." Jackson's hand urged her legs to part. His palm came to rest on the inside of her thigh. "You, on the other hand, might not."

Mouth going bone-dry, Nikki swallowed hard. Her stomach rolled with cramps. No doubt he'd had a lot of time and a lot of damned souls to practice his techniques on. She couldn't say a word, only gulp and wonder what was about to go down with that hand of his between her legs.

She was about to find out.

"Ah, found it." Grinning, Jackson lifted his hand from between her legs. A set of nipple clamps with serrated teeth hung on a braided silver chain. "Know what these are?"

Nikki slowly nodded. Things seemed to appear as he needed them. Jolly.

He dangled them above her. "Administered correctly, pain can enhance sexual sensation tenfold. It puts you on the edge, makes you more aware of what your body is truly capable of."

Nikki's vision blurred. She blinked, concentrating on holding on to her composure. If he expected her to beg, plead for mercy, she wasn't. She might be afraid, chilled to the bone inside, but she didn't have to show it.

I can't stop this. . . .

Further thought fled from her mind when Jackson lowered his head, nuzzling her breast. He sucked the tip into a hard little peak. The first clamp followed.

Nikki grunted at the tight pinch around her tender nipple. Vicious little spikes invaded the sensitive bud bundled with thousands of nerve endings. She felt every one. A tiny sound escaped her throat as the unexpected sensation of pure carnal delight blazed straight down.

Jackson dangled the other clamp above her other breast, letting it brush the tip.

Her nipple responded instantly, coming to a nice hard peak. The sight delivered a hard kick to her libido. Her core throbbed with sudden appetite, wetting the insides of her thighs.

He applied the second clamp. Its serrated teeth bit hard, sending a spike through her chest and down her spine. The pain lasted only seconds, quickly settling into a pleasurable tingle. A pulse of heat settled into both nipples, causing her clit to respond by telegraphing needs all its very own.

Nikki failed to prevent her moan or the shiver tearing through her. Beads of perspiration drenched her as sexual hunger rose fiercely inside, demanding satisfaction. She panted fiercely between little shocks of electricity through her sensitive nipples.

Jackson unexpectedly tugged on the chain suspended between her breasts, pulling her nipples rigid at the same time. He made no effort to be gentle, sensing through her reaction that she wanted to be completely mastered. "Makes you want to come, doesn't it?"

Unable and unwilling to deny the needs of her body, Nikki winced briefly but didn't protest. Hands clenching into fists, she unconsciously fought the ropes holding her wrists. A sensation of burning shimmied down her arms. She welcomed the pain. Rode it like a wave. "God, yes . . ." The rest of her sentence became an incoherent babble. A fine madness ensued as the pain delivered the intended results. Ravening energy buffeted her from all sides. Climax loomed just beyond the horizon of her senses.

Close . . . She was so close she ached.

Jackson let go of the chain, dashing her back to earth. "No, you don't," he warned. "You may not come until I allow it."

Losing the moment, Nikki collapsed back against the mattress. The metal clamps burrowed into her nipples like two molten sets of fangs, branding her forever.

Nikki groaned under her breath, exhaling on a shaft of delightful agony. Fighting to still her racing pulse, she forced herself to take in air. Perspiration drenched her trembling body. "I was almost there."

He smoothed a hand over her belly. "Not yet." Palm sliding lower, he silently urged her to spread her legs, giving him access to her sex. The touch of his fingers burned a blazing, delicious trail.

Nikki caught her bottom lip between her teeth when his thick fingers invaded her sex. With the lightest touch and using just the tips of his fingers, he stroked the length of her creamy labia.

With each caress, a series of soft moans slipped past her lips. The clamps around her swollen nipples pinched, adding a dash of forbidden spice to her pleasure. The more he stroked, the more her need grew. The incredibly fierce sensations whipped her toward frenzy all over again.

He curled the tip of his index finger into her clit. "Feels nice, doesn't it?"

A series of tiny seismic shocks immediately traveled through her. "Mmm . . . yes . . . feels wonderful," she agreed through a shiver. So far the experience hadn't been a bad one at all. Given her knowledge of BDSM, it seemed rather tame. She wouldn't mind a little more at all.

Jackson sank two fingers into her creaming sex, burrowing deep and hard. The jab of savage pleasure was too intense to resist. Hand in hand with the sadistic clamps on her nipples, wave after wave of pure bliss flashed along every nerve ending in her body.

Fingers curling around the ropes binding her wrists, Nikki gasped and thrust her hips upward. "That's damn deep."

He slowly dragged his fingers out of her liquid depth, then pumped back in. The feel of penetration caused flashes of lightning to dance behind her eyes, the thrill of merciless delight spiraling toward the center of her core. Small, helpless sounds escaped.

Jackson plumbed her sex mercilessly. Each stroke pushed her closer toward the dangerous edge. A minute, just another minute, and she'd go over, unable to keep from losing herself in a climax threatening to incinerate her into a million particles like an atomic blast.

Close to screaming with absolute delight, Nikki felt Jackson's fingers suddenly slip away. Palm settling on the rise of her mound, he savagely jabbed his thick middle finger right into her clit.

Going rigid with surprise, Nikki stiffened. Heart skipping a beat, her lungs failed to take in air at the vital moment. She hung, suspended. Rapture slowly evaporated into frustrating disappointment.

Realizing what he'd done to sabotage her, she clenched her teeth. "Shit." Hitching in a lungful of air, she mentally stepped back from the brink. A burst of unexpected anger buffeted her from all sides. She wasn't sure whether it was from embarrassment or sheer frustration. Jackson was playing her the way a cat played a mouse.

The game could go on for hours.

She groaned. *Or eternity.*

4

Nikki suspected Jackson wasn't going to let her come anytime soon. Now she understood why and how pleasure could become an unendurable thing.

The idea wasn't cheering in the least.

The pressure against her clit relented.

Jackson flashed a cocky smile. "I warned you not to come." He tugged the chain hanging between her breasts in punishment. The clamps attached to her nipples stretched the tender nubs. He maddeningly refused to be hurried.

"Ouch!" Nikki winced, unwilling to start again. She doubted she could take much more. "Just fuck me and get it over with."

"Maybe I will." Another tug delivered fresh shocks of pain. "Maybe I won't. I haven't decided yet."

Close to going ballistic, Nikki clenched her teeth until her jaws ached. Her wrists burned from chafing against the damn rope. He wasn't doing it to her again. Get her worked up, then giving her no release. "With no due respect, Jack, why don't you just stick that cock of yours up your own ass? A sick fuck like you should be able to manage that just fine."

Ignoring her insult, Jackson pretended to think. "Maybe a little change will help get you back in the mood." He shifted her body so that she lay half on her back, half on her side. His hips pressed against her, the line of his rigid cock filling the seam of her ass. The position had the extra bonus of allowing full access to her breasts and clit. He could suck and fondle at will.

Nikki gasped at the contact of naked flesh on naked flesh. In the blink of an eye his clothing had melted away and she hadn't even been aware of it. All she felt was his rock-solid hard-on pressing right against her rear. One good thrust would impale her like an insect on a pin.

Her cheeks heated at the thought. He hadn't been lying about his size. He felt huge, definitely hard and ready to go.

"Ah, perfect." A warm palm settled on the curve of one ass cheek. Jackson repositioned his hips so that the crown of his cock pressed for entry against the tight pucker of her anus. "Just the way I like it."

Nikki drew a breath. Held it. *No!* She wasn't ready.

Wretched with mortification, she shut her eyes and prepared for the worst.

Jackson's mouth settled just inches from her ear. "I warned you that I planned to ream your tight little ass."

Nikki refused to open her eyes. She definitely didn't want to think about it.

She clenched her fists, tightening the bonds on her wrists. The rope dug in painfully. A violent shiver shook her, one that left her muscles quivering. Her entire body was drenched with perspiration, her fisted hands moist and hot.

Apprehension constricted her throat, threatening to choke off her reply. "Get it over with."

The pressure of one nipple clamp abruptly disappeared. "Not so fast." A warm wet mouth followed, the circle of his tongue soothing away the ache. He knew exactly what he was doing and how to torment for maximum effect.

Nikki gasped with surprised pleasure. The contact between his lips and her nipple were electric. Frustration was quickly forgotten in the reemergence of desire. She felt another trickle of moisture seep from her covetous sex.

Jackson's hand slipped toward the crux of her thighs. From behind, his hips shifted subtly. The smooth crown of his penis slid through her silky labia.

Lost in a fog of pure sensation, Nikki automatically shifted her hips. His thick shaft slid inside like a hot knife cutting through butter. Strong inner muscles rippled around his length, gripping and holding. Wild currents of pleasure raced through her veins. Raw unchecked lust roared like a tigress in heat.

"Easy," Jackson warned. "Not too fast." He bit down on the nipple he'd freed. At the same time, thick fingers rubbed her clit. Breast, clit, and cunt were completely claimed.

Nikki winced against the brief discomfort. Wrists tied, body half twisted like a pretzel, she could only submit. "I can't take this much longer," she gasped. His hips rocked in tandem against hers, each move sending his cock a delicious inch deeper inside. He filled her, utterly and completely. The knot in her belly tightened. Orgasm hovered just out of her reach, enticingly close. She was close, so infuriatingly close. "Damn you! If I had my hands free, I'd shred you!"

His mouth lifted from the nipple he was abusing. "Is that a threat?"

She snarled. "A promise."

"I don't take threats lightly," Jackson purred right back. The sinister tone of his voice didn't bode well.

Nikki should have known better. *Uh-oh.* The metallic taste of fear rolled over her tongue, down her throat, settling like lead in her belly.

The ropes around her wrists suddenly melted away.

Before she realized they were missing, Jackson had gotten up and settled on his knees. With a neat flip, he sent her face-down on the bed.

Realizing she'd made a serious mistake, Nikki immediately tried to scramble away. She didn't get far enough, fast enough.

Jackson caught her by the hips and pulled her back. He captured an arm, easily twisting it up behind her back. His free hand locked around her waist. He held her tightly, his fingers painfully digging in like a vise.

Fighting against the pain, Nikki cursed viciously under her breath. She was no match for his speed or strength. "You're hurting me!"

Jackson's grip tightened with possessive delight. "I warned you that you made your own pleasure or your own pain here, Nikki darling. The choice was yours." He angled her forward, spilling her long hair around her face. His cock pressed between the tight cleft of her ass.

Nikki's free hand shot out, hand against the mattress to support her weight. His erection nuzzled for entry through the ring of her asshole. She automatically clenched in resistance.

"Don't fight it," Jackson said quietly. "It'll hurt more."

Shaking from the exertion of resistance, she took a deep breath. She was doing a heroic job to keep him from penetrating. "The least you could do is use some fucking lube," she snarled over her shoulder.

Jackson snorted. "Hell doesn't stock that convenience, so we'll simply have to use your own sweet juices." He chuckled. "You lubricated my cock quite nicely."

Nikki mentally cringed. Hard to believe it, but she'd actually begun to get off on his abuse. Even now her wrists were raw, chapped, and burned by the rope, her nipples chafed by the clamps. Not to mention that her nerves were completely frayed by coitus interruptus.

Nikki refused to let her mind linger on the sensations. "Just do it." She wondered what in Jackson's life might have so twisted his spirit that he'd ended up in hell himself. Must have been something pretty damn wicked.

"I intend to, babe. No question about it." The thick head of his shaft pressed, penetrating and spreading the tight halo of her anus. He sunk in an inch, then two.

A hot iron stabbed. Inner muscles giving way to the invading girth, Nikki groaned. She tried but couldn't ignore the overfull sensation. Her fingers clenched. Spasms wracked her. "You're hurting me!"

Tightening his grip on her thigh, Jackson thrust deeper. "I intend to."

Her anus stretched wider to accommodate even more. She gasped, feeling chilly claws twist her bowels into knots. She desperately attempted to crawl away as his hips pressed closer. His grip on her arm kept her immobile. One good twist and her forearm would snap like a brittle twig.

Jackson groaned with pleasure. "I thought that pussy of yours was super tight, but this sweet ass of yours is heaven." Wicked satisfaction darkened his voice.

Nikki hardly wanted to think about his dick buried to the hilt in her butt. With her ass in fiery agony, she twisted and wiggled against the burn. She only wanted the intense agony to end. Bitter tears stung her eyes, blurring her vision. She refused to let them fall. Cry now and she'd be lost. "It doesn't feel that terrific."

Chuckling, Jackson withdrew. "That depends entirely on your point of view." To emphasize his words, he brought his palm down flat against one round cheek.

Nikki yelped. "I'm not into spanking," she snapped.

Jackson's palm connected a second time. Harder. The loud crack sounded like a firecracker going off. Felt like one too. "You don't seem to be into ass fucking either, but you're doing it."

She sucked in a breath between clenched teeth. "Not willingly."

A third smack followed, blazing straight up her spine. "By the time I get through with you, you'll be begging for it all over again."

"I seriously doubt that," she grated back.

Jackson pushed back in. The tip of his penis connected with every nerve in her gut. "Let's see if I can change your mind about it." Shivers lapped at her damp skin. Trying to ease the feeling a little, Nikki braced her knees on the mattress and eased forward. Just a little.

Jackson immediately pulled her back. "Had enough?"

Nikki craned her head around. There was no way this asshole was going to make her cry uncle. "Not nearly."

She clamped her lips into a tight line, determined not to be baited further. Of all the things she might have imagined about the afterlife, she'd never imagined that it would entail having some demon's dick up her rear. She just wanted him to shoot his wad and leave her alone.

No such luck.

Jackson seemed to take her words as a challenge. "Don't worry, babe. You're about to feel every goddamned inch."

Letting her arm go, Jackson settled his weight on his folded legs. Bodies still connected, he pulled Nikki up onto his lap, plastering her back to his chest. His arms slipped under hers. One hand cupped a breast, teasing the distended nipple. The other slipped down her flat belly and settled between her spread legs. Fingers settled on her clit, caressed.

They fit together perfectly, and suddenly everything felt good. The ache and burn in her rear was bearable now. It even felt . . . good.

A gasp followed shock. "Oh, yes."

Erotic fire blazing ferociously through her, Nikki drew a startled breath. The dynamics had changed. It wasn't his weight controlling the depth of his penis, hers was. Still a tight fit up her ass, but not as uncomfortable. Bearable even.

Moaning, Nikki tipped her head back against his shoulder. Somehow during the realignment her hands slipped behind her. Palms settling on his hips, her fingers flexed into his skin, nails digging deep. She didn't want to give in, but her body insisted on taking the bait a second time. Vision blurring with sexual haze, she let a gasp of unintended pleasure escape.

Jackson plucked at her nipple, this time more gently. His hips undulated gently under hers. "I can't get enough of you," he murmured against her ear. Pressing two fingers together, he slid them back into her sex. "I want you, fully and completely."

His absolute possession of her sent a wave of pleasure crashing through her body.

Something in the far recesses of her mind snapped. She wasn't just Nikki anymore. Some strange spirit seemed to have entered her body, taking the reigns and whipping her into an impassioned frenzy.

Caught up in the overwhelming desire to embrace this new arousal, she barely heard his words through the haze of passion surrounding and overwhelming her. Her pulse danced, driven by the fierce rhythm of her heart. The tables had turned, and all of a sudden, she was the aggressor, taking from him what he wouldn't give.

Grinding her ass back against his hips, Nikki forced his pulsing shaft deeper inside her. The length of him, filling her so completely, brought a delicious rush of power. She arched against him, insisting on driving him even deeper. This time she relished the pain, attacking and mastering it with breathtaking swiftness.

Bodies locked together in fierce motion, she felt the pulse of his cock seizing her from inside, drawing her toward the inevitable conclusion of their illicit joining. It was all so primal, instinct driving her toward a single pinnacle she'd come so close to reaching.

As if she'd driven him to the edge, Jackson's cock surged inside her. "Damn you, Nikki," he grated out, then lost his breath as his body convulsed around hers. Hot semen jetted. To get even with her, he simultaneously twisted her nipple and jammed his fingers as deeply into her sex as physically possible.

At that precise second, some sort of magical fusion occurred. Every nerve ending came together, merging and weaving into one magnificent web of pleasure. Winding itself around her body, it clutched her in the grip of a pure and unrelenting bliss. Wave after wave carried her to a higher plane, passing consciousness by for a state that could only be described as paradise.

Nikki arched her back, crying out as the ferocity of orgasm flooded through her entire being. She dissolved into a series of trembling spasms, each threatening to drive the breath from her lungs. Through a long moment she hung suspended.

And then she fell.

Limbs going boneless, she collapsed. Strong arms wrapped around her, lowering her gently to the tangle of sheets.

Nikki immediately stretched out full length, groaning in relief as cramped limbs and sore muscles slowly relaxed. Tiny aftershocks still plundered deep inside her core. She shivered. *Wow.* This was one for the record books. She'd never felt so thoroughly filled, or fulfilled. He'd plundered tits, cunt, and ass without any reservation or hesitation. Being fucked by him had been like being branded. It hurt, but in a good way.

Still trembling from the aftereffects of the most mind-blowing sex she'd ever experienced, Nikki felt spent, absolutely empty. A long sigh slipped from her lips. At the last moment he had let her control the depth and pace of penetration, take her pleasure as she wanted. Who'd have thought there could be such a thing as *good* pain?

"Shit," she said, rolling over on her back. "I've never done anything like that. Incredible."

Brushing her long hair out of her face, Jackson smiled down at her. "Glad you think so."

Looking into his eyes, a delicious sense of completion seeped through her.

And then it hit her.

She'd just had sex with a demon.

And had enjoyed it.

5

Stretched beside her, Jackson's hand lightly skimmed Nikki's bare abdomen. The tips of his fingers traced the hollow between her breasts. "Looks like you survived your first ass fucking." He grinned. "What did you think?"

Nikki's breath caught in her throat. Her butt still ached from the reaming, but not unpleasantly. "It's a wild way to be screwed, but I wouldn't want a steady diet of it."

Jackson laughed and traced one distended nipple. "It's just the beginning of what's in store for you, darling Nikki." He plucked at the nipple, rolling it between thumb and forefinger.

She shivered at his touch. Her nipple anxiously hardened. Need was building all over again. Amazing. She angled her body toward his, hinting. She wouldn't mind a bit finding out what he had in mind. If it was anything like the first time, it would be incredible.

Jackson lowered his head, capturing the peak with his mouth. His tongue rasped against the tender bead, soothing away the lingering ache. His touch was charged with a current that made every move electric.

Mind spinning with desire, Nikki's body pulsed as the wonderful sensations began to build all over again. True, he'd introduced her to pain, but at the end she'd enjoyed it. A lot. She'd willingly share a bed with Jackson Sullivan forever, letting him have delicious sex with her any way he wanted. They were in a place of no limitations, only impulse and desire. Lost in the haze of eternal pleasure didn't seem like a bad way to spend the afterlife.

And he'd promised there would be more.

Teasing each nipple in its turn, Jackson's mouth moved higher, tongue skimming the softness at the base of her throat. Claiming a handful of her hair, he nipped the ridge of her jaw. And then his mouth touched hers. His lips skimmed hers.

Closing her eyes, Nikki parted her lips. She hungered to taste him.

Nothing.

Swallowing a groan, Jackson lifted away from her. "I can't," he murmured, more to himself than for benefit of her hearing.

That was it.

Rolling away from her, Jackson flung himself back against the pillows.

Opening her eyes, Nikki frowned. "What's wrong?" she asked.

Jackson cursed under his breath. "Nothing," he said.

Her brow wrinkled. Damn, she hated being left on the edge. "I don't get it. You were hot and heavy on me a minute ago."

He shrugged. "I changed my mind."

Nikki forcibly held herself back from slugging him right then and there. "Hell of a time to decide you're not in the mood," she grated.

Jackson's tone indicated that he addressed her out of courtesy only. If he had any feelings about what he'd just done to her, he wasn't revealing a thing. He seemed unwilling to commit any sentiment to her presence. "I'll decide who gets fucked and when," he snapped.

His answer rankled.

Nikki immediately went on the defensive, putting up her hackles and pulling out her claws. She sat up. "Don't you mean raped, *jackass*?" She deliberately twisted his name into an insult and threw it in his face. "You just hijacked a major piece of my ass, and now you're all sad. Didn't that make your day, *jack-off*, fucking a virgin hole?"

He tossed his head, clearing a fall of black hair out of his face. Cruelty sparked in the depths of his haughty gaze. "You can hardly cry victim, Nikki," he said coldly. "You're here now because you have that deviant side in you."

Nikki felt her cheeks heat. Looking at Jackson Sullivan, it was easy to forget he was a demon. He might look human, but there was probably not an ounce of humanity left in him.

"So I'm just as guilty as you are?"

"Yes," he said coldly.

"Well, since I'm such a bad bitch—" Nikki reached out, whipping the sheet away from his hips, much like he'd earlier ripped it off her naked body. "I guess you won't mind if I finish off what you started."

"What—?" he started to say, clearly surprised by the turn of events.

Nikki smiled sweetly. "I'm not a one-orgasm girl, Jack. It takes more than one puny climax to make me happy."

A ridge of muscle tightened along his jaw. Despite his outer composure, he was thoroughly vexed. "Are you saying you weren't satisfied?"

She arched one eyebrow and shot an acidic glance toward his exposed privates. "By that?" She laced her grin with more saccharine. "How could I be? You don't have a clue how to use it." Her broadside was unflinching in delivery.

And scored a direct hit. The attraction between them was intense, and undeniable.

Nikki wasn't exactly sure how she was supposed to handle it. She'd have been horrified to land in hell with any other man. But there was something about Jackson Sullivan that electrified her. It was like two magnets coming together: Turned one way, they'd repel one another; turned another way, they couldn't fail to come clashing together.

He clearly picked up on her thoughts. A smile of interest twitched at his lips. "You think you could do any better with it?"

Ah, that's just what she wanted. "Oh, I know I could."

Jackson settled back against the pillows and nodded toward his cock. "Be my guest."

Nikki shook her head. "Nothing I can do until it's all nice and clean. No way its going in my mouth after its been up my ass."

"Understandable." Jackson snapped his fingers. A table holding a basin, pitcher, and several thick washcloths appeared beside the bed. "Better?"

Nikki scooted toward the edge of the bed. "Kind of old-fashioned," she commented, lifting and tilting the pitcher toward the basin. Steaming water poured out.

"It does the job," Jackson said.

She shrugged and dipped a washcloth into the water. "True enough." Wringing it out, she applied the washcloth to his privates, washing every inch and then some.

Jackson grinned all the way through it. "Nice having such personal service."

Nikki flicked the tip of the rag toward him. "Don't expect it all the damn time." Satisfied with her cleansing, she tossed the washcloth back into the basin. It vanished before she could even blink an eye. "Gotta love the concierge service around here," she muttered.

She slid back into her former spot between his legs, spreading his thighs wide enough so that she could stretch out between them. Settling on her stomach, she rested her weight on her elbows. Jackson's flaccid penis was just inches away from her face. His personal scent was rich and arousing, a nice mix of male musk and sweat.

She smiled up at him. "Nice view."

He grunted. "Thanks."

Nikki leaned forward and gave the tip of his penis an experimental lick.

Jackson quivered. The beast stirred, rising up in an arch against the cobblestone ridges of his abdomen.

Nikki licked again.

More response.

Jackson quickly recovered his arousal. A benefit if you were destined to fuck all the way through eternity. His cock filled with blood, taking on a life all its own. Sprouting up from thick black curls, his shaft was solid, long, with a wide, flaring crown. A weave of thin veins webbed its length.

Her heart kicked with anticipation. Moisture trickled from her sex, sparked by a fresh rise of lust. Fingers circling his tumescent organ, Nikki slowly jacked her hand up and down his length. His generous balls were tight against his body.

Jackson hadn't exaggerated when he'd told her he had a lot of cock. He did, a good eight, maybe nine inches. And it wasn't just all length either. His girth filled a woman's hand to overflowing. More than a handful, it definitely wouldn't be wasted either. Need had completely overtaken her senses and wouldn't be stopped now.

Nikki shivered at the sight of his arousal, wanting him all over again. But this time she'd take control. Droplets of precum seeped from the wide tip. Her tongue flicked out, licking them away.

Jackson closed his eyes, moaning softly. "Damn, that feels good."

Pleased, Nikki smiled. His responses to her touch were those of any red-blooded male. "It's about to feel better."

Her lips closed over the plum-ripe crown. Using just the tip of her tongue, she traced the thin seam separating head from shaft. Then she went deeper, taking him all the way into her mouth. She'd sucked more than one cock in her time, and the depths she could achieve amazed men.

Hands pressing into the mattress on either side of his body, Jackson levered his hips upward, trying to force himself deeper into her mouth.

Nikki immediately pulled back. He wasn't going to get this cock sucking so fast or so easy. This time she intended to be the one in control—and delivering the pain.

Turnabout was fair play.

Nikki freed the nipple still captured in the clamp he'd applied. Just as he had, she dangled them above his erect organ.

"Remember these?"

Eyes riveted on the clamps, a sharp hiss escaped him. Tension visibly knotted his shoulders. "Oh, you wouldn't . . ." he started to say.

Their gazes locked. The look in his eyes wasn't fear, or even discomfort, but intrigue. No one had ever turned the tables on him. A silent communication passed between them.

Jackson wanted the pain. Would welcome it.

Savoring his breathless anticipation, Nikki nipped the tip of his cock with one of the serrated clamps. "Here?" she teased.

"Put those teeth there, darling Nikki, and I'll come right now."

She snapped the clamp. "You can't come yet, Jack."

"Use them right," he said.

Nikki clamped both his flat male nipples.

Drawing a sharp breath as the tiny little teeth gnawed deep,

Jackson's head lolled back against the pillows. A long, slow moan slid past his lips. "Mmm . . . I've missed the pain."

Watching every wave of the pleasure spilling over him, Nikki felt her own lust rise again. Her core pulsed with wet hunger, powerfully stimulated by his enjoyment.

Climbing to her knees, she straddled his hips. Her pussy hovered just inches above him. Hands on his shoulders, she pressed him back even as she lowered herself onto his erection. His length filled her, giving her a delicious sense of power as she conquered every inch. She took him to the hilt, seating herself firmly and completely. His reentry into her depth sent a shiver of pleasure all the way down her spine.

His hands slipped around her hips. Big, warm hands cupped her ass cheeks. "Your cunt is a steel trap. If it had fangs, it would be perfect."

She tugged the chain spanning Jackson nipples. "If it did," she breathed, "I'd have your job."

He winced even as he punished her against his grinding hips. "True."

But it wasn't enough.

Nikki wanted more.

Raking her hands through his long hair, she captured a handful of his thick mane. Pulling his head back, her tongue flicked out to tease his lips. Their mouths brushed again.

Jackson turned his head to evade her. "Don't."

His refusal startled her.

Nikki tried again. She wanted to taste him, drink him in as his cock plumbed her rippling depth.

He pulled away. "No." All the while their bodies clashed below the neck.

She captured his face. "Why not?"

Regret flashed across Jackson's face, disappearing just as quickly as it arrived. Or maybe it was a trick of the shadowy illumination. She wasn't sure.

"It's too personal," he said softly. "Intimate."

What? He'd had his dick all the way up her ass, and a kiss was *too personal*?

"We're fucking right now." She demonstrated by lifting her hips off his cock, then sliding back down. "I'd say that's pretty personal, Jackson."

A sudden growl broke from deep in his throat. With a single quick move, he rolled Nikki's body under his, assuming the superior position. He caught both her wrists, pinning them down on either side of her head. His cock pressed against her belly like a hot iron bar.

Face-to-face, he stared her down. "It's not supposed to be like this," he hissed. "I'm not supposed to feel anything, Nikki."

A tiny smile teased Nikki's lips. She deliberately moved her hips under his. "Feel what, Jackson?" she asked innocently.

He tightened his grip on her rope burned wrists. "You," he growled. "Damn you. It's never been this way. I've never felt anyone before. But you—" He repositioned his hips, impaling her with a single hard thrust. "I feel your touch, your heat around me."

Head spinning from the sheer erotic ferocity driving his reentry, Nikki gasped, swallowing her groan. No man had ever plumbed her that deeply. The feel of his entrenched shaft sent a shock of pleasurable sensation through her entire body. Her pulse raced as fast as her heart, threatening to outrun the pulsing organ and burst out of her veins.

Jackson's mouth descended until his lips were just inches from her left ear. His hot breath scorched. "I don't feel you, Nikki," he breathed. "You're nothing to me." His weight lessened, pulling back.

To prevent him from pulling out, Nikki curled her legs around his body, locking her ankles together over his firm ass. She twisted her wrists under his hold. "Prove it," she challenged.

He shook his head.

Nikki persisted. "Let me touch you, Jackson, all over."

His grip lessened a little.

She slipped her arms free. Her hands slipped around to his back. She spread her palms against the wide plane of his back, relishing the feel of rippling muscle under her hands. He was hard and lean, every bit the perfect masculine beast. Her sex pulsed, feeling every last inch of his massive cock.

Jackson looked down at her. His eyes, more green than copper now, burned with lust. "Hurt me," he urged. "Make me feel you, Nikki."

Instinctively knowing what he craved, Nikki raked her fingernails into his skin. She'd always kept them long, strong, and sharp enough to tear skin. She raked down his back. Hard.

Shoulders bunching, his hips rolled against hers. Head dipping back, he closed his eyes and moaned. His cock surged.

Nikki wasn't prepared for the flood of desire that followed. Her body responded instantly to his, wave after wave of sensation pouring through her. Enjoying the feel of his excitement, she raked again. Four thin rows of red marred his pale skin.

Jaw clenching on another moan, Jackson's mouth tightened. His cock pumped into her, slowly at first, then picking up speed as his desire turned to something desperate, punishing. "Do it again. Make me feel it."

Excited by his excitement, Nikki dug harder and deeper into his skin. This time she drew a series of thin crimson tracks. Blood welled. Spilled. Tracked down his spine.

Their gazes locked.

Nikki recognized the hunger in his eyes, a powerful stimulant revving up her own carnal needs. A silent communication passed between them. She felt him fighting to hold himself back, not climax too soon.

She opened her mouth to whisper his name but never got to speak. With a sudden and crushing cruelty, his lips descended to hers. His teeth clashed against hers, and his tongue plunged into her mouth the way his cock drove into her sex—brutally and mercilessly.

The connection was so instant—and powerful—that it took Nikki's breath away. She felt the oxygen being sucked from her lungs but could do nothing about it.

Arms and legs locked around Jackson's massive frame, Nikki forced her nails deeper, summoning every bit of strength she possessed simply to hold on to him. Skin slick with sweat and blood, her otherworldly lover plundered her mouth and cunt.

The friction was enough to send them both crackling into spontaneous flames.

Jackson rode her fast and hard, giving her no respite. Cock grinding until it was buried to the hilt, his lips demanded kiss after ravening kiss. The kisses burned into her mind like acid.

His mouth finally freed hers. "I'm going to come," he grated. A body-shaking bellow broke from his throat just as his cock released a stream of pure fire. Surge after surge of exquisite surrender followed. Hot semen poured like molten lava through the center of her core.

Trembling on the edge of another violent orgasm, Nikki released her hold on the precipice and let herself fall into the glorious abyss of pure surrender. Her body convulsed. Orgasmic energy surged through her, an entity so powerful and so amazing that it threatened to tear her down to atoms and scatter them throughout infinity.

Filled and flooded with a sense of infinite strength and belonging, Nikki slowly drifted back toward conscious thought. Strange, unfocused visions swirled through her mind.

She drew a shaky breath, fighting to bring air back to her lungs, to clear her woozy head.

Jackson lay on top of her, his weight close to crushing. Over one of his shoulders, Nikki's gaze settled on the mass of vicious scratches marring his pale skin. Tracks of blood etched like ink, a crimson portrait of their passion. She'd gotten to him, literally burrowing into his skin.

One corner of her mouth turned up. Now she understood how the power behind inflicting pain could be an incredible aphrodisiac. It was beautiful.

Because I inflicted it.

6

Groaning under his breath, Jackson rolled off Nikki. "Damn, that was—"

Relieved of his massive weight, Nikki sat up, combing her fingers though tangles of long blond hair. Cascading around her bare shoulders, it reached almost to the middle of her back. The stuff was definitely out of control.

"Fucking fabulous," she finished, delightfully sated and still panting a little. Deep inside she still trembled from the incredible orgasm they'd shared. His blood stained the tips of her fingers. Looking at her hands, she believed it was the most sensually erotic sight in the world, as if she'd taken communion of his flesh even as his seed filled her womb.

One corner of his mouth quirking into a sexy smile, Jackson reached for his cigarettes on the bedside table. He selected one.

"Fucking fabulous," he agreed, giving her an artful wink. The tip flared with a brief flame. The scent of dark, rich tobacco filled the air around them with its heady, enticing scent.

Yawning and stretching, Nikki cuddled up against him, laying her head between his flat male nipples and curling a possessive leg over both his. His flaccid penis snuggled in its thatch, its hungers momentarily sated. Her mouth watered at the sight of it. His sweat-musk scent teased her senses, arousing her all over again.

Nikki thought about leaning down and sucking him back to erection, then decided not to. It felt so good just being beside him. Their bodies had fit together so well that it felt like they'd been created for each other. She'd never before met a man who made her shiver and moan the way Jackson Sullivan did.

He was definitely worth going to hell for. She almost found it impossible to believe such a gorgeous piece of hunk was a demon. That boggled the mind. Everything she knew about demons—very little, actually—painted them as ugly, twisted little creatures with glowing red eyes, mouthfuls of sharp fangs, and misshapen bodies. There was definitely nothing misshapen about Jackson. His whole physique had clearly been sculpted by the hands of a loving creator.

As for the postcoital smoke, well, she could use a puff herself. Lifting her hand, she made that gesture so familiar to other smokers.

Taking a final drag, Jackson handed it over.

Nikki positioned the tip between her lips, inhaled, and said, "So if this is hell where'd the cigarettes come from?"

Jackson released a long stream of white smoke through his nostrils. "Contraband from good old earth," he said. "We've got a good supply of booze, and enough drugs to keep us senseless for centuries. We do appreciate mankind and their ability to create all these self-destructive devices."

Nikki took another drag. "Sounds like you've got a perpetual party going on here," she commented dryly. Hell was starting to sound like a pretty good place to ride out eternity. A good-looking man, drugs, and booze. Shit, better than being alive. She supposed that as one of the dead she wouldn't have to worry too much about hangovers or overdoses.

He licked his fine lips. "This is hell, babe. Here we embrace and revel in the forbidden."

"Sex, drugs, and rock and roll sounds pretty fucking okay to me." She pumped her fist into the air. The ashes flicked from her cigarette vanished midair. You couldn't beat the maid service in this place. No doubt the bed would replenish itself with fresh linen if left to its own devices.

She sighed happily. "Are you sure this isn't heaven, Jackson? If I'd known this was waiting for me, I'd have made arrangements to get here sooner."

"I can assure you this is hell." As he spoke, the chiming of what sounded like mission bells rang in the distance. They rang on, twelve strikes echoing through the chamber.

Jackson slipped off the bed before the last chime had faded, moving with an inborn predatory grace. Sinew and muscle rippled across his shoulders and down his back. Aside from drying flecks of blood, no sign of the vicious scratches she'd raked into his pale skin during lovemaking remained. He'd healed completely. Not even a scar remained.

Hardly surprising. He wasn't human.

"What's that?" Nikki asked.

Eyes narrowing, his copper-green gaze slipped on a sinister glint. "We have company, darling Nikki." A single muscle twitched in his jaw. His smile chilled. "It's time for you to meet the rest of your eternal companions."

Eternal companions?

A bitter shimmy went down her spine as the same time a gut-level sense of terror began its spread through her bowels. In the span of seconds, something about Jackson had changed, bringing a sense of revulsion that made her skin crawl and the fine hairs on the back of her neck rise. The air around him shifted and momentarily thickened. The cloying smell of sulfur singed her nostrils.

Nikki struggled to swallow past the lump forming in her throat. This was a surprise. She hadn't expected—or suspected—that there might be other demons lurking in the midst. The blood in her veins turned to icy water.

Demons that might also be wanting to stake a claim on a nice piece of her ass.

This news did not bode well.

At all.

She squeezed her eyes shut for a minute. Damned if she'd be afraid. "So you're not the only one?" Her voice nevertheless sounded a little thin and strained, hardly recognizable to her own ears.

Still smiling that hellishly icy smile, Jackson shook his head. "Oh, no. Our numbers are infinite. There are a lot of very horny men in the parlor waiting to take a turn with you."

Nikki wavered. The shit was slowly seeping past her neck. Soon she'd be in over her head, for sure. "Infinite?" she parroted. Having sex with Jackson was acceptable. Adding two or three or even four? No sweat. She'd participated in a few gangbangs, had gotten off on the thrill of having more than one man at a time to satisfy that lust-laced hunger constantly burning in her core. She couldn't claim she hadn't enjoyed it either. She'd been stone-cold sober and more than willing every time.

He bent over, catching a handful of her silky hair and letting it sift through his fingers. "You're a special one, Nikki Malone. I haven't had a soul like yours through here in ages. It's been a pleasure abusing you." His fingers slid along her cheek, under her chin, tipping back her head. "And it's going to last until the end of time."

Nikki thought a moment. "Guess there's no way I can repent for my sins before this little group sex party gets started?" She eyed his naked body. "Keep this between you and me, you know?"

Jackson snorted. "Oh, don't worry, my dear. I'll have you again. And again." He lifted a single brow. Lust flashed in the depths of his eyes. "We've only just begun our own little affair."

That promise didn't sound very reassuring at the moment. *So what am I supposed to do now?*

The answer arrived with crystal clarity.

There was nothing she could do.

Nikki sighed and tossed her hands into the air. "What the fuck?" she said. "Let's get going."

Pure unadulterated surprise colored Jackson's features. She could have knocked him over with a feather. "That's it?"

Prickling like a cactus, Nikki shot him a look that would have had the punch to knock him dead—if he'd been alive to begin with. "What do you want me to do, Jackson? Cry because someone's going to get a little bit of tail? Shit. It's not like a few dicks will wear me out." She shot him a saccharine smile. "Right now I have a feeling I've got the tightest goddamned cunt in hell. And she who holds the pussy has the power."

Jackson's burst of laughter was unexpected, but welcome. "If no one else," he chuckled, "you do belong here, Nikki."

Trying to appear relaxed, Nikki bunched her fingers into the sheets around her. "So when do I meet the others?"

"We should go now," he said. "They're waiting."

She cocked a brow toward him. "Naked?"

Jackson looked down at himself. "Ah." He made a brief gesture with one hand. Barely had a blink passed and there he stood, fully dressed in a formal black tuxedo, complete with vest and bowtie.

Nikki's brows rose. She'd almost, just almost, detected the moment when the change occurred. *Slick.* And very convenient. She'd like to learn that little trick herself. What woman wouldn't want to be able to snap her fingers and appear fully dressed, with perfect hair and makeup done like a movie star.

Jackson looked like he'd just stepped out of a cover shoot for *GQ*. The tux fit his perfect body like a glove. "It's a formal orgy, I assume?"

"Of course. We're not savages here." He winked. "Just a group of nondenominational pagans on a quest to have a little fun."

"There's a song in there," she commented as an aside. "Who would have thought that demons were fashion conscious?"

"We keep up with everything going on in the modern world," Jackson said.

"I didn't know hell had a direct link with planet Earth."

"Satellite, actually," Jackson explained.

"You're kidding, right?"

He sighed. "Hell isn't all parties all the time. Some days it's absolutely boring. There's already so much that's wrong in the world that no one needs us to throw a little angst into their lives. Humankind seems bent on reaching the end of days as soon as possible. Pity when there's so many forbidden pleasures to be savored."

She shrugged. "Good point."

He held out a hand. "Everyone is waiting. Shall we go?"

Nikki cleared her throat, indicating her own obvious nakedness. "If you seriously think I am walking in a room full of demons naked..." She shivered. "You have another thought coming."

Jackson lifted his brows with wicked intent. "I could always carry you in."

Nikki challenged his warm gaze with a cool one of her own. "Kicking and screaming wouldn't make a good presentation at all," she countered, able to level her tone this time. "No one wants to fuck a hysterical woman."

Brows lifting, Jackson rocked back on his heels, contemplating her. "I thought I already did," he countered cheekily.

Nikki frowned. "I wasn't hysterical. I was just having a moment."

Jackson rubbed his mouth in the place she'd smacked. "And I enjoyed every moment of your moment."

"Don't be a smartass, please. Just get me some fucking clothes."

He considered. "Hmm. *Fucking* clothes. I think I can manage that just fine. Stand up, if you would."

Nikki slid off the bed. She squelched the urge to cover her breasts and privates. Jackson had already and thoroughly ravaged every inch and then some. Her rear still hurt from the invasion of his massive cock.

He snapped his fingers. "Allow me."

Nikki glanced down. "Shit." She speared him with a glare. "Is this a joke, Jackson?"

He'd dressed her, all right. In a hot-pink halter-style babydoll gown, all see-through lace. The confection included a teeny-tiny lace thong and lacy pink thigh-high hose. Her feet were crammed into lace-up stiletto sandals with a heel at least 6 inches high.

Nikki scrunched up her face. Frills definitely weren't her style. "Oh, shit," she groused. "It looks like someone puked pink spiders all over me." She wobbled on the tiny sticklike heels. Her feet threatened to rebel. Whoever had created these devious devices of torture clearly hated women. High heels definitely had to be a demon's twisted creation. The only good thing about them was they made her legs look twice as long, muscular, and very shapely.

Jackson grinned like a wolf on steroids. A certain part of his anatomy was beginning to take notice. "You don't like it?"

Nikki stuck her tongue out at him. "No."

His hand went for the zipper of his slacks. "Open that mouth again and we'll definitely have to be late."

"Like I would want to suck your cock for putting me in this

confection." Nikki kicked off the shoes and began to unsnap the garter. Her clothes were still draped over the chair beside the bed. "I'll wear what I arrived in, thank you very much."

She headed to reclaim them. Might not be as fancy as what he'd put on her, but her faded blue jeans, roach-stomping cowboy boots, and T-shirt were a heck of a lot more comfortable. Nothing plain about them either. Working in bars had taught her to wear 'em right, you had to wear 'em tight. Hustling those tips wasn't easy. Maybe that's why Sammy's hair-brained scheme to rob drug dealers hadn't seemed like such a bad idea at the time. Stealing from scum couldn't be all bad.

Apparently, it hadn't been a smart move.

It had landed her straight in the pit of hell.

She briefly entertained the idea of trying to make another break for freedom. *Yeah, and look what that got you.* Lashed to a bed and royally ass fucked by a man with a super-duper dick.

Not that she minded dicks that would make an elephant jealous.

Jackson caught her by the arm. Sitting down on the edge of the bed, he expertly bent her in half over his lap. The flat of his palm came down hard against her bare ass.

Nikki gasped in surprise, twisting and wriggling hard to escape. "Hey! Quit treating me like I'm two years old."

Jackson ignored her protest and held on, keeping her in place across his lap. "You're acting like one, so you will be treated as such." He delivered another two smacks in quick succession. "Your first lesson in minding your manners, Nikki, is that you will always obey me. Whatever I want to do with you—whenever I want to do it—I will."

Nikki squealed. How undignified! He'd positioned her in such a way that her face almost touched the floor and her rear was straight up in the air, fully exposed. The teeny little thong offered no cover, little more than a piece of floss between her stinging butt cheeks. Pulled tight against her clit, the crotch rubbed in the most enticing way. Her nipples hardened as a velvet ribbon curled around her senses. Sudden, creaming arousal wet her inner thighs all over again. She'd never been spanked before and was stunned at how it made her feel.

Hotter. More intensely aroused.

Jackson smacked again and again. "We can do this all night if you like," he warned smoothly. "I like the way your ass looks, all nice and pink. Matches what you're wearing now."

Nikki considered the options. Stay here and have her ass paddled all night, or she could go and meet the gang.

She relented. "Okay, Jackson. You've convinced me. I'll go."

His hand hovered above her ass. "Dressed like I want you."

Nostrils flaring, Nikki released a pent up-sigh. "Yes, I'll go like this." She couldn't resist a barb. "Tacky as it is. You've got me made up like a dollar whore marked down to fifty cents."

Jackson reluctantly let her go. "And you're only worth a quarter," he smirked.

Nikki glared. "One of these days the tables will be turned, funny boy, and it'll be your ass up for the reaming."

Jackson grinned with delight. "My dear, that is a day I truly look forward to. You know I like the pain." He winked. "A lot."

Stepping back into the torturous heels, Nikki rolled her eyes. "Is there anything that turns a demon off?"

He shook his head. "If there is, I don't know about it."

Peachy.

7

Stepping into the hallway outside Jackson's private suite, Nikki felt a sense of familiarity begin to seep into her mind. She vaguely remembered walking this hall, only heading into the room instead of out.

Jackson glided ahead of her, silently leading the way. Though she could see where she was going, everything around Nikki looked muted, as though draped in thin layers of see-though gauze. Where the light emanated from, she didn't know. It was just there, a low, muted glow that showed everything, yet revealed nothing. She had the feeling if she reached out and tried to touch anything, it would evaporate under her fingers.

Only Jackson appeared to hold solid form. The rest felt unearthly and incorporeal, as if her spirit hadn't fully merged with this place.

The hallway seemed to go on forever. Then it ended as it had begun, without warning. A long staircase spiraled downward, leading down into a mist-shrouded gloom.

Gazing into the distance below, Nikki shivered. "Where will this take us?"

Jackson checked her question with a commanding gesture. "You will soon find out." He smiled back and added, "It is a place you'll enjoy, I think."

His words didn't reassure.

Nikki shivered again, letting go of a heavy breath. Her heart rate bumped up a couple of beats per second. A volatile mixture of emotions knotted inside her. She suddenly felt extremely sensitive toward her surroundings. All nerves, she instinctively divined that this place felt she did not belong within its walls. "I don't think I really want to know."

Jackson plunged down into the darkness. His stride quickly carried him out of her sight. Apparently he wasn't concerned with leaving her alone. She had no other place to go.

Mute and frightened, Nikki hovered at the top of the staircase. She didn't want to go, but neither did she want to be left alone. Negotiating the narrow stairs in stilettos would be treacherous enough, each step demanded care. Trip and she would go plummeting into the darkness. Even now the murk seemed to reach up from its endless depth, seeking to embrace her in smothering arms.

An abrupt image of the town came flooding back to her mind.

She remembered that it had seemed a mirage, little more than a cluster of abandoned buildings; the remnants of its failure to thrive in the center of the godforsaken desert. Once it had a post office, a convenience store, gas station, a small one-room schoolhouse, and most poignantly, a playground with children's toys overgrown and eaten away by the continual blasts of high desert winds.

Only one place seemed to have any current inhabitants: the huge, three-story manor appearing to rise out of the white sand like a beacon. There had been a sign, too, pointing the way. *House of the Desert Sun*, it had read. An oasis or a mirage, she didn't know.

Nikki vaguely remembered carrying Sammy's backpack. No way she would ever part with it. She'd walked through the windswept night, her soul feeling as devoid of life as the derelict town. A shimmering light, like a ray of hope, had pointed her toward the last sanctuary for a weary traveler. The front door had opened and a man had greeted her, one whose name she didn't yet know. Welcoming her across the threshold, he'd shown her the way.

So tired, so cold and heavy with fatigue, Nikki had gratefully followed him inside. As the door closed behind her she'd heard the voices, whispers really, welcoming her.

There all recollection ended and her whole mind felt empty again. If anything, her disorientation was deepening, not fading. Only one thing was certain: She'd come into this place willingly. There were other roads she could have taken, different paths she could have chosen. But no, this place had beckoned. And she'd answered its siren's call.

Destiny, the one that would claim her forever more, lay down that staircase.

I have to go.

Nikki swallowed hard and summoned her courage, not very much at this point. Squaring her shoulders and stiffening her spine, she headed into the belly of the beast.

Her walk did not last long.

Jackson waited below. Seeing her arrive, he held up a hand to take hers and help her negotiate the final few steps. "I wondered if you'd come," he murmured.

Feeling a cold trickle of sweat work its way down her spine, Nikki licked dry lips. "Did I have any choice?" she asked, already knowing the inevitable answer.

He smiled. "No."

Nikki looked around. Four gray stone walls met her gaze from all sides. There seemed to be no place to go but back up the stairs. "Where do we go now?"

Jackson pointed to the solid wall. "There."

Just like that, the wall began to glow. From floor to ceiling, a series of square stones came to light, glowing with white-hot energy. Heat emanated from the stone, radiating outward with a skin-blistering intensity. The fire and brimstone had decided to put on a show.

Screaming in terror, Nikki's hands flew up to cover her face. She was about to fry, sizzling like bacon in hot grease.

The heat intensified tenfold. No doubt about it. There was a serious power surge happening here. Awesome. And impressive. Hell certainly knew how to entertain. If she hadn't quite believed before, this display of underworld fireworks had managed to do the trick.

Nikki clenched her teeth. Another moment and her flesh would begin melting off her bones. Her only hope was that this horrific torture would end quickly.

Just when she believed it couldn't get any worse, a terrible grating sound tore through the chamber. An ear-shattering blast ripped through the stifling atmosphere. The earth beneath her feet rocked, buckling so violently it felt like the stone floor had turned completely liquid.

Groaning, then shrieking, the stone wall broke in half.

And then there was nothing.

Only silence.

And then she felt it.

A breeze.

The kind that cooled the earth after the sun had slipped beneath the horizon.

Delicious. Welcome. Bliss.

Nikki peeked through her hands and could hardly believe her eyes. The wall had evaporated. Paradise lay on the other side.

"I don't believe this," she breathed.

Jackson, apparently unaffected by the whole spectacle of

near apocalypse, looked at her like she'd just lost every last marble out of her mental bag. "What's not to believe?" He held out a hand. "Shall we?"

Without saying a word, Nikki reached for his hand. His strong fingers closed around hers.

He led her into paradise.

The parlor, as he so quaintly called it, looked like some Victorian gentleman's club. The walls were paneled in heavy dark wood, and acres of carpeting stretched out underfoot. Thick heavy furniture was covered in a fabric of the richest scarlet shade. At least a dozen men, maybe more, lounged casually throughout. Like Jackson, they were all beautifully turned out in formal clothing. And like jackals scenting blood, they turned her way, hungry to feast.

Breath lodging in her lungs, Nikki fought to hold back a smile of delight. Holy smokes! It looked like she'd just walked into a Chippendales meeting. These men—not one of them appearing to be over the age of thirty—were the most gorgeous pieces of male flesh that she'd ever had the pleasure to lay eyes on.

And not a single female in sight.

Even as she ate them up with a mental spoon, every damn one of the breathtaking hunks were eye fucking her right back. The air around them, a heady mixture of cigar smoke, fragrant spirits, and rich male musk tickled her nostrils. As in the rest of the strange manor, she could find no source of illumination. Light seemed to seep from nowhere, merging and mating with the shadows.

Blondes, brunettes, even a tawny auburn head or two. Oddly, perhaps significantly, Jackson was the only one with coal black hair, as though his inky mane served as an indicator of what lurked deep inside his mind. Dark, dark things, indeed.

The way the others looked at him indicated he led the pack as its alpha male. Jackson clearly ran the show. The fact that he'd gotten the first taste of the fresh pussy in this place was another tip-off, and by the look on his face he wasn't happy that he had to share his conquest.

Still, the leader must feed the horde to keep order. Unsatisfied demons would probably be a bitch to handle. Sort of like rednecks on payday. They wanted to drink, fight, and fuck after a week spent digging ditches.

Come to think of it, so did she.

The acorn clearly hadn't fallen far from the tree. Nikki's momma was the same kind of wild woman—six husbands, six kids, too many mouths to feed, and not enough room or money.

Nikki had gotten out on her own, young but not so tender to the ways of the world. She did what she had to survive on the streets, to have a place to lay her head at night. Maybe she hadn't made the best decisions or picked the finest examples of men. There really hadn't been many choices. Trailer trash didn't come with any pedigree or degree. Survival meant using hook, crook, or her own shapely ass. This wasn't the first time she'd faced down a room full of horny bastards.

Nikki felt her nipples rise to attention under the skimpy lace. She practically creamed against the crotch of her thong, the insides of her thighs moistening with lust. The sight of all these good-looking men waiting to fuck her delivered an instant carnal kick. And considering the way they were eyeing her, like hungry wolves, it was readily apparent that Jackson had chosen appropriate evening wear. Hot gazes burned right through the lacy nightgown, visually ripping away every last shred.

No doubt I'll soon be naked.

And happily so.

Jackson glanced down at her. "What do you think of the men here, darling Nikki?" he whispered in an audible aside everyone heard.

Nikki gulped. Just looking at all these good-looking men

sent her inner mercury soaring into the red. Adrenaline mixed with heat surged through her veins, searing them from the inside. This was the same reckless exhilaration she'd experienced when tearing through the desert, hell-bent on getting away. Half fear, half excitement, all pleasure.

She licked her lips. "I have to admit that these are some of the most fucklicious demons I've ever laid eyes on."

Jackson held her hand, leading her into the center of the gathering. All turned her way, gazes riveted on her. Center stage now, she was on full display. "My dear," he said smoothly, answering her statement. "These are not demons you are looking at, but angels."

She looked at him with disbelief. "Angels?" Confusion followed. "I-I thought you said this was hell."

Jackson laughed, then clarified. "Fallen angels, Nikki. All of us were cast out of heaven for rebelling against God. Fallen to earth, we are the princes of this world and shall infest this planet until judgment." Laughing, he quoted from the bible, "And the angels which kept not their first estate, but left their own habitation, he hath reserved everlasting chains under darkness." He spread out an expansive arm. "And this is our darkness."

Well, that certainly confused Nikki. "But if you had heaven, Jackson, why would you leave it? Isn't it . . . uh, heaven? Eternal paradise?"

Jackson's brow warped in sudden anger that rippled over Nikki in waves. "Eternal paradise is no paradise when you have no capability to feel any emotion." He grimaced nastily. The light in his copper-green eyes sparked with a menace that wasn't anywhere close to sanity. "Imagine standing by century after century while your Creator lavishes his love on a lesser—inferior—species. *He* loved humankind best just because He'd given them souls."

Nikki's heart thudded in long, jarring beats against the inside of her ribcage. Her mouth felt like someone had wrenched open her jaws and dumped a truckful of sand right past her lips.

Now she knew what he'd meant when he'd said he didn't feel her the last time they'd had sex. But she didn't quite believe that to be true. Jackson *had* felt her, all right. Otherwise, he wouldn't have kissed her so deeply and desperately.

And the idea that he had begged the larger question: Give an inhuman being a grab at human emotions and what would you have?

Chaos.

She gasped out a half-strangled laugh. Not an ounce of amusement colored its tone. "Was it worth sacrificing heaven, Jackson? Falling to sin?"

Jackson's misshapen smile widened, feral and chilling. "Oh, it most definitely was. Coming to earth we learned all about the pleasures of the flesh we'd been so long denied." He gave her a glance that swept from head to toe. "And you know how I like to put that knowledge to use."

Nikki grimaced and thought of her chafed wrists, aching nipples, and abused rear. Yes, she certainly did.

And all the other men in the room had the same idea. They wanted to put their knowledge to use too.

On her.

Looking around at their eager faces, she entertained the notion that not all of them would want to make the experience pleasant or enjoyable in the slightest. They were going to use her, brutally and sadistically.

A remnant of Jackson's earlier warning flashed through her mind. It could all be very painful, or it could be completely pleasurable.

The choice was hers.

Closing her eyes, Nikki let her head drop, willing herself to dig deep inside and find the strength she'd need to get through her first night. She'd reached this point intact. She could go further.

I can take it, she resolved. Nothing had ever backed her down before. Certainly not a bunch of horny ex-angels packing cocks as dangerous as sub-machine guns. Otherwise, a long and miserable time stretched ahead. She was fairly sure Judgment Day wasn't coming anytime soon for the rest of the world.

Jackson reached out, lifting her head so that she had to face him. He flashed that familiar pirate's grin, the one that had so earlier beguiled Nikki when they were alone. His smile said that while he had to share her with others, part of her belonged to him alone.

"The ceremony is about to begin," he said softly.

That one caught Nikki's attention. Her protective antennae swiveled forward, centering and focusing. *Ceremony?*

"What are you going to do?"

"The mark of the beast shall be put upon your skin," Jackson said, his voice dark and gravelly with anticipation.

Nikki breathed a soft sound, somewhere between a whimper and a low moan. She started to protest, but the words died in her tight throat unspoken. The searing heat of bestial hunger burned in his gaze, immediately silencing her with its ferocious intensity.

Sensing her unspoken acquiescence, Jackson smiled. "I suggest you do your best to enjoy the experience of the Claiming, darling Nikki."

Struggling to suppress her fear, Nikki nodded. Tiny beads of perspiration dotted her brow, shoulders, and neck, trickling down between her breasts and shoulder blades. Fear scented the air around her, mingling with the musky smell of sex still clinging to her skin.

Nikki already knew she couldn't hurt them physically. She'd

taken a roundhouse swing at Jackson, and he'd brushed it off the way anyone else would brush away a gnat.

"I'll t-try," she stammered softly.

Jackson noticed the tremble in her hands, the shakiness of her legs. "Don't worry." He grinned. "We'll start out easy on you."

If that was supposed to reassure her, it didn't quite make the cut. Nikki bit back the urge to ask him what he intended to do. That was already clear enough. Anything he—they—wanted.

The mark of the beast.

She glanced down at her wrists, so raw and red from the ropes he'd tied her down with. No doubt here. She'd already been marked once. That hadn't been a bad experience at all, considering the mind-blasting orgasm she'd gotten out of it.

There was something arousing behind the idea of being forced to climax. Having her body so completely controlled appealed to her on a deeper level inside her unconscious mind. How else to explain her erect nipples rubbing against lace, and the ache beginning to bloom all over again between her thighs? Her mind might say no, but her body had said yes every damn time.

Nikki sensed her physical self awakening, slowly readying for the onslaught of a dozen hands, mouths, and cocks plundering her from every direction. The idea made her blood boil with a pure and undiluted lust. Her ravenous desire felt fueled with a darker, more demanding ache. It seared her senses like a slug of straight whiskey hitting the back of her throat.

Her clit swelled and pulsed even more between her legs. She could almost taste their desire, hanging hot and heavy throughout the room like a thick fog.

She cleared her throat. "What do you want me to do?" she finally asked.

"Just stand there." Jackson produced a cigarette out of thin air, already lit and ready to be smoked. He trailed the tip of the cigarette along the length of her bare arm. The red-hot tip grazed her unmarked skin.

Nikki instinctively winced against the burn she imagined he planned to deliver. It took every ounce of strength she possessed to remain absolutely still. She had a feeling it would go harder on her if she tried to resist. She'd already had a taste of how Jackson handled resistance.

Jackson continued his tease. He trailed the tip of the cigarette along the curve of her left shoulder. "Scared?" he asked.

Nikki briefly gritted her teeth together. She forced herself to swallow down the thick lump clogging her throat, threatening to cut off her oxygen. "No."

Jackson laughed. So did the rest of the demons. "You should be."

Nikki clenched her fists tighter, until her fingers dug painfully into her palms. She forced a smile and replied, "What's the point of being afraid? I haven't got any choices here."

Jackson considered. "True." He sucked on the tip of his cigarette, sending a stream of fragrant white smoke directly at her. "You don't."

Fingers tracing the path his cigarette had blazed along her shoulder, he plucked at the bow holding the strap of her gown secure.

Nikki gasped as half of her halter disintegrated, baring one breast. The distended tip was obviously bead hard. Curiosity piqued, carnal interest raised its head and smiled. The slow rise of heat began to simmer inside her core all over again. The primal instinct of the female to be conquered and possessed wasn't worth struggling to resist. Given the way she felt right now—hovering between fear and exhilaration—it would be a relief to get started.

Jackson's wicked grin washed over her. It felt as though a thousand hands moved along with the skim of his gaze, invading every vulnerable spot on her body. "Time for my boys to feast."

His simple look heightening every nerve ending in her body, Nikki drew a quick breath. The room began to spin around her as the hoard of fallen angels advanced from all sides.

Uh-oh.

8

Jackson faded into the background as two of the angels glided her way.

Nikki swore she could smell the desire simmering under their skin, even though they had yet to make physical contact. Looking at them, her slit swelled and pulsed between her thighs. A blonde and a brunette, both stood at least a head above her, and both were drop-dead gorgeous. It was hard to choose which one she would have preferred. Didn't matter, though. They weren't going to give her any choices.

The dark-haired angel slipped around behind her. A big hand brushed the hair off her shoulders, baring her nape. Warm lips nibbled a slow tease along the curve of her shoulder. "My name is Phenex," he murmured softly. "And it is my pleasure to serve you."

The touch of his lips against her bare skin hit Nikki like a thousand-megawatt bomb. A little sizzle crackled between his mouth and her skin, jump-starting a sweetly erotic pulse in her veins. The promise of pleasures to come. Arousal spread through her, hot and fast.

As Phenex nibbled, he pressed his hips against her rear, dragging her back against his straining erection. As the thong left her ass totally bare save for the thin piece of string between her cheeks, she immediately felt his bare skin against hers. His clothing had already melted away. The heat of his cock seared like a hot iron rod.

Feeling Phenex grind against her from behind, Nikki gasped. Damn! These guys didn't waste a second. The hard cock wedged between her cheeks taunted her, intensifying the ache between her legs.

The angel in front of her also took up the cause.

"My name is Dagon," he said. Reaching out, he slid the other side of the halter down her arm. Both breasts were deliciously bare. He palmed both her breasts, squeezing, testing their weight. Steamy lust darkened his gaze. "And it is my pleasure to serve you."

"Nice to meet you," Nikki choked, not knowing what else to say. Gathering her thoughts proved difficult, considering she was locked between two of the hottest men she'd ever encountered. Both with the intention of having their way with her.

Dagon moved closer, bending his head to the level of her breasts. His tongue played around one distended nipple, teasing the peak into full attention. Every time his tongue made another arc around the tip, Nikki felt the heated throb of need in her clit.

This was excellent. Better than good.

Phenex's big hands settled on Nikki's hips even as Dagon unlaced the rest of her gown, then tugged it away from her body. All she wore now was the skimpy little thong, garter, hose, and heels.

"Does it make you hot when a man suckles at your breasts?" Phenex breathed in her ear. His erection nudged deeper between the cleft of her ass, though he didn't attempt to make entry into her tender anus, just rubbed up and down in the most enticing manner.

Nikki gulped her answer. "Oh, yesss . . . ," she breathed. The mass of pleasurable sensations swamping her body felt like a hypnotic drug. She'd gladly overdose just to get more.

Clothing fading away, Dagon slipped to his knees. His palm brushed across the smooth plane of her belly, followed by the brush of his lips. The tease caused her breath to catch in her lungs as he paused to gently tongue the dip of her navel. She whimpered softly at the suggestive penetration.

Mind spinning, Nikki could barely catch her racing thoughts. This was better than she'd expected. As Dagon slipped lower, her head lolled back against the solid support of Phenex's shoulder.

Phenex took the chance to pounce. His mouth traced soft, wet caresses on her neck. His hands slipped beneath her arms, cupping the breasts Dagon had too quickly abandoned. Thick fingers tugged and rolled the sensitive tips. "And do you like it when a man's mouth claims your clit?"

The words had no sooner left his mouth before Dagon's hands tugged her thong over her thighs and halfway down her legs. At the same time, Phenex angled her hips upward with his.

Nikki moaned and shuddered all the way to her toes when Dagon's tongue penetrated then probed the soft inner folds of her sex. Back arching against Phenex's hard body, she grabbed handfuls of thick blond curls and held on.

Seeming impossibly long, Dagon's tongue delved deeply, probing her wet pussy to find every slippery crevice of her sex. His mouth devoured.

Looking down through half-lidded eyes, Nikki held her breath in anticipation as Dagon pleasured her orally. Watching a beautiful man give her oral sex while another teased her nipples and rubbed her from behind was a turn-on beyond any she'd ever experienced.

Dagon's mouth worked liquid magic, teasing the soft petals of her labia, circling her creaming depth. He dipped inside her, but only briefly.

The pressure of her need for penetration rose and rose until she cried out, "Take me—please!"

Answering her cry, the tip of Dagon's tongue flicked upward, curling right into the soft center of her pulsing clit. His tongue against her sex created instant sparks of electricity, flooding her entire nervous system with molten fire. Phenex simultaneously rolled his hips under hers, tugging her nipples into straight high points to double her pleasure.

Nikki grunted in surprise. "Oh, holy hell . . . !" The rest of her words disintegrated into a babble. Lost in the sheer glory of shuddering climax, she whimpered, half crazed with the ravenous intensity of sheer ecstasy. Her pulse banged against her skin, threatening to burst through fragile veins. Orgasm roared through her like a tornado on the ground, tossing and tearing up her senses with ferocious intensity.

And that was only the beginning.

Now that the gates had been loosened, the others surged in.

Still breathless and reeling, Nikki was hardly aware of her body being repositioned, lowered to the floor. She felt the scrub of carpeting against her back, was dimly aware of strong hands grasping her wrists and ankles, spreading her out.

The whispers of names brushed her ears, so many that she could not comprehend or remember them all: Araziel, Gressil, Forneus, Murmur, Nelchael, Sonneillon, Mammon, Sytri. More and yet more until she felt she'd drown in the sea of names they murmured against her skin. Hot, wet mouths and hands caressed every inch of her skin, invading her inner thighs and breasts. Head to head, body pressed to body they circled around her, no one giving an inch to have a turn. The rest of her frilly gown disintegrated, pulled away by eager hands. Cocks strained, pressed, sought entry.

Lost in the haze of their sheer numbers, Nikki finally managed to wrench open heavy eyes. She expected to see a dozen beautiful male bodies, all centered toward the focus of bringing her pleasure. What she saw chilled her blood.

The beautiful angels had disappeared, replaced by a grotesque cadre of horrible misshapen creatures.

Mouth going dry, Nikki felt her guts twist into knots of sheer horror. She looked in terrified disbelief, hardly comprehending the changes. Horns ruled over faces cankered with oozing sores. Skin flayed away; bones protruded in sharp angles. The smell of them sickened, like a corpse bloating and rotting under the hot sun. Red eyes flashed at her, filled with glee. Fangs gnashed over her exposed, very vulnerable flesh. They were just husks, an aberration mocking nature.

Nikki opened her mouth to shriek, but nothing came out. Her vocal cords felt like they'd been ripped from her throat and tossed away. It was one thing to be abused by attractive demons, quite another to be menaced by such ogres.

A commanding voice broke through the ugly mass. "Enough!"

Standing tall and straight, Jackson materialized amid the fray. Unlike the others, his form hadn't changed shape. Naked, he loomed over the group, a vision of beauty among the desecrated. Only his face had changed. A smirk twisted his mouth, as vicious as the glint burning behind his gaze. That alone made him ugly, as terrible and malformed as the other demons.

But that wasn't the thing about him that made Nikki start squirming and widen her eyes. Not at all. What so painfully and gut wrenchingly captured her immediate attention was the dagger he carried. The blade glinted dangerously, a silver sliver of pure menace. No doubt its edges were razor sharp.

Nikki gulped. She had no doubt he intended to use it on her. *The mark of the beast.*

Jackson grinned. "I have not yet introduced myself properly, darling Nikki. I am more commonly known as *Jacsul*, and

I am the deliverer of great pleasure." He lifted the dagger, turning it just so. "And great pain."

Even though she knew there could be no escape, Nikki started to struggle against the hands holding her securely pinned. "I don't deserve this," she gasped, voice hoarse with horror.

Jackson smiled. "Apparently you didn't study your scriptures close enough in life, Nikki darling. Otherwise, you would have noticed the passage that said, *'If their souls should perish in their youth through rashness, their afterlife shall be wounded by the angels.'*" He flicked the dagger against the tip of one finger. Blood welled as he lifted it to taste. "Mmm . . . I look forward to marking your skin . . . tasting your blood . . . possessing your body. It is a ritual I adore."

He'd no sooner spoken the words than the chamber around her took on a strange animation all its own, becoming a dark and cold place of almost no illumination or warmth. Gray dimness, like a heavy mist, solidified around the edges of the wall. The demons holding her seemed to melt away. Ugly, twisted, and gleeful, they cloaked themselves in gray mist. Only the glow of their beady red eyes revealed their presence.

For a moment, everything fell out of focus, like a dream within a dream within a nightmare.

Beneath her back, Nikki felt the floor begin to take on strange animation, almost like it was trying to wriggle away. A hard ridge of stone formed, widening as it lifted her into midair. Taking final solid shape, the stone platform was wide and long enough to support not one but two bodies.

The platform sat level with Jackson's hips.

A spasm closed Nikki's throat when he climbed up to join her. She struggled to raise herself but had not an ounce of strength. What the hell was he going to do with that blade?

Locked against the platform, she was about to find out.

Painfully.

Jackson stretched out between her spread thighs. His mouth

hovered just a few inches above her sex. "One thing I haven't gotten to taste is this lovely cunt of yours—something I intend to have again." He chuckled. "And again."

Nikki drew a sharp breath when he trailed the tip of the blade along the inner softness of one leg. She stiffened when the tip penetrated the skin there. Not deeply, just enough to draw blood.

Jackson's head dipped. He licked up her blood with a flick of his tongue.

Nikki gasped and instinctively arched her back against the hard stone. Clenched fingers dug deeply into the palms of her hands. She didn't want to enjoy this. Her body, however, had other ideas. She felt herself growing damp all over again, and the ache in her clit was fiercer than ever before. "Oh—!"

Jackson grinned and followed with another suckling against the small cut. His tongue soothed away the brief ache he'd inflicted. Then his mouth found her clit through the nest of soft curls covering her mound.

The friction invading her sex set Nikki's insides on fire. Her hips rose, pressing against his mouth in silent plea. The pleasure uncoiling in her gut was so intense that little sparkles began to dance behind her eyes. The pressure of pleasure surged, threatening to erupt all over again like an active volcano. A long, lusty groan tore from the depth of her throat. Hips rising and falling, her body craved the harder friction of a male body.

Jackson abruptly lifted his mouth away, ending the delicious sensations. "Not yet," he warned. "You don't come until I tell you." The heat in his coppery eyes burned brighter than any flame. He inched his body up a little higher, nicking the softness just below her navel. His mouth followed, tasting her.

Nikki gasped. Even as she fought to encompass her senses, she somehow found herself focusing completely on what Jackson was doing. The sight of him cutting her flesh, tasting her as he made love to her was fascinating. And intoxicating. She couldn't tear her eyes off him.

Possessed of a strange, sweet inertia, she gazed at him. Unlike the others, he was still so beautiful. So desirable.

Jackson moved higher, cutting, licking. It vaguely occurred to Nikki that when he'd finished, the scars would create some sort of pattern on her skin. That would be her mark, the tattoo of the beast etched into her flesh. And it would leave no doubt whom she belonged to in the torturous realm.

No, her mind filled in. *Jacsul.* The true name of her demonic lover.

Coming to the level of her breasts, Jackson circled one pink nubbin with the blade. The bud immediately tightened under the assault of the icy silver tip. She drew in a sharp breath as lust stabbed as deeply into her core.

"You don't know how long I've waited for a woman like you," he breathed. "A soul like yours . . . so rare, so responsive." He bent to taste one of her nipples, sucking it deep into his mouth. His mouth entertained the shadow of a smile. "I wanted to keep you, Nikki darling. But I want the energy sacrificing your soul will bestow upon me. One more is all I've needed to become the reigning prince of demons."

Sacrifice.

The single word stood out, a stark alarm sounding in the back of Nikki's beleaguered mind. Her mind began spinning backward, rewinding to the first things he'd told her, trying to recall if he'd mentioned anything remotely close to this. He hadn't.

Desire fled in the wake of pure, unadulterated fear. The awful sound of the word penetrated her brain deeper than any stab he could inflict with that wicked blade. It was something she couldn't let happen. The demons had claimed her life but hadn't yet fully wound their clutches around her soul. If Jackson finished the terrible deed, she wouldn't even be damned. She'd simply cease to exist.

She be . . . *nothing*.

And that wasn't acceptable.

Nikki Malone wasn't ready to cease to be. Existing in hell was better than existing nowhere at all. Life had been too short to be enjoyed. Hell damn sure wasn't slipping through her fingers. Even pain was preferable to nothing at all.

Flashing a smile laced with the menace of his murderous intent, Jackson repositioned himself between her legs. "Sorry, babe. It's all politics." Cock jutting toward his ridged abdomen, he loomed over her. His massive body trembled with the efforts of restraint.

Nikki looked at him through horrified eyes. "Don't—" she started to plead, then stopped herself cold. One thing she'd never done in her life was *beg*. Whined, whimpered, even sniveled a bit now and again, but she'd never begged anything from anyone. She'd always stood on her own two feet, took life as it came.

Seething inside from his betrayal, Nikki decided then that her afterlife would be no different. She may have died. She may have landed herself in hell. But however seductive and entrancing Jackson's lovemaking might be, giving up her immortal soul without a kicking, screaming fight just wasn't the way she wanted to face eternity.

So that he could better control penetration, Jackson settled the dagger vertically across her abdomen, the tip between her breasts, the hilt pointing toward her belly. Hands free, he guided the tip of his shaft to her sex. His hips pressed forward just a little. "I need to feel that hot little cunt of yours around me. A complete connection." He smiled down at the blade. "Then bye-bye, darling Nikki." His voice mocked like salt rubbed in raw wounds.

Nikki squirmed, but there was no escaping. She felt the crown of his cock slide between her silky labia. All she could do was grit her teeth and reject the pleasure of imminent penetration. She groaned under her breath. "Damn you, Jackson. This isn't fair."

Shuddering with raw need, Jackson grinned down at her. His red-hot gaze sparked dangerously. "No one ever said hell was fair." His long, driving stroke penetrated.

"You said you felt me," she said, grasping at straws.

Pulling halfway out, he tweaked a rosy nipple. His evil smile said that's exactly what he'd intended for her to think. Chump.

"I lied. You should know, Nikki, that all demons are master deceivers. We never tell the truth."

Nikki glared up at him. Confusion, then anger whirled like a hurricane inside her. "You stinking bastard!"

Jackson laughed with glee. "It will only hurt once," he said and drove his cock to the hilt. Seconds later, he pulled back out, then plunged again. "But you know that's a lie too."

Gasping for breath at the size of him, she had to bite back a whimper as his massive cock plundered every last inch of her sex. He rode her with a smooth, rhythmic ferocity that made his pale skin glisten with sweat. It felt so good she wanted to give in, let herself go over the edge and embrace the climax insidiously winding like a venomous snake through her core.

Determined not to let her body betray her at this last vital moment, she turned her head. Her arm was stretched away from her body, locked into place by some force she couldn't see. She clenched her fist, fighting to raise her arm.

Nothing.

The chances of freeing herself seemed slim to none.

She clenched her eyes shut and concentrated harder. Logic dictated that if Jackson were truly sucking up energy from her, then she should be able to reverse the current and draw off his.

Her head hurt. Her chest hurt. Geez, come to think of it, there wasn't an inch of her that didn't ache.

Nikki forced her mind clear of all images and all thoughts. Imagining a dark room, she next pictured a brief, tiny pinpoint of pure, pulsing white light. Taking a breath, she opened her eyes and focused on her left arm. She mentally pointed the blazing point of light toward her wrist, visualizing her arm rising from its locked position.

Her arm lifted. A little.

Nikki concentrated harder. More. Her breath came harder. Faster. If she lost control, that would be it. There wouldn't be another chance.

Suddenly, she felt a snapping sensation against her skin. She didn't have to lift her arm more than an inch to know it was free.

Jackson's low moan tore her mind back to the dilemma at hand. Close to hitting climax, his cock strained inside her, more powerful than ever before. Groaning, he reached down and wrapped one of his hands in her hair. Lifting her, his free hand reached for the dagger poised between their bodies. Lost in the passion between them, he seemed not to notice the shift in power.

Nikki recognized her chance. It was all or nothing now.

Her hand beat Jackson's to the dagger's hilt. Sitting up, she angled the long, thin blade upward toward his abdomen. She sucked up fear and did what she had to do. With a quick jerk, she shoved upward. Hard. The blade slid under his breastbone, impaling him. "Feel me now?" she grated through clenched teeth.

That was all it took to rip the smile off his lips. Jackson's mouth opened, but nothing came out.

Nikki fought the gut instinct to pull the blade out. Her stomach rebelled at the idea. She had to go with her first instinct, no holds barred. She swallowed several times, forcing down the bitter burn of acid at the back of her throat. Instead of relenting, she did something she hadn't even suspected herself to be remotely capable of doing.

She twisted the blade.

And shoved it deeper.

Too bad she had to do it. She could have fallen hard for this sexy devil. But when it came to the question of who would come out on top, well, it didn't take a lot of brains to answer that one. Nikki didn't play fair. Never had. And she wasn't about to start now.

Tension throbbed between them for a minute or so.

Belatedly reacting to the incredible stimulus of penetration, Jackson's body convulsed, every muscle in him twitching as though struck by a bolt of lightning. A series of violent spasms wracked him, pushing his hips forward a final time to impale her. His cock blasted, filling her womb with jetting hot semen.

Still not fully comprehending what she'd just done, Nikki gasped and fell back. Her body arched against the stone as her own climax came fast and hard, lifting her up and crushing her with the ferocity of a giant crushing a gnat. Just as she thought she'd be able to catch her breath, a rushing crescendo of subsonic vibrations coursed through her nerve endings.

Then the world went insane, like an atom bomb landing directly on top of her. Everything around her all of a sudden morphed into a weird, distant blur. Sparks of pure energy detonated inside her skull. Rather than ebbing away, the force gathered strength, deepening until she felt that she'd explode from all the pressure filling her. Her soul soared on the outspread wings of dark euphoria.

Waves after wave of glorious pleasure dimmed her sight. She screamed as the ferocious energy roared on and on, reverberating into some unimaginable gut-wrenching infinity.

And then it was over, ending as quickly as it had begun.

The atmosphere around them quivered, then collapsed.

Nikki's dazed brain could hardly process a single thought,

much less two. Reduced and distilled to a shuddering, sated mass, it took a few minutes for reason to return, along with the realization of what she'd done. As her heart slowed down to a normal rhythm, the impact of what she had done horrified as much as it had aroused. Almost. She'd penetrated him, fully and completely.

And it felt wonderful.

Rubbing her hands across her numb face, she blinked, then glanced around to get her bearings. She reluctantly looked up at Jackson. To her surprise, he didn't appear to be dying.

Their gazes locked. Action and consequence simultaneously passed between them. Anticipation sent Nikki's heart into a faster beat. Her nerve endings crackled with anxiety.

Jackson smiled and slowly drew the dagger out of his gut. Incredibly, no blood seeped from the wound. Giving a grimace of disdain, he tossed the blade aside. "Oh, Nikki—" His voice was as taut and ragged as his respiration. "You should have known this wouldn't kill me."

Blood turning to ice in her veins, Nikki gulped. She'd taken her shot and somehow botched it. There'd be hell to pay now. Palms sweating, throat tight with anticipation, she waited. Whatever he wanted to do, he probably would.

Nikki's muscles tensed. Her breasts rose and fell with each hard, panting breath she drew. She doubted she could pull off the escape trick a second time. It had taken every bit of effort she possessed to do it the first time.

Payback, she silently bet, *would be hell.* The idea made her guts knot all over again.

Jackson reached for her, grasping her wrists and lifting her astride his lap so that she faced him. Their lips were just inches apart, his still stained with her blood. He flexed his hips. His pale skin seemed to glow from inside, lit by some erotic force. "You are truly a devious little demon, my dear. Quite worthy to join our ranks."

At first Nikki didn't understand. Then the meaning behind his words dawned on her. "Are you saying I'm a demon now?" Her nervous system still buzzed from the ferocious infusion of pure unadulterated energy invading her body.

His gaze a glittering mass of dancing greens and glowing coppers, Jackson nodded. "Very much so. You survived your baptism of pain, fire, flesh, and blood. Only the strongest can."

Swallowing hard, Nikki felt her lips twitch upward. "That's a good thing, right?"

"Depends on your point of view," Jackson said slowly. "It does make you one of the eternal damned."

Nikki considered his words, then shrugged. "Pretty much the story of my whole life." She mock sighed. "I always have to do things the hard way."

Jackson's cock stirred. "Speaking of the hard way, my dear, we have some unfinished business between us."

"I thought we had finished," Nikki teased.

His smile took on that familiar wicked cast. "We have only just gotten started."

Before she could say another word, Jackson kissed her, mouth covering hers to share the forbidden. His tongue sparred with hers. The sexual tension between them was still there, as strong as ever. If nothing else, it had intensified to an almost unbearable level.

Ordering her body to relax, Nikki sparred right back, as much the aggressor now as he was. The blood lingering on his lips tasted of energy, enchantment, and pure lust. Her stomach fluttered with the realization. Her blood. Her magic. Her lust. Desire blossomed all over again, stronger, more intense.

Hungrier.

Jackson's hand rose to cup her breast, teasing the weight of it, before dragging his thumb across the peak of her distended nipple. His cock hardened. Everything inside her went all liquid again.

Shuddering with raw need, Nikki slowly drew back. Reminding herself to breathe, she reached up, cupping his cheek with her palm. Everything had changed now. She wouldn't be the victim anymore. "So, Jackson," she drawled behind a spreading smile of gratification. "You know this means I expect you to be the one tied to the bed next time."

A grin spread across Jackson's face. "I think I can handle that," he murmured. Then he kissed her, long and deep.

With her entire being, Nikki knew that his kisses would never be enough. She wanted more. And would take it out on him.

One sweet, excruciating lash at a time.

Captive Heat

Jodi Lynn Copeland

1

"Goddamn you!" It wasn't enough he'd been an asshole when alive, Ken had to haunt her from the depths of hell.

This time it wasn't Leia Jenson's mind or body her ex-husband abused, but the pricey pumps she'd flung at the burning backwoods hovel she'd once called home.

Who the hell paid over half a grand for shoes anyway?

A woman trying to outrun her past.

"I don't have to outrun it now, you bastard!" A self-inflicted bullet to Ken's temple took care of that. Not nicely, but messily.

The rotting paneled walls of the one-room shack were splattered with the grisly remains of what had been his suicide scene. Leia hadn't gone inside. She couldn't even stomach the thought of peering through the set of dirt-stained windows, for fear old memories would grab hold. The sheriff who called to tell her Ken was dead and that her ex had left her the shack in his will— apparently to give her a final taste of his sick sense of humor— had forewarned her about the shape of the place. The cop had been scanty with the details. Just told her enough that her mind could fill in the gruesome blanks.

Only the blanks weren't so gruesome.

She was glad Ken was dead. Glad the asshole was finally getting his due. If she'd ever questioned the afterlife, then Leia had to accept it now. Had to believe he was dancing to the flames of the devil's caustic beat.

Which meant he would be too busy to fuck with her shoes.

It wasn't the bastard reaching from the gates of hell to destroy the slingback, gold-sequined Manolo's she'd bought two years ago as a final severance to the pathetic woman of her past. It was the acrid smoke rolling off the shack's dilapidated roof, stinging her eyes and screwing with her mind. Making those old memories surface even though she hadn't gotten any closer than what kicking the barely hinged door in and tossing a gasoline-soaked rag, followed by a pack of lit matches, had required.

Either gray matter was a hell of a fire conducter, or Ken still kept stacks of porn magazines lying around. Her little rag fire had turned to an inferno in minutes.

Flames licked at the small, dirty windows on either side of the doorway, blackening the glass. From Leia's cross-armed vantage fifteen feet away, the heat coming through the open door turned from steamy to sweltering.

Mindful of her bare feet and how stupid it had been to walk even a quarter mile down a decently cleared trail in three-inch heels, she put another ten feet between her and the hovel.

She wouldn't be escaping this overgrown, secluded stretch of woods and returning to her life in the city until the shack was ashes. Looking skyward, past the towering tops of decades-old elms, she attempted to escape the memories.

Hazy purple-black filled a summer sky that had been blue minutes ago. The color obliterated any chance of escape, watering her eyes and fucking with her mind even more. Reminding her of all the times she'd worn the ugly shade on her body, of all the shit she'd endured. The way Ken had handled her, called her a fat-ass good to be nothing but his house bitch and sex slave.

Her ass *was* big. She'd come to terms with her size along with a whole lot of other things the last two-and-a-half years. But she was no one's slave.

Then why won't the memories quit?

An explosion erupted from somewhere inside, knocking the question from Leia's mind. She focused back on the doorway as a second blast followed. Then more.

The first of the windows exploded, spewing fragments of glass for yards as if the winds of hell themselves spurred them on. Panic slammed into her belly as the last of those fragments barely missed clipping her side, and she backed farther down the trail by rote.

Son of a bitch! This was supposed to be an easy means of destroying Ken's meager possessions while severing any final ties between them. It wasn't supposed to be dangerous.

But just as the ties between them had been dangerous from nearly the moment they'd said "I do," this situation became dangerous as hell in the blink of her stinging eyes.

Pure TNT seemed to detonate inside the shack, the caterwaul sound near deafening. Reflex had her hands jerking to her ears. Too late, she realized she should have covered her body. The second window exploded in a blaze of orange and black fury. Shards of discolored glass arced toward her. This time they didn't miss but moved past the lavender silk of her designer shorts and tank combo to slice at bare skin.

Covering her head with her hands, Leia half fell/half dove to the trail. The air whooshed out of her as her breasts and belly collided with the hard earth. The breath dragged back between her lips, even the low air pungent now, and she gagged out a cough. Pain scorched through her thigh. Burning frissons of ache speared upward. She bit her lip against the hurt, tasting blood, savoring that bit of life-confirming metallic warmth as she pinched her eyes shut and waited for the explosions to end.

A deceptive calm descended after nearly a full minute, broken only by the crackle and hiss of the fire. Adrenaline pumping through her system, she gingerly turned on her side. Through bleary eyes, she took stock of her injuries. Dirt and nicks covered her legs, and a chunk of concave glass protruded from the inside of her lower thigh, just past the cuff of her shorts.

Brown-bottle glass.

"Shit. Shit!" Of *course*, the bastard had alcohol inside. Drunkenness had always been the fuel that fed his rage.

Popping sounded to her right, keeping her attention on the present when it threatened to stray to the past. The popping was far too close. Holding her breath, Leia followed the direction of the sound . . . and panic closed in all over again.

The fire was no longer confined to the shack, but eating away at the rain-deprived woods and quickly making its way toward the trail.

Sickness settled in her gut along with bleak reality. She hadn't set out to be dangerous. But she'd been damned dangerous, damned harmful. And there was nothing she could do but run.

Panting, despite her attempts to not take in more of the toxic air, she shoved to her feet. Razor-edged pain rifled up her leg and had her sucking a hard breath between her lips. She pushed the air back out and pushed her feet down the path, ignoring the sting of fallen twigs and bramble as they cut into the soft pads of her feet. Ignoring everything but the need to find help somewhere in this godforsaken nowhere.

She almost made it to her car when another explosion hit. Once again, the sound was too close. She'd come nearly a quarter mile. But it was right there, right behind her, emitting a force strong enough to topple her to the ground and knock her out cold.

* * *

Ken wasn't dancing to the devil's beat. He was sitting right beside the horned demon, enjoying a flask of brandy and a deep-seated laugh over Leia's misery.

Hands ran along her body, and she steeled herself against the physical assault that would follow. Only, these hands didn't feel vile. Even with her eyes closed, she could tell they were much smaller and softer than her ex's—not gentle, but not truly abrasive either.

They moved with efficiency, stroking over every inch of her as they bound her upper body.

Bound?

Leia jerked alert. Ache speared through her with the move, and she realized she'd been steeped in a foggy semiconsciousness. How long? And what had happened to warrant her pain?

Behind their closed lids, her eyes stung like a bitch. She opened them slowly, expecting to find a paramedic tending to her, strapping her to a gurney until he was certain she wouldn't harm herself by moving. Bile rose up in her throat, and a dry, wheezing sound left her lips as she saw her freakishly diverse surroundings.

No paramedic saw to her welfare. No straps hooked her to a gurney. She stood in the center of what appeared a cell carved out of the barren earth while a white-haired midget worked the underwear down her dirt- and blood-caked legs.

Horror and confusion clamped together as a tight ball in the pit of her stomach.

This can't be happening.

She closed her eyes and shook her head. Opening her eyes revealed the same irrational scene. Thick green, flowerless vines circled just above and below her exposed breasts. Another set hooked around her arms, pulling them behind her back, thrusting the ample mounds of her breasts upward and outward. A ceiling of moss and tree roots leaked in light from overhead, and dirt walls surrounded her. Six feet at most separated her from reaching out and touching those walls.

Three of those walls. The fourth wall was at least fifteen feet away and shrouded in darkness. Anything could lurk back there.

Death. Freedom. Another white-haired midget.

Desolation taunted from the fringes of Leia's conscience. Her breathing went ragged as she strained to see through the dark, to see what may well be her fate. She couldn't even make out shadows.

What was this place?

"Where am I?" The tremulous question scratched at her throat, low and husky, not her natural voice but a side effect of smoke inhalation.

Oh, God. The fire!

How quickly the flames had gotten out of her control, escaping the shack to attack the woods, came slamming back to her. The blaze had been fast on her heels. The final explosion directly behind her.

She'd considered death lie waiting in the darkness, but was she already dead?

No, she couldn't be. Not and feel so alive, so aware of every touch of the midget's warm fingers as they caressed her ankles and then lifted her bare feet from the cool ground to remove her underwear. She couldn't be dead and feel so awash in sensation—terror, disgust, and an unfathomable intrigue—as the midget looked up and revealed herself to be a four-foot tall, generously endowed, nude female.

Female, but not human.

Elfin ears, multi-pierced with ruby studs, protruded from beneath the waist-length waves of her white hair. Stark-blue eyes and blood-red lips contrasted dramatically with a ghostly pale face. The female's lips curved with unmistakable sensuality as she straightened with a thick length of vine in one hand. Her other hand reached out, below the swell of Leia's belly, toward the juncture of her thighs that was now as naked as the rest of her.

Small fingers cupped her mound, and Leia's heart kicked against her ribs. Gasping out a strangled sound, she attempted to step backward, to fling the perverted little bitch off her. Her feet made it a few inches before they were left to tread in place. No vines restrained her lower half, but she could feel something cold and hard pressing against her wrists. A pole of some sort lined the crack of her ass.

Bound and staked. *Helpless.*

She gulped down a hard breath, fighting off the desolation that bulldozed forward this time as hysteria. But shit! Being at the utter mercy of anyone's touch was the makings of her worst nightmares.

Was she dead after all? Was this hell?

The female squatted, bringing her heated gaze even with Leia's sex. Eagerness shimmered in her eyes as two of her fingers pushed through Leia's blond bush, lightly penetrating her slit. "Shall I bind her here as well?"

Past the panic, revulsion boiled in Leia's blood. She clenched the muscles of her sex and shifted her hips away from the assault, only managing to wedge the pole snug between her butt cheeks. As if oblivious to her resistance, the female took her fingers deeper, probing the inner walls of Leia's pussy, handling her with damning efficiency once more. Fondling her until the panic began to ebb to something far more fearful.

It was as if the female somehow knew her body intimately, knew exactly where to touch to have sensual warmth building against Leia's every want to stop it.

But, no, she wasn't responding to this. She *hated* it!

"Don't touch me, you bitch!" Rasping the words, Leia heaved at the captive vines, wrenching until her arms burned with the effort.

The female didn't even look up.

Her fingers continued their violation, pumping into and petting Leia's sex. One finger pulled out suddenly, lifting the hood of her clit and stroking the bead, and arousal pitched through Leia as a fireball of erotic sensation. She clamped her lips down around a moan. Her pelvis's blatant thrust wouldn't be stopped.

Lifting her hands away, the female leaned back and let out a lusty laugh. Her breasts shook, calling attention to erect nipples pierced with ruby studs that matched those that lined her ears. "Her clit is ripe. A crotch vine would serve her well."

A crotch vine? Is she mad?

What of Leia herself? What was wrong with her body to respond so eagerly? Either she was still unconscious and having a nightmare, or somehow her mind was being controlled, her feelings skewed.

Squeezing her vaginal muscles as tightly as possible, in the hopes of hindering further penetration, she forced herself to concentrate. The female was talking to someone . . . or some *thing*. Whichever it was waited in the darkness.

Her skin tingled with the unknown. Her mind and heart raced with the idea she really was in Hell and it was Ken the blackness harbored. Ken somehow controlling her body. Ken about to lay a final siege to her body and soul.

Narrowing her eyes at the darkness, Leia feigned bravado. If she were already dead, cowering would be futile. "Are you too much of a chickenshit to show your face?"

The thing stepped out. Not a thing, though. Not Ken either. But another man.

Or, quite possibly, a god.

Developed flanks escaped a leopard-print loincloth. Above

the low-rise waist of the loincloth, sun-drenched flesh covered a chiseled torso. Raven black hair curled over a rock-solid chest. Straight locks of the same shade hung freely around a lean face, the blunt ends brushing along wide shoulders and rolling in glistening waves over rounded biceps. He was the kind of hard-bodied guy whom fantasies were built around. The kind of guy she would never have a chance with.

Like a panther on the prowl, every move he made was pure grace. Every inch of his tall frame and the unyielding line of his mouth emanated danger, darkness. Vengeance burned in his obsidian eyes as he moved closer.

Ignoring Leia's question, he nodded at the female. "Not until she's cleaned and shaved."

With the deeply spoken words, the female's fingers pushed back between Leia's thighs. She'd forgotten about keeping her sex clenched while taking in the man she presumed to be her captor, and the female easily slipped inside her sheath.

"She's not dirty here." Working her fingers against disturbingly aroused tissue, the female flashed a licentious smile. "Just wet."

"Your thoughts are as good as mine, Aubrie." His expression stayed firm, but wry humor clung to the words. With a flick of his wrist, he indicated Leia's crotch. "You may have a taste."

Horror returned as a maelstrom. Leia's eyes flared wide, her gaze zipped downward. Aubrie's warm hands settled on her upper thighs and pried her legs apart. The female shoved her pale face against Leia's sex, nuzzling the lips of her labia past her pubic hair before flicking her wet tongue into her slit.

No! Goddammit no!

The words reverberated in Leia's spinning mind. She fought against her bindings, attempted to clamp her knees together, knowing already the moves were pointless. Having learned well that fighting the invasion only made the pain that much more acute. Only, the pain wasn't acute. Truly, there was no real pain. No bile churning in her belly. Just a moist pulsing in her core that spoke of traitorous, hungry urgency.

Grinning, Aubrie came up for air, her vibrant red lips slashed in a debauched grin and glistening with juice. "Delicious. Such a tight pussy. Silky inside."

Her mouth returned instantly, fitting over Leia's sex, tonguing up into her sheath. Swirling with darting licks, she brought her free hand to Leia's ass, puckering the hole as she stroked the supple flesh of her right butt cheek.

The female's licks turned to forceful sucks, and her grip on Leia's left thigh increased. Blistering heat chased up Leia's body, into her neck and face. Salon nails bit into her palms with the fisting of her hands. Needful pressure built in her core, trembling her legs and blurring her vision with tears, those born of her own shame as much as that of loathing for her handler.

Why couldn't she feel pain? *That* she could endure. Instead, she fought a violent war with the tightrope edge of climax.

She wouldn't come!

She didn't want to come. Could never in such an insidiously powerless situation. It wasn't *her* mind ruling her body, making her crave trappings forged in cruelty. Someone was trying to take over her thoughts.

That someone had to be *him.*

Leia lifted a glare at her captor—evil cloaked in a tauntingly gorgeous package. "Get me out of here, you bastard!"

He didn't move. Just stood with booted feet and powerful legs braced apart, arms hanging at his sides, looking bored as his minion continued to assault her. "You may call me Sebastian," he spoke in a dead-calm voice, "and I suggest you enjoy it while it lasts."

"Enjoy being raped?" Leia spat the words out, wanting to spit in his face as well.

"Rape doesn't make your body flood with desire. It doesn't

speed your heart with anticipation and leave your pussy clenching for release."

No matter the want to do so, or the fear that coursed just beyond the unfathomable desire, she couldn't deny the truth of
his words. Whomever or whatever was at the source of her
cravings, she yearned to yield to them.

Aubrie's tongue stabbed back up inside her sex, taking Leia
off guard and stealing her focus from Sebastian to gape at the
female. Aubrie's eyes locked with Leia's as the female licked and
suckled at her. No malice thickened the air between them, only
want—raw, intense, chasing a mewl of ecstasy up Leia's dry
throat.

The fingers of Aubrie's right hand slid past the pole at Leia's
back to caress her anus as the force of the tonguing increased.
Leia's sex clamped down around the impaling. Hot cream filled
her core in a rush. Rapt by the desire in the female's eyes, panting with her own needs, Leia thrashed in the vines, all but heedless to the chafing of her wrists against the pole as she ground
her cunt against Aubrie's face.

The female's fingertips slipped away as the pole rode deeper
into the crevice of Leia's ass. It felt like a stiff cock rubbing
against her, threatening to take her in a way no man had dared
in years.

Yes. Please. Put it inside me.

Aubrie's gaze broke away as her tongue changed course and,
in turn, broke whatever carnal enchantment had come over
Leia. She gasped with the unholy direction her thoughts had
run, the depraved way her body behaved.

She had to be in Hell to believe she enjoyed losing total control, to think she wanted to be taken so roughly by any nature
of being.

Had to be!

Struggling to ignore Aubrie's tonguing, Leia lifted her head
and again met Sebastian's face. Arousal emanated from his eyes.

Or so she believed until she blinked and saw only dark fury. "Am I dead?"

"Is that what you want?" Unlike the cold steel of his gaze, his voice remained calm. "What you hoped would happen when you set flame to my home? I could kill you. It would be justified for the pain you've caused."

"What h-home?" The words trembled out as wicked sensation balled in her belly. Not mounting terror, as it should be for his threat, but the continued need to explode.

God, the want to come . . .

"*This* is my home." He spread brawny arms to encompass the small, dirt space surrounding them. "This room and the land above us. All of it would have been destroyed, along with countless lives, if I hadn't stopped you."

Was *he* the explosion that knocked her out? With the size of his fist, one blow could accomplish that easily. He *could* kill her.

Desire finally tapered with the ice-cold wash of reality. Her belly rolled as the fear rose. Shame for her senseless actions scorched the tender skin along her throat and high into her cheeks. "I d-didn't mean—"

"Enough!" Sebastian moved forward to tug at Aubrie's hair.

Lifting her hands and mouth from Leia's body, the female stepped back to regard him. Overt affection and reverence filled Aubrie's eyes as she met his gaze from two feet below. "What shall I do next, Master?"

"Begin her cleansing." Contempt curved his lips down as he again looked at Leia. "You look hideous."

Fat. Plain. Ugly.

Acidic words Leia heard from Ken's mouth a thousand times returned on a haunting wave. Worse than the shame was the weakness. Her cheeks stung with the heat now, the knowledge of how huge and repulsive she looked displayed so blatantly.

But, fuck no, she wouldn't let herself go down that nasty road. She wasn't that feeble woman anymore.

She had a fat ass, but so what? More than one man had been eager to get his hands on it the last two-and-a-half years. Few had succeeded, but that didn't stop the want. Aubrie clearly enjoyed her full figure. Sebastian could go to Hell . . . if they weren't already there. "Kiss my fat ass!"

His gaze coasted down her body, lingering hot on her breasts and crotch before sliding to her hips and butt. A sly, wicked smile touched at his lips when his eyes again met hers. He stepped forward with purpose, one hand outstretched, fisted.

Nerves spun upward to tackle Leia's moment of brass. She pinched her lips together, wishing she'd have kept her mouth shut. Kept her legs open to Aubrie. Kept her ass back in the city instead of returning to the woods to torch Ken's shack.

Anything to avoid Sebastian's fist.

2

Denying her urge to fight the vines that bound her, Leia waited, breath caught in her throat, blood pumping madly between her ears as Sebastian stopped a foot away. His hand continued toward her, infinitely slow. Each millisecond seemed to pass by as a full minute. The same ugly memories from back at the shack surfaced against her will, intensifying her fear, the impulse to cower.

She stayed firm, solid, refusing to surrender.

In the end, his fist didn't pound into her. His fingers uncurled to fill with a breast and squeeze the nipple so sharply she couldn't stop her squeak.

Or the resounding surge of damp awareness between her thighs.

Humor shone in his eyes, lightening the shade that didn't look quite so black this close, while lending a gentler appeal to his smile. "I plan to kiss every inch of you," he vowed, "starting with your ass, just as soon as you're washed and healed."

Leia swore she was past body-size issues, and yet, that he

wasn't repulsed by her stature, merely her filth, was nearly as relieving as avoiding the brunt of his fist.

Then both were forgotten as something about the unexpected warmth in his smile rang familiar. "I know you."

Sebastian's fingers jerked from her nipple on a rough tweak. The smile vanished, coolness retaking his eyes as he stepped backward to stand next to Aubrie and make the fair-skinned midget look diminutive.

"You *don't* know me." Biting the words out, he exchanged a look and a nod with the female, then moved around to Leia's side.

Nerves started a new, furious dance in her belly. His entire left half was blocked from view. He was as good as cloaked in darkness again. Only, this was worse. In the darkness, he hadn't been able to touch her. Up close, he had touched her, though not in an overly painful fashion.

Here, now, his hand slapped down hard, large, splayed fingers swatting across her still-sensitized right butt cheek. "Shut up, behave, and listen to Aubrie."

Leia swallowed her yelp. The ache caused by his hand would have been minor if not for her earlier injuries. She now became intensely aware of those injuries, of the continued dry ache of her throat. Equally as aware that she didn't know Sebastian but recognized Ken's immorality in him.

"I'm not a damned dog!" She ground her teeth around the last word. She had friends in the city she could speak bluntly with, but this man was no friend.

What he *was* remained to be seen. Until she knew, she would be wise to weigh each word carefully.

He stepped back into view, and her entire body tightened with expectation. He didn't touch her again, didn't even bother to meet her eyes in reprimand. Just stood halfway between Leia and one of the dirt walls, back to looking bored as he watched

Aubrie produce a damp strip of white cloth and an earthen bowl of minty smelling translucent green gel from somewhere behind Leia.

The female squatted in front of Leia, and she constricted her sex instinctively. Aubrie let out a short laugh, letting her know the move hadn't gone unnoticed, but then brought the cloth to her legs. She scrubbed along the length of Leia's legs, leaving the nicks and the gash from the chunk of bottle glass burning as savagely as if she'd poured salt into the wounds.

"The pain is well worth the pleasure," Aubrie offered as she worked.

"I'm fine," Leia lied through gritted teeth, because she had a feeling the pain and pleasure Aubrie spoke of went well beyond this moment.

Then the unaffected facade was lost as Aubrie coated her legs with the gel, stopping the burning on contact and bringing tears of thankfulness into Leia's eyes.

Smiling, the female brought her fingers to Leia's mound, covering the blond curls with the gel. Here, the gel cooled as well, and it left her mound and the outer lips of her labia tingling with raw sensation. Gratitude was forgotten as her pussy moistened with fresh arousal. Stiffening, she clenched her sex harder and focused on the dirt wall beyond the muscle-and-flesh wall of a devilishly gorgeous man clothed only in a loincloth and workboots.

Cold metal touched against Leia's mound, scraping gently. Every ounce of the desire she'd fought back surged into her core. She leaned forward to view her crotch past her belly and caught Aubrie shaving off her pubic hair with a straight razor.

What next, the crotch vine or nipple piercings?

It could be either, probably both, and she would be powerless to stop them. Closing her eyes, she did the only thing she could: She tried to get her breathing under control while she waited for the humiliation to pass.

Given the adoring way Aubrie regarded him, Sebastian couldn't be completely heartless. Eventually, this situation would get better. It had to.

"I'll finish."

Leia's eyes opened with the sound of her captor's deep voice to find he'd moved up next to Aubrie. He was close enough she could see the muscles move beneath his glistening skin, smell the sweat lifting off his big body as if he'd just fought a hard battle. Hear the sound of his not-quite-steady breathing.

"Yes, Master." Aubrie's lips tilted into a salacious smile as she stood and handed the razor to him. And then, suddenly, it wasn't a small nude female standing before Leia, but a small nude male with a fully aroused cock bobbing for attention.

With a chuckle, Sebastian spanked the erect flesh. "You may go play."

Releasing a moan of pure pleasure, the male disappeared into the wall of darkness.

Leia's sex fluttered with the sound, the sight of the two males' intimate behavior. Again, she was left to wonder where she was, and if nothing was considered taboo in this place? And if not, if her captor didn't believe his actions toward her were immoral, what did that say of where he and his minions would stop with handling her?

Would the humiliation stop? Was there even an exit to this hell?

Panic bulldozed forward once more. Breathing hard, she twisted futilely in the vines. Weighing her words wasn't possible. "Where the hell am—"

Sebastian slipped a thick finger between her thighs and into her sheath, cutting her off short. "Aubrie is a skin-shifter. Female or male as the mood suits." Pulling his finger free, he sucked the shimmering skin between his lips. "A delicious pussy, indeed. I'm going to take great pleasure in fucking it."

* * *

"I'd rather have burned alive in the woods than be fucked by you!" Ice shot from Leia's green gaze, belying the fear Sebastian could guess ruled her mind.

Only guess, damnit.

He couldn't read her emotions the way he'd once been able. Even so, her body's desire was obvious. The vines looped around her arms, drawing them submissively behind her back, kept her breasts thrust out slightly. Raw want had the plentiful mounds surging higher, the nipples blood red and erect. The slickness of her pussy spoke of what she craved deep inside: long-forgotten and carefully suppressed yearnings.

How hard he had to focus to appear aloof and keep his cock from hardening beneath the loincloth spoke of his own cravings, his own suppressed yearnings. Those he harbored for her were never forgotten. They would also not be lived out tonight.

If he was smart, not ever.

He'd never intended to fuck the woman he found torturing the land and nature he ruled over. He thought solely to put the fear of God into her, let Aubrie toy with her long enough to ensure she'd never set foot in the woods again, then let her go. The loincloth had been intended to up the savage facade. Had he known the woman's identity immediately, he would have believed a business suit more menacing.

The pricey clothing that had never been Leia's style was stripped from her body now, and he knew her identity well. He also knew he couldn't release her so easily. Just as he couldn't yet reveal that she did know him, even if they'd never actually met.

Quelling the urge to slip a finger into her sheath for a second taste of her succulent juices, Sebastian concentrated on bringing the razor to the fine strips of blond hair lining the mouth of her sex. "You're not what I guessed."

Her hips shifted, pushing her ass back against the wooden support rod that extended from ground to ceiling of the underground holding area while bringing the plumped-up lips of her pussy dangerously close to the blade.

"Who are you?" Haughty command mingled with Leia's nerves.

Ignoring her question, he finished the job of freeing her mound to its natural soft and silky state, the way she'd always kept it in the past. Resting the razor against the side of the bowl of Camaloe, he coated the pads of two fingers in the translucent green gel. The breath whistled between her teeth as he covered her sex with the gel. He didn't think she physically hurt here and needed the herb's healing power. But rather, he knew she sexually hurt here and the gel's icy nip would make the ache all the more intense. "I expected weakness to match your cowardly actions. You're not weak."

"No," she spat back, "I'm not some sniveling piece of ass, so let me the fuck go."

So much stronger in spirit than when I convinced you to leave.

He wanted to smile his approval of her boldness. But where her spirit had grown, her body had fallen prey to her mind's need to forget.

Dipping a finger into the Camaloe, Sebastian shoved it between her legs and deep into her pussy. "You're strong. You just don't know it yet."

Leia's breasts thrust forward, her sex clenching. She squirmed as he moved his finger inside her, coating her interior walls. "I know what I am," she ground out.

"I'm not going to fuck you." Before his cock took control of his mind and he made a tragic liar of himself, he slipped his finger from her body and straightened. "I'm going to keep you."

There was no need to guess at her fear now. Terror widened her eyes, and she thrashed in her bindings like a woman set on escape solely for the purpose of his demise.

In his mortal years, he'd been a man who thrived on control.

He'd pitied few, never his lovers or those women he intended to become his lovers. Leia was different. He knew her past and those scars that kept her from remembering and embracing the racier desires of the flesh she once reveled in. For her, Sebastian felt both guilt and compassion. Even if it wasn't intentional, she'd helped to save him in a time when he felt his middle life was for shit. In repayment, he'd turned his back on her when she needed him most.

He'd been getting too damned close. To her mind. Her body. He'd wanted to reveal himself, wanted to make her his at any cost.

He'd walked, and she'd suffered the consequences of months of abuse.

It was time to make up for that failing. Time to show Leia the half life she'd fallen into, just as she'd once done for him.

Casting off sympathy, he stepped backward, toward the wall he'd come through. "Those aren't normal vines. They won't break. They could hurt you if you keep fighting them."

With a huffing breath, she quit her struggles. Despair crossed fleetingly over her face before the icy veneer returned. "You'll never get away with this. The sheriff knows my plans for today."

"He knows you were going to set fire to that shack?" Sebastian smiled—a mix of amusement and arrogance—as he stepped into the blackness. She'd never been able to lie worth a damn. "I might not get out much, but I do know there's a fire ban on."

"I have friends in the city who'll come looking for me. When they do, and they see what you've done to me, you'll pay."

"Even if they could find their way down here, they couldn't see me."

The color drained from her face. "I *am* dead."

"You're alive. I'm not. I'm also not dead." He also couldn't stay here and begin reminding her body of all the dark, extravagant indulgences it had forgotten beyond what the Camaloe and his power over the herb would accomplish.

He'd managed to get the fire Leia had set under control before it took out more than a fraction of the 200-acre woods. But he hadn't managed to flush all of the wildlife out of harm's way. Some of those injured had been treatable. At least one other wasn't, and Sebastian could sense the fox's pain as intensely as if it were his own. He could ease the animal's passing.

Even if it meant enduring death by another's hands again himself.

3

Leia let her body go limp against the pole, allowing the thick vines around her chest and arms to help support her. With Sebastian gone, she had no reason to feign courage, or toss out scathing words and threats that could well come back to harm her. She could be afraid. Cry. Kick and scream. And then get over the feeble-ass pity party and figure out how the hell she would escape these vines that weren't normal without injuring herself further before her captor who was neither dead nor alive returned.

Laughter over the incredulity of her situation bubbled up. Before it could escape, words echoed from the recesses of the dark wall. "I'll be back. Don't come without me."

She drew ramrod straight as the laughter died in her throat, replaced with soul-wearing agony. He wasn't gone. For the better part of five minutes he'd been standing there silent, somewhere in the black abyss, watching her. Waiting.

For what?

Her to break down in hysterics so he had some final fodder for his twisted sense of humor before he left to do Satan only knew what? Probably spank Aubrie's erection a few more times. Or maybe the midget would be in female form, and Sebastian would toss her over his lap and pleasure in paddling her pussy from the rear.

Leia's own pussy, chilled and hypersensitive from the gel he spread over and into it, throbbed with the iniquitous thought.

Glowering into the blackness, she groaned. If it was the last thing she did, she would regain control of her body's desires.

"That you think I could want to—" Speech left her on a sharply indrawn breath.

Holy Jesus! Something was inside her, moving around in her sex, expanding, pulsing. Fucking her like some imaginary dildo. Some dildo that was every bit as efficient and knowing as Aubrie, stroking up into her in a way she couldn't ignore.

"That's the Camaloe. And my influence over it. Don't come without me, slave." Demand edged the order. "You won't like the consequences."

Slave.

Icicles of rage skated along Leia's spine. The blunt edge of salon nails pinched back into her palms while hatred burned through her.

She was no man's slave, damnit! No man's. No creature's. "You might as well kill me now. I'll never be your slave."

Once you enjoyed it.

She shook off the phantom thought. It was no more her bidding than her amorous response to Aubrie's handling had been, or the dampening of her sex was now.

She would *never* enjoy being Sebastian's slave, but she also would never lay her life on the line, the way she'd intimated. She expected him to recognize that truth and call her on the lie. He didn't respond. Didn't speak another word.

Body strung taut with tension and vines, Leia waited for some sound, some shadow. Some dark, sensual god of a man who wasn't quite human to emerge from the blackness. Seconds ticked on, drawing out into minutes. The Camaloe thickened until it filled her vagina to completion. The fucking sensation ceased, leaving her sex feeling stuffed full yet strangely empty and aching.

None of it she wanted.

"Stop being a chickenshit and get out here!" The daring words worked once to call her captor out of hiding. This time he didn't appear. This time it seemed he really was gone.

For the first time, the earthen cell felt truly like a chamber. Dank. Isolated.

Leia fought off a shiver, knowing it was about nerves and not the weather—this time of year the temperatures never dipped below the seventies. And isolation was a good thing. It meant time for thought.

For strategizing her escape.

She let the tension drain from her body once more, relying on her bindings and the pole at her back for support as she studied the walls surrounding her. From what she could see of the three nearest, they were nothing but hard-packed earth. No chance of escape there even if she could somehow break free of the vines. Which left the mysterious fourth wall, or the ceiling.

Tipping her head back, she studied the maze of tree roots and moss several feet above. Earlier, sunlight had bled down from small openings, coloring the moss in soft yellow browns and greens. Now the light was faint, the overhead canvas looking dark and dead. Night was falling.

Her first night here?

She'd assumed as much, but who knew how long she'd been unconscious? Maybe it was a second or third night. Only, wouldn't Aubrie have undressed her and tended to her injuries before this? And wouldn't her body hurt more from the strain of standing, not to mention being fettered?

How long would it even take for someone to come looking for her?

Would anyone come?

She did have friends in the city, colleagues at the museum where she'd been lucky to find employment after discovering she had an excellent eye for Art Nouveau. But anyone who cared enough to seek her out? Damnit, she hadn't even told anyone where she was going. Hadn't dared to open that black hole of humiliation.

She might as well be dead, because no one was coming for her. She was going to die down here, rot away little by little while a midget and her master took turns screwing with her mind and body.

Frail thoughts littered with bleakness, but Leia couldn't stop them. Couldn't stop those that came directly on their heels. These ones dark. Foreboding. Thoughts that made her belly roil with nausea and her mind threaten to purge every vile moment of her brief, married life with Ken.

Just when her racing mind would have spun too rapidly to bear without screaming, the Camaloe resurged inside her. The pace wasn't an insistent pumping as it had been before, but gentle, hypnotic. Lovely really. Cooling her insides and yet somehow warming her, too, filtering delicious heat from her pussy outward. Spanning calming sensations along her nerves, soothing her frayed thoughts.

She rocked gently with the lulling pace, feeling her vagina soften and moisten. Her clit tingled with want, but the pace wasn't enough to bring her to climax.

Just enough to ease, to comfort.

Her eyelids flickered shut.

Leia forced her eyes back open, her body stone erect. To sleep in these unknown circumstances would be insane. But darkness was flooding her cell fast now, drawing long shadows on the visible walls, and she was so tired . . .

The odds of escape would have to be better with a fresh mind. Yes, she had slept for some quantity of time after being knocked unconscious, but that couldn't have been restful sleep to feel so weary. Not like the kind of sleep pulling at her consciousness, making it impossible to keep her eyes open and her mind alert a moment longer.

Rolling her shoulders back against the pole, she heeded the warming sensations lulling her from deep within and gave in to the call of exhaustion.

Husky laughter rolling from her lips, Leia dashed barefoot out the door and into the summer sun. Anticipation and wild thrill kept the laughter coming and her blood flowing hot as she ran.

She loved it when Ken played these games. Acted the part of master to her sub.

She didn't dare to look back, but she could hear the soles of his workboots pounding against the wood floor as he followed her out off the little one-room shack they were slowly remodeling. Their home was tiny now—smaller still it seemed nestled so deeply in the woods—but one day it would be bigger. One day the walls would be painted a charming yellow and echo the giggles of a half-dozen kids.

For now, it was all she could do to focus on running through the endless rush of trees and wildflowers, over the tangle of brush and roots that lined the forest floor.

Pulse racing, body on fire for what was to come, Leia made it nearly to the edge of the stream where they collected fresh water before arms closed around her middle.

Viselike. Unyielding. Wonderful.

Gasping out a sound that was half anxious screech/half delighted squeal, she felt Ken's grip go lax. He knocked her off her feet then. Knocked her to the ground—cheek kissing the grass-mottled earth and rigid nipples poking into the dirt through the flimsy cotton of her tee—and left her lying there beside the stream, floundering like a fish, while he came over her lower thighs.

With his knees pinned against the backs of hers, he fisted her short jean skirt in one hand and jerked the loose material up past her ass. "No panties." The sun warmed her bare skin as the flat of his palm connected with her butt, swatting the cheeks and leaving a delightful sting. "What'd I tell you about not wearing panties, slave?"

"S-sorry, Master. I forgot." As if she could ever forget the white-hot thrill of those erotic promises of his. All the wicked and delicious ways he would punish her should he catch her pantiless again.

"I'll have to make certain next time you remember." Glinting command and dark promise edged his words, lifting goose bumps on Leia's skin.

The weight of his body left hers, quickly replaced with the weight of a lone booted foot against her back. Instinct had her fighting the pressure on her spine, struggling to push herself off the ground and away from the tickling sweep of scattered grasses against her lips.

Instantly, she stilled with the swooshing hiss of material sliding against material. The unmistakable crack of leather split the afternoon air.

"Oh." Her pussy fluttered expectantly.

Tension and excitement balled together in her belly. From the corner of one eye, she caught the movement of the tail of Ken's belt whipping into the air. Slowly, it arced downward, lashing out, licking into the soft flesh of her buttocks. Not hard enough to leave its mark on her body, just hard enough to leave its mark on her growing need.

Yes. Yes. Yes!

Stinging heat spiraled down from the tender tissue to the gathering well of juices in her cunt. Giving up the fight to plant *her palms on the ground, she fisted her hands at her sides and waited for a second irresistible lashing.*

The belt flicked higher this time, the leather licking at her ass with a decadent nip she felt all the way to the tips of her throbbing nipples. She squirmed on the ground, biting her lip to keep from pleading for release. The pleasure was so much more intense when she let that first biting pain build into a slow, keen, darkly sensual ache.

But Ken wasn't letting it build, not this way.

"Did I tell you that you could move? You do nothing without my command. Nothing!" His boot lifted from her back, and his knees returned to the backs of hers. Rough fingers took hold of her labia and parted her sex from behind. Something stiff and slim and hard, she quickly recognized as the tail of his belt, pushed up into her sheath. "Fuck this belt, slave. Show me how much of it you can take."

He fed it inside her, doubled it up, and spread her until her pussy burned and a hot ball of electric sensation stormed through her from the sheer intensity.

Without warning, the other end of the belt whacked down across her exposed ass—fast, solid, hard. She jerked, and her nipples scraped along the ground, triggering a chain reaction in her pussy, throbbing her clit. "Oh, God."

The belt came again, the doubled-up tail pumping into her creamy sex in tandem. Tension dragged at her eyelids until they were clamped shut. Her face pressed tight against the grass. Her hips stayed in place by some magical force other than herself. She wanted to move them. Wanted to grind her cunt against the hard earth.

I need to come. So badly.

The pressure of Ken's knee changed until she could feel his lower stomach pressing against her back. His breath teased across one of her earlobes, hot and tawdry, chanting a near-silent warning, "Don't you come."

"I can't stop," she risked wailing, risked one little wriggle of her mound against the forest floor. *"Not when you treat me this way."*

The pressure shifted again as he straightened. She expected to feel the lash of the belt for her insubordination, hoped for it. Needed it to gain that final release. The tail end of it jerked from her cunt instead, and she whimpered.

Strong hands took hold of her wrists, gripped them, yanked her arms behind her back. Damp leather cinched around her wrists in the next instant, trapping them in place together at the small of her back.

"You're mine. All mine. I'll treat you however I want to treat you." Fingers shoved into her sex from behind, pumping up into her slick walls, sliding between her labia to caress the hard, aching pearl of her clit.

Now she would come. Now she couldn't help herself.

"Don't come without me, slave." Demand edged the order. *"You won't like the consequences."*

Oh, but she would. She always did.

With her ass and pussy afire, Leia panted an elated sigh against the ground. Even if their home never grew to more than one room. Even if they weren't blessed with children, so long as she had this man by her side, this man who catered to her most intimate fantasies and every secret dream, she would never have a want for more.

Sebastian's senses prickled with keen awareness as he stepped into the clearing that surrounded his home. With the spirit of the fox alive and pumping wild in his blood, he moved past the sedate log structure to the four-by-four slate of unremarkable flint emerging from the foot of a wildgrass-dusted hill.

Typically, he relied on Aubrie or another skin-shifter's loyalty and unabashed hedonism to keep his body engaged while he waited for the dying drags of an animal's soul and its power over him to wane. Tonight, even before he transferred through the flint, and the dirt that lay beyond it, into the holding area, Leia's ragged breathing echoed like a tempest in his ears, rousing his nearly half-decade-old want for her and her alone.

One booted foot on the hard-packed soil that was the cell's floor, his cock went rigid beneath the loincloth, and every nerve stood on end as his body primed to pounce. Nocturnal eyes of the fox cut through the darkness of fallen night to view her naked, erect form. His jaw tensed with how closely she resembled the woman he remembered—the one who snubbed materialism as fully as she embraced the darker side of ecstasy.

This was *his* Leia.

A true vixen, she writhed in the vines, all but shoving her bare, stunning breasts toward him. One arm had managed to work its way partially free of its binding. The fingers of that hand fondled her pussy from behind. With no hair blocking the view, he could easily see the slickness of her sex, the juices streaming down her inner thighs. How fiercely hard and red she'd worked her clit.

All while she slumbered.

The Camaloe had done its job, healed her minor injuries while starting her on the path to remembering. Now he must do his own job.

Ignoring the yearning the scent of her arousal stirred in his blood and the innate urge to leap at her and take her down, not as prey but lover, Sebastian moved forward.

As if she too were somehow caught up in the fox's spirit, her senses attuned as his own, her eyes opened with his first step. For a moment, her fingers continued to fondle and her gaze hung on to the mask of lust. Then the ice returned, her body going rigid. He'd yet to light the lantern that hung from the dirt wall behind her. While he could see her past the blackness, she shouldn't be able to see him.

"I know you're here." Leia's voice came cool with a touch of unsteady.

Sidestepping several feet confirmed she knew no such thing. She might be able to detect a change in the space's chemistry, but her attention remained fixed on the wall that doubled as a gateway to the outside world.

Wearing a smug grin, he continued over. "Good dream?"

Her head snapped around with his proximity. Her chilly gaze nearly even with his own, she jerked the fingers from her sex to join their still-secured mates behind her back. "Yes, I was dreaming that you were the one in vines."

Sebastian darted soundlessly behind her to slap a palm across a dimpled butt cheek. "Don't lie to me, slave."

The breath wheezed out of her with the whack. She jerked forward, placing nearly a foot between her body and the support rod. "Damn you, I wasn't lying!"

He filled the space she'd vacated, slipping behind her, pulling the softness of her rosy ass flush to his thighs. Pumping a finger into the slick valley of her sex, he coasted his lips along her neck up to her ear. "Bullshit." He gave the lobe a punishing nip. "You'd never get this wet in the role of master."

"The vines were wrapped around your neck."

Where Leia's words carried bite, the shifting of her hips in time with his propelling digit spoke only of want. Her pussy contracted as he changed course, caressing her clit with the rough pad of his finger. Erotic sensation spirited through her, building tight, wet need in her core while starting her pulse into a mad scurry.

And he felt it all.

For one brief, incredible, breath-stealing moment, Sebastian had back the fragile connection of mind, body, and emotion he'd once shared with her. When it came to detecting emotions in animals and those beings that were not of human origin, the empath gift was something to alternately value and scorn—if he couldn't sense their suffering, he wouldn't feel compelled to lighten it by taking on their pain himself. Leia was the only human he'd ever been able to read. Reestablishing that link full-time, knowing precisely what her body wanted and her mind refused to share, could only aid his quest.

He released a dark chuckle as her death threat caught up with him. "It's good to see Ken didn't kill all of your fight."

Leia went stiff, and for another fleeting moment, he knew the panic slicing through her as if it were his own. "How do you know about Ken?"

Fuck, he hadn't meant to share that knowledge so soon. Still, it wouldn't have to hurt anything, so long as he revealed only what suited the cause.

Sebastian shifted his body, letting her feel the hard ridge of his erection against her upper ass. The knuckles of his free hand stroked along her neck, down the side of a breast. "I know most everything there is to know about you, Leia. I know what he did to you. I know when I'm through with you"—turning his hand, he palmed the globe and gave the nipple a subduing squeeze—"when I've reminded your body what it craves, you'll be on your knees, worshipping at my feet with gratitude."

"*I* know that I *hate* you."

"Then you don't want my touch." Only, even without needing to read her emotions, he knew that she did.

He'd been gone longer than intended, seeing to the fox's end and surveying the area the fire had affected to ensure no others had been caught in its path. His influence over the Camaloe would have worn off while she slept, leaving her feeling empty and hollow inside. Aching to be filled.

She would be filled again, at his discretion. For now, Sebastian pulled his fingers from her body and went to the wall a handful of feet behind her.

A storage chest butted up against the wall. He opened it to find the razor and bowl he'd used earlier in the day had been cleaned and returned to their place in the chest by one of the skin-shifters, likely while Leia slept. Grabbing a lighter from a corner pocket of the chest, he lit the gas lantern that hung from the wall.

Dim light danced off the lush curves of her body, highlighting the flare of her hips and ass, and the dips of her sides. From her earlier comments, she'd allowed Ken's taunts to convince her that she was overweight. She *was* bigger than the women Sebastian had been attracted to when alive, but then when he'd been alive he'd been blind to a lot of things. Now, thanks to Leia, he saw truth, and he saw her for what she was—a centerfold blond bombshell.

Returning to her side, he took hold of the wrist that had come free of its binding. A silent incantation had the remainder of the vines uncoiling from around her breasts and arms. Without the vines and the rod to help her stand, her knees buckled. He caught her before she went down, steadying her on her feet, then pushed her toward one of the opposite walls.

Leia moved a step forward, then stood fast, turning to look back at him. In her eyes, wariness mingled with resentment. "What are you going to do with me?"

"Let you go to the bathroom. You've been down here for a number of hours. Your bladder has to be full."

She glanced toward the gateway door that was shrouded in darkness now more than ever. "There's a bathroom down here?"

"Do I look like a savage who defecates where I lie?"

"You'll hit me if I answer that."

His question had been meant as teasing. Her answer tightened his gut into painful knots with the memory of seeing her again, nearly three months after vowing to keep his distance. He'd come upon her in the woods, sobbing silently, bruised and battered from her asshole of a husband's filthy touch.

Christ, how he'd wanted to hold her. . . . Bodily, he'd kept his distance.

Not a second longer.

Grabbing her chin in his hand, Sebastian jerked her face toward his. Her eyes appeared huge, luminous pools of green, and fear filled every inch of them, tugging at his heart. "Many things I'll do to you, but never will I raise my fist in violence."

Slowly, the fear receded. "I meant you'd spank me again."

At least Leia seemed to agree now that his swats weren't in the name of hostility. Taking the perception as a step in the right direction, he pulled her to the opposite wall and nodded at the hole dug out there.

Mortification filled her face. "You expect me to pee in a hole in the ground?"

"There was a time you'd have done so gladly."

The shame lifted, replaced with demanding curiosity. "How do you know me?"

"I told you, we've never met." Inclining his head once more, he placed a palm on her bare shoulder and applied commanding pressure. "Go if you're going to."

She moved into a semisquat position before idling to press back against the weight of his hand. "I can't do it with you watching."

"Then don't. Either way, you have thirty seconds."

"What then?"

"Then the Camaloe returns." He gave in to a wicked grin, one both for show and that revealed his true anticipation for revealing the highly sensual, naturally exquisite woman lying dormant within. "The gentle pace you enjoyed earlier, the one that soothed you to sleep, that's gone, slave. From here on out, you work for the right to rest."

4

He's going to sleep with me.

The idea of Sebastian lying next to her, touching, possibly holding her while she slept should pale when compared with the degrading things she'd endured in this underground cell and those forthcoming, far more despairing ones he'd hinted at. But the words continued to rally through Leia's mind, the idea making her skin feel crawly as she gracelessly squatted over the hole carved out of the dirt.

No matter her struggle to shut his presence from her mind, Sebastian's gaze heated the back of her head. At least the lighting was dim. That small measure of comfort eased through her enough to fight off the weary strain in her thighs and relax her bladder. The arousing effect of the Camaloe obviously masked the urge to pee, because she hadn't realized how badly she'd needed to go until a sigh of relief slipped between her lips.

"I'll take that as a thanks."

Leia almost laughed at the arrogance in his words and tone. Allowing her to piss in a hole in the ground, such a gentleman. *There was a time you'd have done so gladly.*

She frowned with the reminder of his accurate words. There'd been a time when she'd have turned down her now-toasted Manolo's and shredded designer clothes for the joy of bare feet and faded denim, and been damned glad for it.

How could he know her so well if they'd never met? He couldn't.

Unless he'd known Ken . . .

It would explain so much. Particularly, how Sebastian could know to speak the same demanding words Ken had spoken to her that day near the stream, when he'd used his belt to alternately paddle and fuck her.

No, that day never happened. That was just a dream, conjured up as a side effect of the Camaloe. Ken had been a decent guy once, but she'd never been a woman who thrilled in pain. No matter what Sebastian believed, she never would be.

Leia started to rise only to feel his hand return to her shoulder, splayed fingers pressing her back down into the squatting position. His free hand came between her thighs, wiping her with a damp towelette, as if she were as helpless as a baby.

Humiliation like nothing she'd experienced with her ex scorched her cheeks. She jabbed her teeth into her lip to keep from railing into him. But, goddammit, that was it! By his accounts, this was her first day in this cell. Even if his vow not to raise his fist in violence was sincere, she wouldn't spend another hour here, enduring his future plans and playing along with his wicked games.

Lifting his hand from her shoulder, he commanded like some high and mighty asshole, "You may rise."

She obeyed, rising to a standing position while her pulse began a frantic beat, then darted for the black abyss that was the mysterious fourth wall. There had to be a door hidden in the darkness. An exit she *would* reach first.

Escape. Freedom. *Dear God, no midgets please.*

"You only serve to hurt yourself."

As if he'd taken possession of her mind, Sebastian's words echoed through her head seconds before they reached her ears. Mentally batting them away, along with the thunder of her heart, she kept running.

It seemed forever her feet plodded against the dirt, her bare breasts jostling until they ached from the movement and fatigue pulling at her limbs.

How could the cell suddenly have grown so big? Minutes had passed, at least five, and she hadn't even reached the darkness yet.

Her breath wheezed out. A searing pain started in her side. Sweat dripped into her eyes, hazing her vision.

Hell, she wasn't *this* out of shape.

Afraid to look back, even more afraid to keep going without knowing how closely he followed, Leia glanced over her shoulder. Shock toppled her. Sebastian stood unmoving less than two feet away, arms hanging at his sides while warning reflected in his dark eyes. The hole she'd relieved herself in was just as close.

Not possible. Not *freaking* possible!

Incredulity had her feet halting without warning. She crashed to her knees, her hands hitting the dirt next, fingers outstretched but not supportive enough to stop her descent. Her face connected almost as an afterthought, cheek kissing the cool ground, naked ass thrust in the air.

She lay prone on her belly, floundering like a fish, with her master directly behind her. Just like that day with Ken at the stream.

And like that day with Ken at the stream, wild thrill chased through her, moistening her pussy with anticipation while her nipples abraded the hard earth.

Damn it, no! That was just a dream. She didn't want this. Wasn't aroused.

Yet, her sex quivered as she waited for Sebastian's knees to come down against the backs of hers, the feel of his workboot pressing against her lower spine. The push of his strong fingers deep into her sheath, driving her insensate with need.

She waited for reasons she couldn't fathom, could only think to blame another for continuing to control her desires. Waited for nothing.

He never touched her. Never spoke.

Fury balling that was as senseless to Leia as her arousal, she pushed her palms against the dirt, intending to stand. Fingers shoved into her hair and yanked her sharply to her feet before she could make a move. Shards of ache rippled through her head as fury turned to alarm. The pain evaporated then, and the potency of his big, hard body so near had arousal threatening to outweigh panic.

It made no fucking sense. Only escape did.

Panting for air, she looked ahead, into the darkness, to the exit that had to be so close. Would she make it this time if she ran? Would he let her go if she tugged hard enough?

"Don't do it, Leia." The heat of his breath sizzled along her nape, eliciting shivers along her spine. "The risk isn't worth the reward."

It was if the reward was freedom.

She wrenched hard, jerking her hair from his grip as pain shot through her scalp and into her temple. Her feet huffed against the ground, bare soles attacking the hard soil. This time the blackness drew closer. Sweet relief jetted through her.

She was going to make it. Going to get out of this hell.

The blackness enveloped her. Tears of gratitude welled in her eyes.

Yes. Yes, please. Just let me get out of here.

Fingers wrapped around her ankle in the next instant. Dread swallowed relief whole, recklessly pummeling her heart against her ribs. She went down fast and hard, the breath sailing out of her as she slammed onto her belly and breasts.

"I told you no," Sebastian reproved.

"I told you I *hate* you." Adrenaline had the words growling out even as it kept her moving, crawling. One hand to the next. Inches. Bare inches until her fingers touched down on something hard. Not wood but . . . dirt?

The mad beat of Leia's heart came to a standstill as disbelief rocked through her and, for a second or two, she forgot to breathe. A wall. It felt like a wall. No, it couldn't be. It could not be another damned solid wall.

It is.

The silent confirmation repeated in her head, not her own thought but placed there by another. By *him*. And yet, somehow, she knew it to be the truth.

"There's nothing here." Her words came out feeble, frightened. Desolate. She couldn't stop it, couldn't stop more tremulous words from following. "But h-how do you come and go? How d-did I get down here?" She angled her neck in an attempt to view the night-blackened moss and root ceiling. It had to be the answer.

"It isn't," Sebastian supplied, as if he was once more in her mind.

The lantern light behind them grew brighter. Rays of light pierced through the darkness, until she could see the width of the wall her palm rested against. The fingers gripping her ankle released, and he came up on his knees to place his hand against the wall beside hers. Only, his fingers didn't remain flat. His hand moved into the hard-packed earth as easily as if it were sliding into finely sifted sand.

Skin, bone, and muscle eased into the wall until his arm disappeared nearly to his shoulder. Leia's throat constricted with harsh reality, acquiescence dodging her mind's disbelief while sickness ate at her stomach.

There truly was no exit from this hell. She was trapped for as long as he willed it. And he really was what he claimed, neither alive nor dead. "You're a ghost."

"No ghost. Just a master. *Your* master." He spoke words, something short, soft, foreign. Something that had her arms jerking behind her back without her consent and more of the damnable vines binding her wrists together. "Playtime's over, slave."

"You don't need Aubrie." Leia's voice shook with the observation as Sebastian took hold of her joined wrists and hauled her to her feet.

He spun her around and slid his gaze the length of her delectable curves. Feeling the effect of ogling her naked body as a needful throbbing in his groin, he deliberately misunderstood her. "You're offering me sex?"

Anxiety flooded her eyes, and she darted her gaze away. Within seconds, she looked back, coolness in place of her alarm. "To *bind* me. You don't need Aubrie or anyone else to physically tie me up. You can do it with your mind."

"I've learned, Leia, to not take anything for granted. You never know when someone might take an arrow to your heart."

"You were murdered?" She gasped as incredulity and compassion took over her thoughts.

The fragile connection between them was growing stronger, his ability to read her coming more frequently. Without knowing her emotions firsthand, he'd never have believed she could feel pity for him, not after just discovering how truly trapped she was, not so soon at all. Much as he savored that connection, he didn't want her damned pity. It called upon his own, made him weigh her inner fears, and that she might not yet be ready to move on with the remembering.

Sebastian spun her back around and pushed her toward the wooden support rod. "I had it coming."

Leia stumbled with the force of his shove, the emotions storming through him making it harder than intended. She righted herself before she went down, feet moving double-time to keep her body stabilized as she continued to the rod. Reaching it, she turned back to eye him with wild wonder. "Jesus, what were you like to believe you deserved to die?"

"Heartless. Controlling. Manipulative."

"Even being murdered wasn't enough to change your attitude?"

He chuckled with the implication. "I can be all of those things still, but I'm not the man I was. Now, my pet, it's time that we see to your needs."

Wonder was forgotten with the narrowing of her gaze. He could see the venom lurking in her eyes, feel it surging through her body for his intimating she was no more than an animal for his keeping. Still, she remained quiet, subdued as she backstepped the last foot to the support rod and waited for the vines to reclaim her body.

The vines came around her. Not above and below her breasts, securing her to the rod as before, but a neat, thin, soft strip of it around her neck.

Leia's eyes flew wide. "You can't!"

"I can. You're mine. All mine. I'll treat you however I want to treat you." Purposely, Sebastian spoke the words he'd heard Ken use that day at the stream, over four years ago. That day he'd seen Leia for the first time.

She'd been such a life force. Naturally wild and beautiful. Unencumbered by the trappings of greed and materialism.

In her, he'd seen what he'd never been: free.

By way of her thoughts and actions, he'd come to understand all that he'd taken for granted. He'd learned to value the nature he'd been left to protect, to see the wonder in the landscape, and not just the profit to be had in paving it down to make way for another development. Because of her, he'd come to know true, unaffected happiness.

Because of him, she would once again know the same.

Leia blinked and then shifted, rubbing her naked thighs together, telling him how quickly his words thrust her, mind and body, back to that day with Ken, that erotic memory, or for now what she believed a devastatingly wet dream. Questions filled her eyes, but she didn't ask them, didn't speak a word, just turned her attention on the ground.

He couldn't read her emotions now, could barely see her face between the length of her blond hair falling across it and the shadows cast by the lantern light. Her subdued behavior was so far off from both the chilly front and turbulent inner fears she'd exhibited so far that he could guess she was sorting through her thoughts, trying to separate the truths. Time would be her best ally in that regard.

Time left alone.

Leaving her free of the support rod, Sebastian moved to the chest behind her. Aware of how often his body suffered while aiding those beings harmed in nature, Aubrie kept a fresh supply of Camaloe stocked for his use. Squatting, he pried the lid off an earthen container and coated two fingers in the gel.

After replacing the lid, he stood and turned to find Leia watching him. Her attention went to his fingers, the translucent green gel shimming there. Caginess flashed in her eyes. Shaking her head, she shuffled backward. "Please don't."

Damn, but he knew how much the pleading cost her. How frightened she had to be to allow it. With her wrists bound behind her and no viable means of escape, she could barely even put up a fight.

He couldn't let that get to him.

Sebastian repeated the thought, sating the compassion once again churning through him as he heightened the stakes in his favor by summoning a length of vine that extended from his hand to her collar. A brisk tug on the vine had her body propelling toward his.

She whirled into him full force. Her breasts crushed up against his chest, her pelvis pressing intimately into his thighs.

Terror sparked in her eyes. "I can't breathe!"

Having served its purpose, he dismissed the vine, though not for fear of her life. This close he could feel the tepid air leaving her mouth, feel the hasty but strong beat of her heart. This close he could sense the juices welling in her core with the charge of electric excitement pushing through her body.

Between fear and ecstasy lay a very fine line. He had no doubt Leia was in the throes of crossing it.

Sliding his hands up her body, Sebastian cradled the softness of her breasts in his palms. So long he'd wanted to touch them, to hold her this way. Relishing each beat of her heart against his, he rubbed his thumbs across her nipples until they flooded with vivid color and pouted for so much more. When it was his mouth he ached to provide that much more with, to take the tender, scarlet tips between his lips and suckle hard, he turned the cooling nip of the Camaloe on them.

"Oh." Sultry breath cruised past her lips as her hips shoved against his.

Bringing his lower half back several inches to safety, he pushed his gel-coated fingers into her body. "I need to go to the surface for a while." Her pussy sucked at his fingers, taking them deeper inside her slickness. Biting back his groan and the raw want to slam back against her slit and give her the hardness of his cock, he lined her inner walls. "This should keep you busy until I return."

Hating the move even as he made it, he pulled his fingers free and stepped back. Reducing the lantern light with his mind, he made his way toward the wall that was once again cloaked in darkness.

"A word of advice, slave." For the sake of his rock-solid dick, he didn't look back at the postergirl for ecstasy he knew she would make. "The more you resist your body's desires, the harder the Camaloe will fuck you. It won't stop for your pleadings. It won't stop until I will it to do so. Be a good pet, give in to your wants, and I just might let you sleep tonight."

Leia snarled at the wall that was once again encased in blackness. The cell felt bleak again, empty, and somehow she knew that Sebastian was gone. That he hadn't stayed behind, lurking in the darkness, waiting with baited anticipation for her to come undone with uncontrollable desire.

Smart move. He would only have been disappointed when she failed to deliver the show of orgasmic proportions he was expecting.

The Camaloe filled her as it had before, hardening until her vagina felt stuffed full, then starting into an insistent pumping. As he'd cautioned, this time there was no relief. This time it flexed inside her, contracting and expanding, pulsing. Flickering sensual ache throughout her pussy and into her limbs.

But she wouldn't come. She would damned well not climax when she was nearly convinced that it was him making her body want to do so. Want, period, at the hands of a stranger, of a controller. Of a man who insisted on calling her slave and holding her captive in a barren cell with no exit.

How could she come in those circumstances and ever respect herself? How could she have degraded herself by pleading with him not to coat her sex with the fresh Camaloe?

How could she want to fondle herself so maddeningly bad?

The Camaloe drilled into her sheath now, dodging up inside her like a frantically vibrating bullet. Only, this was no ordinary bullet. This bullet came equipped with a tongue. Its touch near sandpaper rough, it licked against her highly aroused tissue, lashed up into her core, and then darted back out again to circle the hard nub of her clit.

So real that if Leia wasn't looking down at her shaved sex and well aware she was alone in this cell, she would think someone was between her thighs, eating at her cunt.

She'd had a handful of lovers since Ken, but always she'd been in control. Always saw that things never went beyond her comfort level. Everything that happened here today went well beyond her control, into the forbidden. Into a dark, sensual place she didn't understand or want.

Liar.

"I'm not lying!" she bit back to no one. Or someone. Whoever the hell it was who kept sticking these phantom thoughts in her head.

Sebastian. Aubrie. Ken from his vantage at the devil's right hand.

Who didn't matter. All that mattered was she didn't want—

"Ahhh God!"

Electric sensation zapped through her like a bolt of sexually charged lightning as the Camaloe accelerated to an even greater speed, an unreal setting. Nothing replicable by human technology. The imaginary tongue moved with it, licking fiercely up into her pussy, whipping at her interior walls, mastering them, attempting to master her.

Succeeding.

The breath wheezed out of Leia, parching her throat while her sex grew unbearably tender, wet. Hungry. Her hips shoved forward, grinding at nothing but air.

She needed contact. Needed to feel Aubrie's skilled mouth on her again.

Or Sebastian's.

Yes. Those firm lips. Those arms corded with delicious muscle banded around her. His long, thick ebony hair sliding between her finger as the length of his steely erection slid into her from behind.

Touching her. Taking her.

The Camaloe, cool at first contact, heated to near burning. Her cunt quaked with the sudden change. Her legs trembled. She rocked as she'd done earlier. Now it wasn't a gentle or soothing or lovely sensation, but dark and needful and dangerous.

Dangerous to her peace of mind, to her sense of self.

What was she doing, wanting to give in, aching for it?

But, really, how shameful would it be to submit? He'd instructed her that the fucking sensation would only heighten if she fought her desire. She couldn't take any more than what she was already being given. Couldn't handle a harder, faster pace without her pussy splintering apart.

Somehow she'd partially escaped her bindings while she'd dreamed before, and her fingers flexed with the need to do so again. To bury between her labia and finger herself to a final completion before she lost her mind along with her pride.

Damn it, she couldn't do it. Wouldn't.

She didn't need to. The imaginary tongue did it for her. Ending its stabbing game inside her sheath, it covered her clit. Pressed hard at the tender bud. Harder.

Currents of heat and pleasure sizzled down her thighs, erupted in her core, and raced her heart with pure relief. She rocked back hard, until she felt the rod at her ass again, pressing firmly between her butt cheeks, calling forth Sebastian's wickedly sexy face, and his solid cock rubbing along her anus, shoving up into her asshole.

Oh, yes. Yes. So close. "Almost."

"Hungry?" A deep male voice sliced through the fog of ecstasy.

The tongue ceased its sensual torment. The Camaloe followed, shrinking inside her until it was nothing but a glimmering, needful ache.

Sebastian appeared before her clouded vision. His lips weren't firm as they were so often, but wearing the wickedly sexy grin from her illicit imaginings, the one that made her feel so certain they'd met before. Coupled with the low lighting, the grin carved shadows along his cheekbones, making them appear leaner than ever, him hungrier—not for food but something far more primal.

It was food in his hand, though—a covered silver platter of something that watered her mouth and flared her nostrils from the first inhale.

Leia's gaze cleared as the cutting edge of lust receded, and she realized he'd changed his clothing while away. He wore jeans now. Simple faded blue jeans and a black T-shirt. Attire she'd seen on any number of men and never felt affected by it.

The way the material molded to his chiseled body, exuding his sheer strength and dark beauty, affected her more than the wild look afforded by the loincloth. This look made Leia feel both intimidated and feminine by comparison.

Feminine ...

It was something she should feel naturally, given she was a female, yet she didn't often believe the word fit her sizable frame. Even less did she feel soft and small ... and cherished. An odd thought, yet somehow, as he stood there grinning, with friendly warmth lighting his typically obsidian eyes and holding food made specifically for her consumption, she did.

Damn his black soul for making her feel that way.

But she could use it. If any part of him truly did value her, then he wouldn't allow her to starve. If she refused to eat, he would have to let her go.

5

Sebastian sat the platter of food on the chest against the wall, taking his time in removing the cover to give his body a moment of reprieve. Changing his clothes had been a wise choice. If he'd been wearing the loincloth when he walked in on Leia, collar bound and so obviously near to orgasm, his cock would not only be sliding past the leather, but quite likely be buried inside her.

Pushing out a frustrated breath, he grabbed the platter of steak, broccoli, and a water glass, and turned back to her. "Sit down."

As she had before, she acted subdued, sinking down to sit cross-legged with her back against the wooden support rod and her tethered wrists resting against the rise of her rear. Her focus remained on the ground.

Hell, that was a mixed blessing. Sitting as she was now, her labia parted, he could see up into her pussy, see how deep pink and creamy the Camaloe had left her.

Food. She needs food, he reminded himself sternly.

Going down on his knees beside her, Sebastian rocked back on his haunches and stabbed a forkful of steak. "Open up."

Leia's gaze stayed downcast, her body still. Her mind wasn't so silent. He could see clearly the game she played. If there was one thing that hadn't changed when he moved into his middle life, it was his thirst for a challenge. This challenge he knew well he would win; still, he felt the white-hot adrenaline rush of opposition.

Bringing the fork to his mouth, he took hold of the tender meat with his teeth and pulled it from the tines. He didn't need those things considered basic essentials by mortals to survive, hadn't felt the pangs of hunger or the pull of exhaustion in nearly a decade. Still, he could appreciate the meat's succulent flavor, the juices that exploded over his taste buds. He let her know all about it with a groan of immense satisfaction.

Her lips quivered. Her nostrils flared. He was on the verge of laughing over her obstinacy when she looked up at him. There was hunger in the depths of her green eyes, oh yes, but it had as much to do with lust as famine.

"Dead people eat?" she asked.

"I told you, I'm not dead." Stabbing another bite of steak, he brought the fork to her mouth and pressed the tips of the tines against her lips. "Don't make me slice your mouth open. Eat."

You would do it, too, you bastard.

So stunned by how clearly her thought came to him, Sebastian almost missed that she took the meat into her mouth. He didn't miss that she spit it back at him. Steak and saliva bounced off his chest, and he fought an internal war of appreciation for the bold move and displeasure for how completely she disobeyed him.

The displeasure won out. It had to.

Balancing the platter on his thigh, he summoned a whiplike

vine into his free hand. Understanding dawned in Leia's eyes and mind, along with raw terror, seconds before the tail of the vine licked at the bare, rounded flesh of her belly.

Her mouth fell open with her gasp, and he shoved another forkful of steak inside. "Eat, Leia." Rough demand centered the words as he flicked the vine back into the air. "You need the energy." More important, he didn't want to have to swat her for real. The vine's lash had been little more than a stinging caress. He could change that, if she made him.

Disgust filled her for the action, but to his relief, she chewed— the bite of steak in her mouth and then two more. He brought the glass of water to her lips, letting her take down several long drinks before setting it back on the platter.

"You can conjure up anything at your will?" she asked as he stabbed a spear of broccoli.

Her voice was almost even, almost sedate. It calmed Sebastian's heart when he hadn't even realized how quickly it had raced. Earning her trust mattered. Making her like him along the way shouldn't. Much as he would tempt his chance of moving on by killing for that very thing, he couldn't have a future with Leia. She had a long life ahead of her. His was well past him. "I don't conjure up a thing. I merely transport items that exist in nature and use my influence over them as needed." He slanted a look at the vine whip. "I won't hesitate to transport something much larger and more painful than this vine, should I deem it necessary."

If only I could withstand the pain . . .

Still weak was her thought. She didn't yet understand her tolerance for the right kind of pain, her pleasure for the same. She would.

As the bite of broccoli slid off the fork and into her mouth, he summoned the Camaloe back into action. No soft pulsing that kept her aware of the herb's existence inside her sex as had been the case while she ate those first few bites of steak, but an insistent expanding and contracting that brought every sexual nerve in her body on end by the time she was done chewing.

Her mind told him that . . . and her moan.

Leia's eyes narrowed accusingly as the husky sound left her and her ass jerked off the ground, shoving her open pussy blatantly forward.

With a feral grin, he pushed another bite of meat into her mouth. "You always have loved your steak."

"It's not the damned steak," she ground around the meat.

She took that bite and several more down with huge, desperate chomps as he continually upped the Camaloe's pacing. In truth, nothing filled her but a thin layer of gel and his imagination, yet Sebastian could see her pussy spreading, parting wider with each wild pump. Her ass bucked off the ground again, and her arms wrenched at the vines securing her wrists together. The effect the move had on her breasts, making them jostle and dance, was too great to ignore.

He swatted the tail of the vine against one heavy mound. Red blossomed in its wake, brightening the flesh and puckering her nipples on contact. Her lips parted, hot air streaming out. Words threatened to follow.

"You won't speak another word without my approval!"

"You ass—"

The vine arced up, coming down between her thighs, to her parted juncture, where her pussy was swollen and ripe. She sucked in a violent breath and juices gushed from her sex. "That's what happens when you disobey me, slave."

Lust, raw and intense, sizzled in Leia's blood. Loathing gleamed in her eyes. Her cunt contracted wildly, more as he took the Camaloe from cool to warm, then warmer. In her mind, the gel grew in girth, filling her, fucking her in a way no mortal man ever had or could.

Her ass ground against the dirt, her thighs jerking up off the ground. He swatted her cunt with the tail of the vine, harder this time. Her eyes snapped closed and her head went wild, thrashing side to side, whipping her hair around her flushed face. "Stop! I can't take any more."

She could, though. So much more.

Coming to his feet, Sebastian increased it all. The speed of the Camaloe, the pelt of the vine whip. The heat pooling in her core, seeping its way outward and upward, into her belly and chest, until he could sense the incredible weight in her nipples. Feel how hard she fought the urge to come. Fought her own sensual nature.

"Just keep talking," he goaded.

I won't come. I won't.

She chanted the words in her mind, again and again. Even so, shudders quaked through her. Tension pulled at her from every angle, red hot and electric. He could feel it leaking off her, feel it inside his own body, in the hardness of his dick, in the violent beat of his heart.

He brought the vine down against her thigh. She squeaked and then mewled. "You had your chance to come freely while I was away. Now you won't come without my permission. Who am I? You may speak."

I won't come.

Don't fight it. You want this.

No.

Yes.

Body and soul dueled in Leia's mind until it seemed she wasn't even aware he was still with her. "My name?" he demanded, bringing the vine to her other thigh.

No.

Yes. Yes!

"Sebastian." The word whimpered out. Her eyes opened a fraction.

He saw it there. Need. Recognition. And finally, surrender.

Liberation from the guilt that plagued him from the first lick of the vine filled Sebastian even as he brought the tail whipping down between her labia to strike against her blood-red clit. "Wrong. Who am I?"

"A bastard."

No malice existed in the response. Still, it was disobedience that he met with another swat to her clit. "Try again. Who am I?"

"Master," she supplied in a low, needy, drugged-sounding voice. A voice that ensured she'd well crossed the line from fear to ecstasy. "You're my master," she spoke breathlessly. "Please. Please let me come."

He kept his sigh inside, just barely. "You may come, slave."

He couldn't keep his body anchored. Couldn't leave the job to the Camaloe and the erotic lash of the vine. Leia's eyes were closed again, her mind far gone with passion. She'd remember the exquisite pleasure and all that led up to it, but little about the final details. He used that knowledge for his own greed, allowing himself to go down on his hands and knees on the dirt, to bury his head between her fleshy thighs, and his tongue to spear up inside her cunt and lap at her cream.

"Uhhh . . . so real." Her hips shot up. Her pussy spasmed forcefully around his tongue as orgasm spiked and then sizzled through her.

Too real, Sebastian silently agreed while he devoured her luscious juices, lick for gluttonous lick. But if this was all he would have of her—all that he *could* have of her—then he had to take more.

Pushing two fingers into her hot, wet cunt alongside his tongue, he took her higher with teeth and lips and hands. Met her there as she fell from the crest of climax and took her right back to the screaming edge of orgasm.

The breath squealed out of Leia as she fought for air, for reprieve. Her hips attempted to rear back while her sex continued to grip his tongue tight. "I can't take any more," she sobbed.

You can. You have before, and you will again.

Without pardon, he tongued her sweet pussy, fucked her channel to the limit with the tips of his fingers, and thrust her right back over the edge, into a place where the lines of pain and pleasure mercifully blurred.

And she weathered it all. Weathered it for long moments with her eyes closed tight and a euphoric grin broadening her lips. Against his every burning desire, he pulled out of her body and came to his feet before that euphoria lifted.

The rapturous look passed too soon. Her eyes came open to fill with accusation. Worse, though, was the shame he could sense settling over her.

"I didn't want that," she snapped. "Any of it. You plant feelings in my mind, make my body think it enjoys it when you treat me like your slave. That doesn't change the fact that I hate you."

Fuck, the want to pull her into his arms . . .

Sebastian laughed instead. "As much as I enjoy the ego stroking, I'm simply an empath who can read the occasional mind to go with feelings, not a sorcerer who wields passion as his magic." Squatting beside her, he took her chin in hand. "You want everything that I do to you, Leia. *Everything.* And you don't hate me. Far from it."

He released her chin, and with an uttered incantation, the vines were gone from her wrists and a mat lay beside her on the dirt. Taking hold of her arms, he trailed his thumbs over the thin skin of her wrists, lifting away any ache the vines may have caused. "Sleep, slave." His fingers went to her thighs, slipping past to caress the tender, dewy folds of her labia. "Morning comes early and I have many a pleasurable thing planned for you and this most luxurious of pussies."

Leia jerked awake with the sound of someone behind her. *Sebastian.*

Damn it, she'd been so relieved when he'd left her alone to sleep last night, and now something that felt too much like delight filled her to think he'd returned.

He was turning her into another person. Someone she didn't know. Didn't understand. Didn't like.

Don't you?

Preferring to face her captor rather than the answer, she rolled on the bed mat. It wasn't Sebastian who looked down at her but Aubrie. The elfin-eared, white-haired midget was in female form and naked once again, her smile as brilliant as the red of her lips. Her gaze didn't meet Leia's own but fell hot on Leia's crotch. Leia was well aware that the scent of sex clung to her skin. Given how eagerly Aubrie handled her yesterday, it was probably all she could do to abstain from a morning tonguing.

Unless she didn't plan to abstain . . .

Belly tightening, she shot to her feet. "Where's Sebastian?"

"He has a full morning. He asked that I take care of you."

Take care. So much those words could mean. And if they meant the worst, would Leia have a chance of fighting Aubrie off? "Do you have his powers?"

"I'm as mortal as you are, just not of the same race." Aubrie's gaze lifted, meeting with Leia's own. "Would you care to use the toilet before breakfast?"

"You mean the hole in the ground?" The remnants of desire died from Aubrie's smile, replaced with amusement, and Leia added, "Do I get to wipe myself? What about breakfast, will I be allowed to use a fork that I operate?"

"Sebastian does those things because he cares for you."

So seriously the words were spoken, but no way could they be sincere.

You felt cherished by him last night.

Only for one blind, stupid second. After that she felt . . . something else. First, sympathy to know he'd met such a violent end. And then . . . and then something else. "All he cares about is getting off on my misery."

"Skin-shifters are mortal, but one thing they can't do is lie." Again, so seriously were the words spoken. Maybe Aubrie just didn't know him that well. Or more likely, Sebastian had taken over the midget's mind as completely as he'd taken over Leia's, and she believed she was speaking the truth.

"What about Sebastian? Is he allowed to lie?"

"Yes, though doing so would not bode well for his situation. As you can guess, He frowns upon liars."

Leia frowned at the inflection on the word *He*. "*He?*"

Aubrie looked up at the moss and root ceiling, where the rays of morning sun were once again peeking through. Leia realized then that the female's thoughts were focused well beyond the forest floor. Past the Earth as she knew it and into the heavens.

"The Camaloe worked well." Aubrie's fingers touched down, stroking the inner curve of Leia's thigh.

Leia's attention jerked back to the cell, to the small hand caressing her as its owner beamed over the magical herb that had become the bane of Leia's existence. It worked well, all right, to blind her once more and steal away any chance she had at fighting off the orgasm. And another orgasm on top of that one. Both stronger than anything she'd ever known.

Both incredible.

"Your injuries are healed," Aubrie clarified. A salacious smile pulled at her lips as her fingers traveled higher, up Leia's thigh to brush against her shaved mound. "You're right, though. It also serves other purposes well."

"I have to pee." Honestly, with the arousal moistening her sex over the memory of last night's orgasms, Leia wasn't even certain she could pee. She'd force it out if she had to. Anything to end Aubrie's advances.

"I've left a bowl of warm wash water and a towel." Aubrie

gestured to the items sitting a few feet from the makeshift toilet. "I'll be back soon with breakfast."

Elated over the thought of cleansing her body of dirt and sex, Leia didn't bother to note how Aubrie left the cell. She hurried to the bowl of water. The bowl was six inches deep and another six around, reminding her of those times in the winter when she and Ken had had to bathe from a bowl of stream water heated over the woodstove. Simple living that, in the early part of their relationship, had led to simple pleasure.

God, her life had changed so much the last couple years.

For the better?

In some obvious ways, yes. But had she let materialism become her? Had her attempt at erasing the violent months she'd spent with her ex shaped her into a woman she didn't know or like even more than what Sebastian was doing to her?

The questions wrapped around Leia, stewing at her mind as she used the hole in the dirt to relieve herself and then washed from head to toe. The questions still consumed her thoughts when Aubrie returned with a covered platter, like the one Sebastian had brought to her last night, in her hands.

Leia's stomach growled with the delicious smells coming from the platter. She realized aloud, "I'm famished."

"Eggs Benedict." Aubrie lifted the cover off to reveal a glass of orange juice along with the promised dish. "Sebastian made it for you before he left. He said it was one of your favorites."

"Did he know Ken?"

"I couldn't tell you. I've never heard the name."

"He was my—" *Abuser.* "Never mind." Even if she could voice the words she'd never spoken aloud, Leia wouldn't reveal them to Aubrie. "What is Sebastian's situation? If he's not alive or dead or a ghost, how can he exist?"

"He's in his middle life. His fate was undecided when he died."

"Fate? Like whether he goes to Heaven or Hell?"

"Mostly, yes."

"Mostly?"

"I can't say more." Aubrie held out the platter of food. "Eat before your food cools."

Accepting that nothing she could say would make Aubrie reveal more and not about to give the midget a chance to do the feeding, Leia took the platter and sat cross-legged on the mat. After taking a drink of juice and setting the glass near her thigh, she forked a bite of hollandaise-glazed eggs into her mouth. A dusting of green herbs covered the sauce cresting the egg-and-bacon–covered muffins. For all she knew, it was what Camaloe looked like in its native form, and eating them would send her into a state of uncontrollable lust. Right now, she didn't care. Right now, as the rich scents cloaked her senses, her stomach growled so intensely it was as if she hadn't eaten in days.

Aubrie sat on the ground several feet away, mirroring her cross-legged stance. Ignoring the way the midget's gaze coasted over her naked body, Leia dug in and ate and drank with relish. If she could say nothing else nice about Sebastian, he was an incredible cook.

Five silent minutes later, with a sated smile, Leia handed the plate and glass back to Aubrie. "Thank you. It was wonderful." She glanced at the plate, which she'd given serious consideration to licking clean, and a touch of embarrassment slid through her. "Guess that explains my fat ass."

"You have a beautiful body," Aubrie assured as she set the plate and glass aside, and came to her feet. "One that responds to pleasure the way every human would be lucky to have happen." She went to the chest against the wall.

Leia had tried to open the chest before falling asleep last night, in the hopes of learning what other fates might await her inside. The lid wouldn't budge. Aubrie merely lifted the front edge and the lid rose without hesitation.

Pulling out a length of vine, the female grinned. "You'll love this."

"What is it?" Leia asked uneasily. It looked like any other vine, and in that way she could guess it was another tool to be used against her.

Against, truly?

"Ecstasy," Aubrie supplied, contradicting Leia's panicked thoughts, agreeing with those darker ones that were escaping her mind more and more.

Those darker ones that had her sex dampening as the midget returned to her. Leia had all but forgotten about the collar around her neck. She remembered it now with clarity as Aubrie harnessed the vine around her middle and then drew it between her thighs and tight against her labia before securing the tail end firmly to the collar.

6

Sebastian stayed away until the shadows were long on the holding-area floor, darkness nearly fallen. Throughout the day he'd honed in on Leia's thoughts and emotions, more often than not able to make a clear connection.

She'd been waiting for him, hours now, torn between placing a name on her wait: whether it was impatience because she was eager for whatever sensual game he might choose to play or because she feared that game and her response to it, and wanted it over with.

He hadn't been torn over a thing.

He knew damned well why he'd kept his distance. Why tonight he had to push her even further until she was left with no questions, only pussy-drenching facts. Then he could release her. Then he could get her away from him, before he forgot they had no future and made her his by taking her in every way imaginable.

As she had yesterday, Leia seemed to sense his emergence through the dirt wall. She shot up from the mat to glower at him. "Where have you been?"

Sebastian grinned arrogantly, loving what her expression revealed even as he hated it. Loving how exotic she looked with her hair mussed and the vines looped around her neck and waist, and threaded between the folds of her sex, even as he hated that, too. "Missing me already?"

Am I? The way I jumped to my feet like a good little pet would make it seem so. But no, that was just because I've had nothing to do for hours but stare at dirt. And think. And be too damned conscious of the crotch vine's constant rubbing against my clit. My freaking soaked clit!

The frown left her face as she eyed her sex. *How can something meant to constrain be so arousing?*

Shifting her gaze to the ground, she sank back onto the mat, knees curled under her. "Never."

Biting back a broader grin, he crossed to the chest against the wall and sat down. "As I said yesterday, this is my home— this holding area and the woods that is over us. It's my job to take care of it and see to the welfare of all that live within it."

"You don't see to all." The resentful words came snapping out of Leia's mouth. Immediately, her head jerked up, regret for voicing her feelings overt.

Sebastian's grin evaporated. His body tensed as the painful knots that always emerged with thoughts of her abuse slid into place.

With shadow-hooded eyes, he called out to her courage, dared her to speak of his failure to keep her safe. "Who or what have I missed?"

"I . . ." The need to place blame on his shoulders was wild in her eyes, the clenching of her hands in her lap. Censure filled her mind. Not for him, but rather for herself and what she viewed as her own pathetic actions those months where she'd endured her ex's wrath.

Courage losing out to shame, she looked back at the ground. "No one."

He frowned at the top of her head. That response wouldn't do. The time for her weak thoughts had long since reached its end.

"Are you certain, slave?" The dark question rolled from his lips as he stood. Summoning the vine whip, he arced it out, enlivening the tepid night air with a blistering crackle.

Once more, Leia's head shot up. Wildness returned to her eyes, not fearful this time, but dark green and hungry with lust. She eyed the tail of the whip—that same tail that had licked at her belly, her thighs, her cunt—and he could sense her sex, already so wet and needful from the erotic play of the crotch vine, go molten.

I don't really want it. I've never wanted it. Have I?

Long seconds, she considered the silent question only to fall to the safe side. "You're not seeing to my welfare now."

"I've seen you cleaned and fed. Allowed you to sleep and use the bathroom. I've given you two unforgettable orgasms, with plans to deliver more of the same. How is it that I am not seeing to your welfare?"

When he put it like that . . . But no, sleeping on a mat in the dirt and peeing in a hole were hardly things to relish. Soul-stirring orgasms and amazing cooking also changed nothing. "I don't want to be here, in this godforsaken cell. I want my life back."

"That, slave, is precisely why you *are* here." Sebastian lashed the vine whip out again, this time directly in her path.

The tail swatted against her breasts, one generous globe at a time. Twice in succession. Leia gasped for breath as the thin tail flicked her nipples taut and red before moving lower to meld with the vine cinched around her waist.

A snap of his wrist had her jerkily propelling to her feet, her body zipping toward his. Last night, he'd done much the same. But last night her hands had been bound, keeping them from splaying out in front of her in wait of the impending crash. And last night, the crotch vine hadn't been in place. The hard tug of the vine around her waist spiked forceful pressure downward to where that same vine nestled between her labia.

"Ooh . . ." The cry left her mouth as a ragged sigh. Her hands moved from preparing to brace for impact to cupping her mound, attempting to tug at the vine holding her pussy captive. *Ah, God! Heat. Wet. Hurt.* "Too much. It's too much!"

Mentally dissolving the vine he'd used as a rope, Sebastian caught her in his arms. "Wrong, slave." The words whispered, dark and decadent, along the sweaty skin of her neck. Sitting back on the chest, he pushed her onto her belly over his lap. "Not nearly enough."

Not now when he had the most succulent of treats inches from his hands—her ass, plump and rosy, the crack lined enchantingly with the vine that continued to her sex.

He palmed the roundness of a butt cheek, pleasuring in the silky texture. Liquid excitement trickled from her sex to dampen the thigh of his jeans.

Squeaking out a mewl, Leia tightened her cheeks. *Yes, please. No. Maybe. Maybe I'm losing my freaking mind.* "I don't know what the hell I want anymore, so just do it already! Spank me."

Even as his body panged with needful ache, he sighed his relief for her words of acceptance. Words he would love to take her up on. But that end would be far too fast and easy. As high as the relentless rub of the crotch vine had her, a handful of swats and she would climax. Tonight, orgasm would come at his hands, but also at those of reality.

Sebastian continued the coast of his palms along her ass, cupping and squeezing the supple flesh. Circling the sweet spot of her asshole. Petting the highly sensitive flesh inches from her cunt.

Hot breaths panted from her lips. Her heart beat a staccato rhythm. Parting her thighs, she shifted eagerly as he moved his fingers past her perineum to fondle the rear of her sex and begin what had to be her final lesson in remembering. "There are things that happen in our lives that make us blind. Things that are so horrific we choose to shut them out. We erase entire months, years. Our dearest dreams, our darkest desires. That happened to me. And that happened to you. Someone opened my eyes. And now, slave, I'm opening yours."

"I didn't erase—"

He cut off what would be an unintentional lie on Leia's part, with first the shove of two fingers into her pussy, then the lengthwise press of a newly summoned short, smooth stick between her lips. Hand on her jaw, he forced her to bite down and clamp it between her teeth.

The eager shifting of her thighs turned to trembles of fury. Rage seethed through. Rage she took out on him with the biting press of her nails into his legs.

What the fuck—You bastard!

Inwardly, Sebastian smiled, so pleased with her continued bravado. Outwardly, he pulled his fingers from her sex and smacked her ass hard. One time for punishment, and one time to take her higher and make her ache for more. "Spit it out and just see what a bastard I can be."

She hesitated, breathing deeply, loudly through her nose before allowing the smallest of nods. He rewarded her by taking the crotch vine between thumb and forefinger, and strumming the engorged pearl of her clit. "That's a good pet."

A sound between harrumph and husky moan escaped around the stick, and he continued the idle strumming with a wickedly knowing smile. "I was a developer before I died. I wasn't an empath then, but I could still read people, spot their tells. Their weaknesses. I was the best at what I did. Everyone knew it. If a company was after a piece of land an owner was adamant about not selling, they would come to me, have me do the dirty work. I did it, for a hefty fee." His smile grew thin, condescending. "I had all that money can buy. And then I died at the hands of a landowner who wasn't any too pleased about being blackmailed into selling his property, and I realized what a joke my mortal life had been."

He laughed without humor. Even after all these years, the sting of what an unseeing prick he'd been smarted damned badly. "I had nothing but what money can buy, and the things I bought never made me happy. Something you know all about." He allowed another punishing swat, one that left her cheeks fanned with deep pink while it elicited a whimper and a wriggle. "Eight hundred dollars for a pair of shoes when we both know you'd rather go barefoot."

Tsking, Sebastian gave the crotch vine a tug. Her pelvis ground against his thighs, connecting her juicy sex with the solid ridge of his erection. He curbed his groan even as hers pushed past the stick. *Damn you, they were more than shoes!*

Pulling the crotch vine taut, he demanded, "Tell me."

No! Leia checked the grinding of her hips as her fury resurged, along with it the shame. *You can leave me imprisoned here forever and I won't share a word.*

"Because I didn't protect you? I allowed Ken to beat you?" Self-disgust he couldn't keep inside colored the words. He'd called her weak, but he'd been just as weak. Just as fearful.

How can you know that? How can you hear my thoughts?

He couldn't be weak now, couldn't cave to her sudden rush of panic. Keeping the crotch vine pulled taut, he worked it back and forth across her clit. "Nothing is withheld from your master, slave."

And nothing was her response.

She didn't think, didn't feel. Didn't even moan or whimper when he increased the tension on the vine, all but torturing her clit with the intensity of carnal pressure. Wetness soaked through his jeans after nearly a full minute. At first, he'd thought she come silently, inertly. Then the emotions barreled through her, hot and raw, embraced in a war between revulsion and gratitude, and he knew it was tears of confusion swimming in her eyes, drenching his thigh.

God, I hate you.

"So you've said," Sebastian acknowledged, keeping his tone stern while he fought the urge to comfort. "As I've said, you don't hate me, Leia. Sometimes, though, I hate myself. I hate the weakness that made me stay away while Ken abused you." Just as he hated the weakness that resurfaced against his will now, giving him pause for his next move.

Crushing that frailty with a mental vise, he grabbed hold of the vine around her waist and hoisted her off his lap. The pressure from the vine sliced downward once more, pressing fiercely against her clit and raising another long, keening whimper around the stick as he planted her on her feet. He left her standing for the space of a heartbeat—a beat he felt thick and sour in his throat. Then he shoved a hand at her back and sent her sprawling for the dirt.

Leia saw the dirt coming long before her body connected with it. She would have had time to protect herself, to avoid a painful collision. She would have if her mind, body, and soul weren't condensed into the tiny bud of her clitoris, consumed with the need to come. She landed as she had last night, prone on her belly with her breasts, already so heavy and aching with arousal, taking the brunt of the pummeling. The breath hissed from her mouth. The stick came out with it, spitting onto the dirt.

Sebastian's weight came over her, his knees pressing hard against the backs of hers. She expected him to growl at her, to shove the stick back between her lips while he produced his vine whip and swatted her for her disobedience. Instead, his torso pressed against her spine, muscles so solid and firm and sinfully, deliciously good.

Bringing his head low, he brushed aside her hair. The ends of his own hair teased along her nape as he whispered hotly, "This is how I earn your forgiveness for my failings. By reminding you what was. What should never have stopped being. What has always been more than a wet dream."

The press of his upper half lifted, the shivering warmth of his breath leaving her neck, until only his knees trapped her in place.

His knees, his words, and his actions.

"No panties," he uttered in a sickened tone.

A mock sickened tone, Leia recognized. Acknowledged. Trembled as her blood fired hotter in wait of what she was suddenly so certain would follow.

The flat of his palm connected with her butt seconds later, swatting the cheeks and leaving a sting. Not a delightful sting like that day with Ken at the stream. But a needful one, a hungry one. An urgent one.

"What'd I tell you about not wearing panties, slave?"

Was that day at the stream not a memory? Was it real? And what of the phantom thoughts? Were they not phantom at all, placed there by Sebastian or any other, but her own dearest wishes, her own darkest desires?

She didn't know. Wasn't sure of anything any longer. Not more, at least, than the white-hot thrill of unspoken promises pushing through her. Not promises made by her dead ex, but those made by this undead god of a man.

Her pussy liquid with need, her mind almost desperately demanding her to play her part, she panted out, "S-sorry, Master. I forgot."

"I'll have to make certain next time you remember." Glinting command and dark promise edged his words, lifting goose bumps on her skin.

The weight of his body left hers then, quickly replaced with the weight of a lone booted foot against her back. She didn't want to fight back—not knowing the lash of a belt would fall faster if not for her struggles. She did it anyway, stuck with the choreography of recent dream or latent memory, fighting the pressure on her spine, struggling to push herself off the ground and away from the tickling sweep of dirt against her lips.

Material swooshed against material. On cue, Leia stilled. It wasn't the crack of leather that split the air, but the unforgettable short, quick snap of his vine whip.

"Oh . . ." Her pussy surged, no minor fluttering of expectation, but the deep, delicious furling of near-imminent orgasm.

Unbridled tension and excitement burst through her, clawing at her belly and breasts, blistering an inferno of wet, pulsing heat in her core. From the corner of one eye, she caught the movement of the tail of the whip flicking into the air. Slowly, it arced downward, lashing out, licking into the soft flesh of her buttocks. Not hard enough to leave its mark on her body, just hard enough to leave its mark on her unbearably growing need.

Yes. Yes. Yes!

Stinging heat spiraled down from the hyper-tender tissue to the pool of juices flooding her cunt. Catching her lip in her teeth, she fisted her shaking hands at her side and waited, accepted, knew he'd been right all along.

She loved this. Loved every darkly sensual moment of this game.

Is it a game? Or does Sebastian believe it more?

The whip rose higher this time, the downward thrust licking at her ass with a decadent nip that coursed from her scorching sex to the tips of her throbbing nipples. She squirmed on the ground, biting her lip harder to keep from pleading for release.

But why? Did she even care if he thought it more than a game?

"Did I tell you that you could move? You do nothing without my command. Nothing." His boot lifted from her spine, and his knees returned to the backs of hers. Rough fingers took hold of her labia and parted her sex from behind. With Ken, the belt had followed. With Sebastian, she wanted more. Real. Him.

"Please don't," she cried out.

Wry laughter edged with rough lust spilled into the air. "You want this, Leia. You want every inch of this whip inside you, fucking you to explosion."

"No, I want you. I want every inch of your cock inside me, fucking me to explosion."

Sebastian's breath dragged inward, the sharpness of the sound echoing as an urgent pulsing in her cunt. His hands went still for several seconds where she knew pure, pulse-thundering desperation. Then they returned to action as if she hadn't spoken, pushing the tail of the vine up into her sheath.

"Fuck this whip, slave. Show me how much of it you can take." He fed it inside her, doubled it up, and spread her until her pussy fired from scorching to blistering, and a hot ball of electric sensation stormed through her from the sheer intensity.

She knew to expect the other end of the whip coming down on her ass, and still it managed to take her off guard as it whacked solid and fast. Punishingly hard. Mind-spinningly good. She jerked, and her nipples scraped along the ground, triggering a chain reaction in her cunt, throbbing her nearly numb clit with the most exquisite of painful pressures. "Ah, God."

The vine came again, the doubled-up tail pumping into her drenched sex in tandem. Fierce tension dragged at her eyelids until they were clamped shut. Her face pressed tight against the dirt. She couldn't keep her hips in place the way she had with Ken. Couldn't halt the want to move them, to grind her mound against the hard earth.

The pressure of Sebastian's knee changed until she could again feel the press of his torso against her spine. His head bent, moving past her nape to tease the ends of his hair and his breath across her earlobe.

Hot and tawdry, he chanted a near-silent warning, "Don't you come."

"I can't stop!" Leia wailed, wriggling her cunt against the dirt. Knowing in that moment, when not a single touch of shame filled her for her unabashedly carnal behavior, that no one had planted desirous cravings in her head, no one but her maker when he created her. "I have to come now, with or without you!"

The tail of the whip jerked from her sex, triggering the orgasm she could no longer hold back. It washed over her, huge and violent, shaking her deep inside, past pleasure, past pain, to the recesses of her mind, her body. Past a place where she could keep her eyes open and plead with him to fill her with his cock, join her in orgasm. To a place where she could cling only to the unknown, to the unsteady. To the maelstrom of memories unraveling in her soul.

Since Leia taught him to value the simplicities that life had to offer, Sebastian had always been able to find peace in nature. Tonight, he found no peace in the woods that surrounded him, the moonlight cutting down from overhead to bathe the forest floor in myriad colors. Tonight, he knew only the weakness of leaving Leia, lost and blind, in the clutches of orgasm.

Frustration churned through him, eating at his gut. Discontent clung to him like a first skin, stifling his breath. Not that he needed to breathe.

He was dead. Not technically, but near enough.

He could fuck her, the way she'd begged, but to what good? To make his already near-reckless want for her deepen? To make her want for him grow as well?

He couldn't do that. He could only see that his words and actions tonight had registered with her as completely as he believed they had. He could only let her spend one last night alone, asleep on the mat in the holding room, and then let her free come morning.

Giving his tension time to ease, Sebastian walked on. Minutes. Hours. He had no idea how much time had passed. He only knew that when the pain came, it was near crippling in intensity.

It ripped through him, leaving his abdomen feeling torn apart. Stealing his breath in those first moments when his mind fully aligned with the creature this pain came from. The animal's thoughts came to him slowly . . . undeveloped . . . helpless.

Christ, a baby.

Able to guess at the sickening scene that would meet him, he followed the shattering call of his senses, moving swiftly through the bramble and copse. Seconds passed by as agonized minutes before the thicket finally let up. The cub lay feet ahead, a jagged-tooth bear trap clamped down around its small body, nearly shredding it in half.

The frightened clacking of the yearling's teeth was almost nonexistent, lending little hope for survival. Approaching cautiously but quickly, Sebastian dropped down on his knees and felt for the cub's life source. Air feathered through its tiny lungs, waning with each breath until there could be no mistaking the animal was beyond help.

Weakness coursed through Sebastian for what was too damned many times tonight. He'd learned to respect death and value the cycle of life. Still, he knew more pain from the need to end the cub's suffering than what pain actually transferred into his body from bringing that end about. Cradling the cub in his arms, he soothed its mind as he'd already begun with its body.

A noise trapped between high-pitched moan and heavy breathing sounded as the last of the yearling's spirit lifted into his body. A familiar noise. A noise that had Sebastian's heart pummeling in his chest as he whirled to stare into the eyes of a fully grown black bear. Many times he'd come across the mother bear while traversing the woods. Always, she'd recognized and respected him for what he was, her ruler. Her protector.

Tonight, she reminded him of Leia in those first long hours that he'd held her captive. Too far gone with distress to see truth past misery.

The bear saw only vengeance, in shades of furious red and black. And Sebastian saw only finality, in shades of hazy orange, as the bear bounded at him, slamming into him with 500 pounds of fury. Ripping into him with hooked claws, tearing at muscle, flesh, and bone.

Making his first death by an arrow to the heart seem almost humane, almost painless by comparison.

7

Over an hour had passed since Leia came down from the grips of a life-altering orgasm to crawl onto her bed mat and curl into a weak-limbed ball. Exhaustion and tenderness pulled at her from every angle. Darkness had long since flooded the cell with black.

Still, she didn't sleep. *Couldn't* sleep.

Last night, she wanted nothing less than for Sebastian to lie next to her and hold her while she slumbered. Since the day she found the strength to leave Ken, she hadn't allowed any man to stay in her bed longer than it took to screw. Tonight, she ached to feel Sebastian's strong arms around her, holding her captive in the truest sense. And tonight, he was gone, left without a word. Without even waiting for her climax to end.

"I should hate him."

Hell, she'd tried to convince herself that she *did* hate him for the cruelty of his handling. Tried to convince him of the same. But Leia didn't hate him. Not after what he'd done for her—opened her eyes to the reality his handling wasn't cruel but, rather, everything she craved. And not after having heard the anguish in his voice when he spoke of his failure to protect her from Ken's abuse.

If Sebastian had known her ex-husband, it wasn't from an amicable standpoint. The two men could be no less similar, her feelings for them no further apart. Ken she would never regret was dead. Sebastian she regretted only not knowing while he was alive, when missing him served some purpose because they at least stood a chance at a future.

Tomorrow, he might return to her. But soon their days together would end. Just as she could always somehow sense his presence before he entered the cell, she knew he wouldn't keep her with him much longer. He would set her free to return to the city. To the friends and colleagues who knew nothing about the real her. To a life she'd built knowing nothing about the real her either.

Vowing to change that the moment she was free of this cell, Leia closed her eyes and once more attempted sleep. Eventually, her fatigue must have won out. The next thing she knew, she was being awakened by the plodding of feet and a chorus of keyed-up voices.

Brilliant light filtered through her eyelids, snapping her to alertness. Without moving, she opened her eyes to survey her surroundings. As when she opened her eyes the first afternoon in this cell, her surroundings were nothing she could have guessed. Dirt walls still encompassed her, but near to a dozen short, nude, white-haired skin-shifters now filled the cell with her. Unlike that first day, not one touched her. Not one even seemed to realize she lay curled up on the mat in the cell's far corner.

Currently a mixture of males and females, they moved about the small room conversing in excited voices while gathering strips of cloth and earthen bowls from the wall chest. The bowls, of what she could now see was Camaloe, were set in a wide circle on the ground. The skin-shifters stood around that circle, holding hands and rocking their bodies side to side as they chanted in some low, foreign tongue.

The chanting grew louder, their swaying faster. The air warmed, thickened, crackled with tension. For an instant, Leia considered she was about to witness some archaic orgy. Then she caught the unease that weighted each of their vivid blue eyes, and sickness rose up in her belly. Sickness she recognized all too easily for having experienced it days on end for months in row when she'd endured Ken's drunken wrath.

Her ex-husband was gone, not stuck in some middle life awaiting his final judgment—that much she was now certain of—but straight to Hell. Something else surged her panicked sickness. Some*one* else. For the skin-shifters to be in her cell in such an anxious state and without Sebastian at their lead, that someone had to be him.

Shoving to her feet, Leia demanded, "Where's Sebastian?"

Even with the force of her words, not a single shifter looked her way, instead carrying on as if she hadn't spoken. She bit her tongue around that insult.

Son of a bitch, she would *not* be ignored.

Rage and desperation tangling in her mind, she darted her gaze around the circle of pale-skinned midgets until it landed on Aubrie's once-again female form. Hurrying to Aubrie, Leia took hold of the female's arm, breaking the circle as she spun her around. "Where the fuck is Sebastian? What's happened to him?"

Something changed then. Something in the air. Leia knew even before Aubrie nodded past her with huge, solemn eyes that Sebastian had arrived. Tonight, now, she could sense more than his presence.

She could feel his suffering.

The sickness in her belly turned to a coiling of pure dread. Slowly, she turned to face the dirt wall that served as his doorway. Her heart galloped into her throat at the gruesome sight there; the man who looked nothing like her sinfully sexy captor, yet she knew with sickening clarity could be no other.

"Please, God, no." The prayer whispered out on a shaky breath.

Without words, the skin-shifters surrounded Sebastian's far bigger body, lifting him off his booted feet as a unit and placing him on the ground the same way. They labored over him feverishly, tearing away the remains of his tattered clothing, applying fresh strips of cloth, cloaking him with Camaloe. Stealing all but flashes of his body from Leia's sight.

She could still see it vividly in her mind, though.

So much blood. So goddamned much blood covered his shredded body. Skin gaped open in some spots and hung in limp patches in others, revealing that the muscle and bone beneath had suffered the same dire consequences as the rest of him.

For long seconds, she could only gape and gasp and fight the bile churning in her throat. Then survival kicked in. In many ways, he'd saved her, given her back a life she hadn't known she'd been missing. She owed him for that, owed him nothing less than everything.

Leia attempted to shove her way past the laboring midgets, only to be knocked backward and thrust onto her butt in the dirt. Snarling, she leapt to her feet. God saw fit to gift her with a big ass, and right now she saw clearly His logic. With her ample hips and ass paving the way, she pushed back into the pack, this time refusing to be deterred.

She emerged on the other side victorious and nearly smiled over her feat. Nearly until her gaze fell on Sebastian's mangled form. He lay less than a foot away. His eyes were closed, and long black lashes fanned their undersides. Sweat consumed his body while his breathing came far too shallow. She could only guess the skin-shifter's circular chanting had somehow guided him back here—no way could he have made it on his own.

"Get out of the way! You can't help him!" Aubrie shouted.

Leia met the female's eyes and growled, "I'm not going anywhere."

Small but strong hands grabbed hold of her arms from behind, yanking them painfully behind her back. "Leave, human. You're not wanted here," a male voice retorted.

More hands joined those first ones, jerking her backward, dragging her across the dirt, away from Sebastian.

Madly, she twisted her torso and wrenched at her arms. "Goddammit, let me help!"

The hands kept pulling, blunt fingernails digging into her flesh, gouging at the soft tissue until she could see no more than his bared feet. *Please,* she pleaded with her mind, praying he could still somehow read her thoughts. *Please let me help you.*

"Let her go. Let her see what I am."

Sebastian's voice was low, thready, and still she recognized it. Still, her pulse spiked with hope. He was conscious. He was asking for her.

Again, she thrashed at the arms holding her in place. "Let me see him. Let me see him!"

The hands released. The pack of skin-shifters parted. She raced those few precious feet to Sebastian's side. Falling on her knees in the dirt, she dipped her fingers into a bowl of Camaloe. Coating his torn body with the herb that healed her in more ways than one, praying all the while she wasn't hurting him further with her ministrations, she met his eyes. "What happened?"

"I killed someone." Malice reflected in his voice.

Leia's hands shook as she applied the herb to another wound, and his muscles lurched beneath her touch. Holy Jesus, how could he ever recover? "You're hurt so badly."

His eyes narrowed. "I said I killed someone, Leia. How the hell can you care if I'm hurt?"

"How can I not?" Such little time they'd been together, and

yet, somehow, she felt she'd known him far longer, remembered him from another time. He'd been adamant about the fact that they hadn't met previously. He'd also been adamant about the fact that he would never raise his fist in violence. She believed that first a lie, the second honest truth. If he'd killed someone tonight, it had been done in self-defense. "Tell me how to fix this."

Sebastian's glare remained intact, his lips firm and unyielding for nearly a minute. His mouth curved then, slowly and slyly, into a devilish grin that lent an edge of danger to the air while it raised the fine hairs at the back of her neck. "You want to make it better?"

"Yes." No matter the sudden bolt of fear coursing through her, she would do anything to heal him. At her nod, his hand came up, sliding past her cheek to grip her unkempt hair with brute strength she couldn't believe he still possessed.

A madman's laugh, high-pitched and manic, rolled from his mouth, echoing off the cell walls as he forced her gaze to fall on his cock. Not limp or injured like the rest of him, but solid and thick with arousal. "Then suck my dick, slave," he goaded. "Take it all the way inside. Show everyone what a good little pet you are."

Leia sucked in a stunned gasp. Humiliation burned through her body, blistering her cheeks. She hadn't given a thought to her nudity from the moment she'd awoken to find herself with equally nude company. Now, she realized how exposed she was. How many eyes watched her every move. Eyes that still held concern for their master but, now, also open desire.

"Do it!" Sebastian roared, his grip on her hair intensifying to the point shards of pain tore through her skull.

To hell with the skin-shifters. To hell with this ultimate invasion of privacy. If it meant sacrificing her pride after only just getting it back, she would do it. "Yes, Master," she uttered almost silently. Then she took his member between her lips.

He moaned with that first contact, low, long, and keening. A sound caught between pleasure and pain, heaven and hell. Moving her mouth up and down his steely rod, Leia licked from oozing tip to throbbing base, loving his hot taste and silky texture even as she felt guilt for enjoying herself in his moment of need.

Taking the sac of his testicles in one hand, she gently massaged his balls. She risked releasing his cock then to feed his nuts into her mouth, savoring the taste and texture of those too. Crisp pubic hair teased her upper lip and nose, raising a sneeze out of nowhere.

Her mouth worked around his balls as the sneeze released, her lips opening and then clamping down hard without intention. Sebastian grunted, and his battered thighs went taut, muscles contracting around her upper half, locking her body in place between his legs.

The action was so reminiscent of every other sensual game he'd played with her, Leia's pussy pulsed with expectation. Meeting his eyes with apology in her own, she brought her mouth back to his sex, gobbling his cock up and sucking it deep.

Without acknowledgment, he jerked his gaze away. "Heal her, Aubrie."

"But, Master, she's not injur—"

"Do it! The right way."

Past the deliciously erotic pumping and pulsing of his shaft in her mouth, Leia detected the caution in Aubrie's voice. Warning threatened at her mind. No time did she have to reflect on that warning before the female's fingers moved between her thighs from behind, probing the shaved lips of her pussy, then pushing briskly inside.

Not with fingers, but with tongue.

Like the first time Aubrie ate at her cunt, the female seemed to know her body intimately, knew just where to lick and suck to have her sex slick and heavy with want. Instinct registered the urge to fight back, to block the invasion. Sebastian's staying grip and the upward shove of his hips in time with the downward thrust of her mouth wouldn't allow her to listen to that instinct.

He needed this, needed her.

Leia repeated the stabilizing thought in her mind again and again as the female's tongue, teeth, and lips feasted on her pussy, and electric sensation built like a tempest in her core. Sebastian's cock moved faster between her lips with each of Aubrie's heightened pumps. The female slipped a finger inside Leia's sheath, working it together with her tongue, and heat chased through Leia like a wildfire, racing her heart and boiling her blood.

She knew wildfires. Knew how dangerous they could be. Knew it was a wildfire of her own creation that had her here now with Sebastian. Sucking his cock with relish, moaning around his hard flesh for each of Aubrie's feverish moves, she paid him back for putting out her fire, for giving her back her life. And he paid her back in kind by shooting his cum into her mouth.

His seed slid down her throat, hot and silky, and coupled with Aubrie's continual mouth fucks, more ecstasy than Leia could bear. Panting around his cock, she gave into her own orgasm, coming around Aubrie's tongue as wave after wave of pleasure rippled through her.

"That's good, isn't it? The feel of Aubrie's tongue in your pussy, making you come and then sucking you dry?" Sebastian's voice was hard, his tone mocking.

Playing a game. Playing another game, Leia thought distantly, oblivious to her surroundings as her heart boomed and mini-tremors rocked her to the core.

"Bet you didn't know your tastes ran that dark, did you, slave?" he continued in the acerbic tone. "You like it rough. Like it when a guy swats you around a bit, when he jams his dick up your asshole." Aubrie's tongue jerked from Leia's sex, and a hand swatted across her ass, hard, stinging. Not bringing to life dark passion but brutal pain that squeaked a cry from her lips. "You're just another dirty girl. A toy made for a man's amusement. No amount of running's gonna change that."

The hand he gripped her hair with released to take hold of his cock and pull it from her mouth. He bounded to his feet then, bounded up and knocked her backward, making her topple Aubrie in the process. Bounded as if he'd never been injured at all.

Past his bitterly taunting words, Leia remembered with shameful clarity how injured he'd been and how, in the wake of pleasure, she'd forgotten all about it. Despite his behavior, his body was still torn. Blood still caked his bruised and battered skin, and lay thick and acidic on the air.

He seemed oblivious to his pain now. The sense of his suffering was gone from her mind as well. As was Sebastian gone from her sight, as he stalked to the dirt wall and moved directly through it.

Forgetting his jeers and her shame, she shot to her feet and darted to the wall, pounded at the solid earth until her knuckles stung. "Goddammit, come back!"

A small hand settled on her upper arm. "He's not in the right mood, Leia." Aubrie spoke in a voice mingled with lust and compassion. "He can't listen right now. Can't respond to you as the Sebastian you've come to know."

Then who the hell could he respond to her as?

Fear for his safety lodging emotion in her throat, she turned to regard Aubrie and was taken aback at the sight of the other skin-shifters. Not only did she forget Sebastian's injuries, but she'd been so rapt in pleasure, she'd forgotten the other shifters were even in this cell.

Embarrassment rose up anew. Disregarding the slow burn in her cheeks, Leia addressed the group as a whole. "How can you just let him go? There's so much blood."

"It's not his," Aubrie explained. "Sebastian's heart beats like a mortal, but no blood flows through his veins. He can't die in the traditional sense. He can only move on."

"Then the blood . . . It belonged to the person he killed?"

"The bear, yes."

Bear? "He was that crazed over a bear? I thought he killed a human. Or one of your kind."

"Bear, human, or shifter doesn't matter to Sebastian. He's the protector of this land. It's his job to keep all safe. When he fails to do so, when an animal dies, he feels it's his duty to take on their suffering. In a way, he becomes that animal. Not in body, but in spirit, in actions."

The emotion in Leia's throat thickened as the grim possibility in Aubrie's admission caught up with her. She swallowed hard, fighting to keep her voice from trembling. "Will he move on tonight because of his injuries?"

Aubrie looked to the wall he'd left through. When she looked back, uncertainty filled her eyes. "He should be okay. Later tonight. Or by morning. Will you?"

"I don't know." How could she when Aubrie looked so unconvinced of her words? When even if Sebastian was miraculously okay, she now knew with certainty their days together would soon come to an abrupt and final end?

Earlier tonight, Leia knew she wouldn't like leaving him. Now, she acknowledged that she would hate it, and that she would do everything in her power to see that moment never came to pass.

8

Sebastian had no right returning to Leia, tonight or ever. She wasn't his, the way he'd once taken such great pleasure in pretending. After the merciless way he'd treated her earlier this night, handling and taunting her in a manner befitting her asshole of a dead ex, the mere thought of his touch would likely sicken her.

He had no right returning. But he had to go to her anyway.

Not bothering to dress, he slipped through the back door of his log home and traversed the short stretch to the slate of flint emerging from the hillside. He'd loathed killing the black bear, but thoughts of Leia wouldn't allow him to lie idly in wait of his next life while the animal ripped him limb from limb. If he hadn't returned, one of the skin-shifters would probably have seen to her release. Probably hadn't been good enough, not where she was concerned.

The enraged bear's spirit was out of Sebastian now. With his body healed and his senses his own, he could detect Leia's heightened breathing and anxious thoughts before he cleared the dirt wall and stepped onto the holding-area floor.

Immediately, her head jerked up. Eying him head to toe, once and then again, she rose from the bed mat. Flickering light from the wall-mounted gas lantern shone in her eyes, drawing out joint forces of trepidation and relief. "Sebastian." His name slipped quietly from her lips. "You came back."

Christ, she looked so worried. So upset to think she might never see him again, that no one might ever see him again for the extent of his injuries. Just as he had no right returning, he had no right opening his arms to her, or even believing she would want them. He opened them anyway, opened them and hoped like hell she filled them.

She didn't move. Didn't do anything more than stare at him for long seconds while his heart slammed into his ribs. Then, slowly, a smile curved her lips.

Crossing to him, Leia hugged his body close. "I was so afraid for you."

The words whispered hot and moist against his chest, and it struck him for all that went on the last days, for all the times he'd watched her in the grips of passion over the years, they'd never been this intimate.

Sebastian wanted to drop his mouth to hers and kiss her with every ounce of the tenderness he'd been forced to deny. Instead, he just held on, just accepted he was lucky to be getting even this close. "After the way I treated you, what right do you have to be worried about me?"

She tipped her head back, chin digging against his chest. "Most of it I loved. What I didn't enjoy, you couldn't help."

"What makes you so sure?"

"Aubrie told me about the bear and how its spirit entered your body. Even if she hadn't, it wouldn't have mattered. I know you'd never hurt me, or anyone else intentionally."

She sounded so positive, her thoughts so strong and self-assured. If it weren't for knowing their futures could never be intertwined, he would have admitted his love for her then and there.

But he knew what the future held. And he knew he could never admit how long ago he'd fallen for her.

Releasing her, Sebastian crossed to the wall chest and sat down. "I've been deceiving you, Leia. I deluded you into thinking you're a submissive who needs a master to make her feel complete. You aren't. Binding you, forcing you to call me master, holding you captive . . . It was the only way I knew to make you remember the truth of your desires. You like the darker side of ecstasy—thrill in it until your body's little more than a dripping wet pussy—but that isn't all that you are. All that you need."

Leia nodded, acquiescence filling her eyes as she started over. "You're right, it isn't. Not now. Not tonight." Going down on her knees on the dirt at his feet, she took his hands in hers. "You've opened my eyes, Sebastian. Allowed me to see clearly what my body craves. Right now, there's only one thing it wants. One man."

Hell, he shouldn't even consider the sensual offer simmering in her eyes, the unconcealed emotion and lustful thoughts that accompanied it. But how could he say no? How could he turn down this lone chance to make love with her?

He couldn't.

Pulling her to her feet as he came to his own, he led her to the mat in the corner. The natural and free Leia he'd first come to know wouldn't have a single problem making love on a mat. How completely the Leia with him now had reverted to that Leia of years ago, he wasn't certain. "I have a house. With a real bed."

"Tomorrow we can use it." Slipping her hand from his, she lay back on the mat and opened her arms to him, her legs. "Today I want this place. *Our* place."

There would be no tomorrow for them. No *ours* of any kind.

Choosing to ignore that abhorrent reality, Sebastian went down on his knees and crawled between her legs. So sweet and pink and damp her pussy was for him. This time, he didn't stop to consider his actions or fight guilt, but brought his mouth to her opening and tasted her essence. Stroking his fingertips along the soft skin of her inner thighs, he licked at her labia with lazy swipes, luxuriating in her taste. Delicious. Creamy. A taste he could easily get lost in.

He loved her sex with his mouth for long, languid minutes, until her cunt pulsed seductively around his tongue and her hips bucked up with her moan. He turned his lips on her thigh then, kissing a warm, wet path from inside to front to outside.

Leia released a sound caught between squeal and giggle. "That tickles."

Ticklish. He'd never known that about her. He liked that added familiarity, too damned much.

Turning her onto her belly, he concentrated on making good on his vow from that first day by brushing his mouth over a dimpled butt cheek and kissing the supple flesh.

Sighing, she came up on her hands and knees. Her legs parted several inches, exposing the tight hole of her anus and the swelling folds of her vagina. "Will you take me this way?"

It wasn't a question filled with reservation but hope. A sign she was ready to embrace her darker desires, to admit she needed more than vanilla from her lovers. In answer, Sebastian brought his lips to the union of her buttocks and kissed his way down her crack.

His mouth pressed against the rosette of her asshole, and she reared back against his lips. "Yes. Please. Fuck me with your mouth, Master."

He was no longer her master, never had been, and she knew it. It was just a game she played now. A dark, delicious game that throbbed his solid cock as he moved his mouth to the rear of her cunt and slipped his tongue inside.

He milked her pussy, pumped into it with long strokes—first gentle, then forceful. Gentle again when Leia whimpered and her limbs trembled as if she might come. With the push of his tongue into her silky passage and the press of his lips around her clit, he took her to the edge, again and again. Never quite letting her fall over it.

Pulling her hips forward when he would have again slowed the pace, Leia panted, "I need to come. I need to!"

He didn't need to come. Like sleeping and eating, it wasn't an essential of his existence. But he wanted to come. Wanted to push into her and lose himself completely.

Sebastian didn't do that yet. He refused to end their time together so quickly. Instead, he brought his mouth back to her crack, his lips to her anus. Palming her shaved mound, he slipped two fingers into her pussy in time with the push of his tongue into her asshole.

Gasping, she contracted her sphincter muscles. "Ahhh . . ."

Relaxing those muscles, she moaned again, a lulling tremor of sound he felt as a needful twinge in his groin. His pulse clapped like thunder between his ears as he eased his tongue farther into her tight passage. Feasting on the tender, moist tissue, he used his fingers to devour her cunt, stroking the slick inner walls, pumping up in time with each thrust of his tongue, finally allowing her to fall over that edge and bathe his fingers with the gift of her cum.

Her hips propelled with the force of her climax, her ass thrusting back to work his tongue faster inside her body. His own orgasm clawed at his gut and spine, tightening the skin around his dick and snugging his balls. He held on to his need, held on and let her ride out her climax. Then he let her take the lead, let her have control over him in a way he'd never allowed a woman, in his mortal life or his middle one, to do.

Juices trickling down her inner thighs and the heady scent of her arousal thick in the air, Leia came up on her knees. Playfulness glinted in her eyes as she smacked his hip. "Get on your back, slave."

Unable to stop his smile—not so much over her actions but how far she'd come in such a short time—Sebastian went. He lay on the mat, and opened his arms and legs to her, the same way she'd done for him. She didn't pace herself as he had, but jumped onto his lap and impaled her pussy with his cock.

She inhaled on a sharp breath, eyelids flickering partway closed, and her stunning breasts jiggling like the best kind of aphrodisiac.

He filled his hands with the plush mounds. Drawing the erect, rosy nipples between his thumbs and forefingers, he applied pressure and twisted until she squeaked, taking her right back as his captive. "Now, who's the slave?"

You, Master. Always you.

Maybe. Maybe not. For now, he went with it. Grabbing her around the waist, he brought her onto her back on the mat and pushed his cock deep inside her once more. He lifted her ankles to his shoulders and slid deeper still, to the recesses of her sex where she was molten and liquid. Where he could feel each beat of her heart deep down within.

Where he would gladly stay nestled forever.

Neither circumstance nor Leia allowed it. Squeezing her muscles tight around his cock, she arched her hips. He took hold of her ass cheeks and met her halfway, pumping downward with her upward thrust. They fell into a rash, wild unison. Bodies slamming together, skin sliding against sweat-slicked skin. Mouths stealing for air as primal instinct took over.

The thrash of her hips stilled suddenly. Ripe color flooded her cheeks. Pinching her eyes shut, she cried out, "Now. Now!"

Her pussy clamped down, squeezing his cock as she restarted into a feral bucking. Cream flooded out, surrounding his shaft, drenching it. He gave in to his spent control, flooding her body in return, coming into her with a violent surging of his hips and a blistering inward curse.

Sebastian let her sex continue to contract around his with the aftershocks of her orgasm. He let himself stay right there and hold on to her, pretend she could still be his.

A half-minute's worth of forbidden fantasies filled his mind before she opened her eyes to smile sleepily up at him. "I never knew the ground could be so comfortable."

The fantasies burst, and the cause of his curse—a damning bleak reality he could no longer ignore—took hold.

Sliding her ankles off his shoulders, he set her feet on the mat and scooted backward, away from her centerfold curves. Away from her emotions churning hot through her body and mind. Away from the only woman he'd ever truly given a damn about.

Rolling to his feet, he stood and headed for the chest against the wall. He'd asked Aubrie to stock a fresh set of clothes for the day he chose to release Leia. He pulled out the white shorts and pale pink T-shirt now, wishing the skin-shifter wasn't always so eager to do his bidding and resolute about doing it right.

Without meeting Leia's eyes, he tossed the clothing at her. "Put these on."

"Why? Is something wrong?"

Concern weighted her voice, and he had to tune that out too. Had to not even attempt to read her thoughts. "Yes."

"Another animal?"

"No animal. You, Leia. It's time for you to go."

"*What?*"

Against Sebastian's will, his head snapped up with the force of the word. Denial lifted into her eyes. He steeled himself against that denial, steeled his voice so she couldn't mistake this for another game. "You're going home. Back to your city with its high-rise buildings with white marble floors that echo the clack of your eight-hundred-dollar heels."

Denial turned to staunch objection. Glowering, she stood to cross her arms. "I won't go."

So strong now. At least this time when he sent her away, he would know she took both her lost memories and her lost courage with her.

"You have no choice," he snapped back.

Leia didn't move, just continued to stand and glare at him. Out of options, out of time, he strode to the mat and jerked the clothes up. He shoved them at her. "Get dressed!"

Her nostrils flared, but otherwise she didn't flinch. "I don't want to go back to my damned heels, and I don't want to wear these clothes."

Son of a bitch. Why did she have to make this harder than it already was? Grunting, he dropped the clothes to the ground and grabbed hold of her around the middle. Hoisting her over his shoulder, he strode to the dirt wall that served as a doorway to the outside world. "Then you'll leave naked."

Her breath feathering hot and tauntingly against his neck, she pounded at his back. "Don't do this, Sebastian! I belong here. With you."

"The choice isn't yours to make."

The pounding ceased. For a moment, her attempts at swaying him did as well. Then she continued in a quiet voice. "The heels were a metaphor. They represented my severance from Ken. From the way he . . ." Pausing, she drew an audible breath. "From the way he abused me. From my finding the strength to walk away."

Shit, he knew what that admission had cost her. Knew she'd never voiced the words aloud. He knew it didn't make a damned bit of difference. Holding her tight against him, so her body would move through the dirt as easily as his own, he took her through the wall and deposited her on the other side. Daybreak was nearly upon them, soft fingers of pale pink and orange light spearing the horizon. He loved this time of morning. He knew she used to love it as well.

Now, only blind fury filled her.

Sebastian took a step backward, one foot and leg easing through the flint and the dirt beyond that. "Good-bye, Leia. Don't let your mind convince you the last days were just a dream." He moved the rest of the way into the wall then, away from the loathing in her eyes. But not away from the sound of her voice.

Her fists pounded against the flint. "Goddamn you! Let me in, you chickenshit."

He kept moving, kept going until he was back in the holding area. Always before, this place had felt like a second home to him, natural and hushed, a place to think, to escape. A place where he'd indulged in countless fuck sessions with Aubrie and the other skin-shifters—both those meant to stay his feral urges while he waited for an animal's spirit to leave him and those sessions meant solely for pleasure.

A place that felt empty now, lifeless and dank.

He didn't need to sleep. But he went to the mat and lay down anyway. Waited with his eyes closed and his mind devoid of further thought as the minutes turned to hours so that he could be certain Leia was gone.

"Master?"

Leia? No, the feminine voice wasn't even close to hers. "What is it, Aubrie?" Sebastian asked without opening his eyes.

"It's time."

"Time for what?"

"To move on."

Eyes speeding open, he shot to a sitting position. "Christ, you can't be serious. Now? Today of all the fucking days?"

Aubrie cast her attention to the ground and nodded solemnly. "I'm sorry, Master. I only deliver His bidding."

The irony was, a week ago, he would have been thrilled to have her deliver the news. Now that Leia had returned to his life, he could barely stomach the thought. So long as he remained here on Earth, there was at least a chance they could meet again. "How soon?"

"By nightfall." Her gaze lifted from the ground, trolling slowly up his body, lingering hot on his exposed cock. A carnal smile curved her vibrant red lips. "Shall I gather the skin-shifters to give you a proper farewell?"

A week ago, the offer of a final orgy with those who had become like family to him would have been well received too. Now he couldn't even work up the energy to get aroused. "Thank you, but I need to see that things are left as cared for as possible."

"Another will take your place."

Rising, Sebastian started for the dirt wall that doubled as a doorway. "And they'll hate the duty as much as I did when I first came here."

"Yes. But in time that will change."

It would, too, he knew. Someone would come along to change that next man's jaded viewpoint on being dumped into a middle life, just as Leia had done for him. Would that other man ultimately fail the person who helped him see truth? Would he be standing here after a decade, realizing his middle life was ending on just as shitty of a note as his mortal life had?

Despite her exhaustion, Leia didn't sleep. As was true last night, she couldn't sleep for missing Sebastian. The difference this morning was she had a bed beneath her naked body—a mattress that felt like pure ecstasy at her back. And the difference this morning was that Sebastian wouldn't be returning to her.

She'd held out hope when she found his home. She'd never

seen it before, and yet, one step inside the sedate log structure and she knew it was his place. She could sense him. Sense his presence and hold out hope that, eventually, he would return.

But hours had passed since she'd come inside and helped herself to a modest snack. Another hour since she'd lain down in his bed and inhaled his scent lifting off the sheets. She couldn't sleep, and he wasn't coming back. She might as well just go. Accept what had to be.

He was a freaking dead man, after all. No, not dead, just not alive. Just not able to give her a chance at the future she craved beyond logic.

"Leia?"

Leia's thoughts came to a standstill with the deliciously familiar deep voice. Almost afraid to look for fear it was her mind playing tricks—phantom voices this time—she glanced toward the bedroom door. Her heart raced at the sight of the wickedly sexy undead man standing there.

Oh, God. It wasn't her mind playing tricks.

Sebastian's gaze narrowed. "What are you doing here?"

He didn't look happy to see her. Well, screw him. She was here and she wasn't leaving, even if it meant locking them both inside this bedroom and throwing away the key. Maybe they had no chance in the long run, but they could have a damned fine time in the short run.

Sliding to the edge of the bed, she eyed him past lowered lashes. Courage that she'd forgotten she possessed drove her to her feet, had her sashaying across to him, thrusting her breasts out while her lips curved naughtily. "I told you I'd be here." She planted her palms on his chest, thrilling in the play of hard muscle beneath her fingertips. "I said tomorrow we could use your bed, remember?"

Sebastian's breath drew in. Desire lightened his eyes, taking away his hard look and making her think once more that she'd known him well before this.

He lifted her hands from his chest to move to the end of the bed and sit down. "How long have you been here?"

Leia frowned at the question. At the realization of how peculiar he was acting. She thought he wasn't happy to see her, but now it seemed something else was at work in his mind.

Forgetting the seduction game for now, she offered, "Almost five hours. I wandered around for quite a while, trying to find my car. I couldn't find it, and somehow I ended up right back where I started. At least, I thought it was where I started. I've never seen your house before."

"It wasn't visible to the human eye. Just as I wasn't unless I chose to be so."

Wasn't? "What's changed?"

"I don't quite—" Stopping short, he stood and went to the dresser near the door. He lifted a pocketknife out of the top of the dresser and flipped open the blade. Leia gasped when he dragged the edge of the blade across his palm. Blood oozed past the freshly cut skin, pooling quickly in his palm and dripping onto the rug beneath his feet.

Sebastian looked up at her dazedly, then back at his hand. "I've moved on."

Dread coiled in her belly. She wanted to be with him, but at the cost of death? "But if you have—if this is Heaven—then I'm dead too?"

"This isn't heaven." Opening the top dresser drawer, he pulled out a pair of socks and wrapped one around his cut hand. Fisting his hand, he looked up at her. She'd seen him smile a handful of times these last days, but never had she seen him look this truly content. "It just seems that way when I come home to find you draped naked over my bed."

"I don't understand, Sebastian."

"I don't really either. Aubrie always said I was in my middle life, and that when my fate was determined I would move on. I assumed she meant to Heaven or Hell. But it appears she meant on with my life. My *mortal* life."

Leia's breath caught. "You're alive?"

"My hand's stinging like a bitch, and I feel like I haven't slept in a decade." He laughed in that blithe way only a man who'd just returned to life after a decade of being undead could do. "I'm alive."

She wanted to laugh too. Wanted to hold his wondrously naked body close and show him exactly how ecstatic she was about his mortality. She couldn't without knowing more. "Do you still want me to go?"

Sobriety entered Sebastian's eyes. "I never wanted you to go in the first place. I thought there was no other option. Fucking a guy in his middle life might not be so bad, but I can guess it would really suck ass when you woke up one morning to find that guy permanently gone from Earth."

When he put it like that, it was hard not to smile. Only those missing answers kept her mouth firm, her heart beating too hard. "It would if I cared enough to miss you."

A tortured-sounding sigh left his mouth. He came closer. Close enough he could pull her against him and hold her captive once more if he chose to do so. "I failed you three years ago, Leia. I turned my back on you when you needed my protection most. But I didn't desert you entirely. When I came back and saw what Ken had done to you, I helped you find the strength to leave."

"You came into my mind and gave me courage." Yes, it made perfect sense. Why she felt so sure she knew him. Why after months of taking Ken's shit, she'd suddenly been able to find the strength to accept that love shouldn't come at the cost of unending pain and decided to leave him.

"No," Sebastian refuted her observation, "I can't give you what you don't already have. I can only make you see how strong that courage is." A small smile tugged at his lips. "I can't even do that anymore. I'm just a mortal now. I hunger. I bleed. I love."

"We *have* met before."

"Not technically. I've known you for years." The small smile turned to a full-fledged grin. "In some ways, I know you better than you know yourself. But you've never met me."

"That's where you're wrong." Leia tapped an index finger against the side of her forehead. "You've been up here. You were for years, and then when I left, you weren't there any longer. I missed living my fantasies, knowing the woman I truly am, but I missed you just as much." She glanced around the room, then back at him. "Unless there's someone else, I'd like to stay here with you. Get to know you even better. See how well you handle this whole master/slave game when you can't just chant a few words and make a vine come out your ass."

Humor flashed in his eyes, but he didn't laugh. Rather, the grin fell from his mouth. "Who else do you think there would be? Aubrie? We had our fun, sure, but that's all it was, just fun. A way to pass the years."

"I meant the person who opened your eyes. The one who made you realize what a joke your first mortal life was. Was it a woman?" At the time he'd spoken of that person, Leia had been overaroused by way of a crotch vine—not exactly in the mindset to even consider what they might mean to him. Now it hit her with belly-twisting clarity that the person was probably female, and that he probably cared for her deeply.

Understanding dawned in Sebastian's eyes. He took a step back, looking out the bedroom window before looking back at her and nodding. "It was a woman. And you're right, I should give her and me a chance, because I love her."

The breath wheezed past Leia's lips. The force of his admission stung more than any of the licks of his vine whip had. For his sake, for what he'd done for her, she nodded her encouragement. "Then you need to track her down and see if she's available and feels the same for you."

Another few seconds passed, where he continued to eye her somberly, and her stomach felt acidic. Then a wry smile formed on his lips and his uninjured hand shot out in the air toward her. That hand ended up hanging limply in the air, and his smile vanished. "Shit, this is going to be hard to get used to."

"What is?"

"Not being able to chant a few words and make a vine come out my ass. I was trying to yank you over here to see if there's any chance you feel the same way I do."

Because he loved her just as much as he loved that other woman? Or . . . "Me?" she questioned as the teasing in his words registered. "*I'm* the woman who opened your eyes? But how?"

"By being you. Natural. Free. Beautiful. The reason I wasn't around to know Ken had grown so cold and cruel was because I couldn't handle seeing you anymore without letting you see me in return. Without telling you how much I love you. I ran, Leia. I got scared, and I ran fast and hard."

He'd run. Just like she had, this man who came off as being so big and strong and tough had run. It was so far off from anything she could have guessed of him that first day in the cell, laughter bubbled up the back of her throat.

Checking the sound, Leia moved directly in front of him. Close enough there was no space left between them. She could feel his heart—his mortal heart—beating against hers. Feel the decadent hardness of his torso pressing against the softness of her breasts. Feel the slow rise of his cock against her mound.

Her pussy fluttered with that last feeling, and it took real effort to keep her voice sedate as she noted, "Now, you're strong."

"Yes, as are you."

"And we're not going to run anymore?"

Sebastian's grin returned, this one wide and sexy, and just a little bit dangerous. His hands came around her, cupping her butt and giving the cheeks a squeeze. "Not unless I'm chasing you down so I can paddle this gorgeous ass for not wearing panties."

Leia laughed, feeling alive, feeling really and truly alive for the first time in years. Smiling back at him, she ground her sex against his. "I can handle that. I can handle staying right here for the rest of my life."

Liaison

Anya Howard

1

Dearest Alain,

As it is you alone of our circle who has contacted me, I must decline the invitation to the reunion of our alma mater with especial regret. Of all the young men of our mutual society, you were my only friend. More so, admittedly, the only individual, until recently, who ever shared the intimate details of my mind and heart. It is for my affection, and the knowledge of your inner soul with its enviable honesty, that I hope you accept the expenses found in this missive and grace me with a visit at your convenience. A map I have sent along for your journey, and I wait with expectant heart to renew our friendship. But as you have always been kind in writing, and enduring the long intervals between my responses, allow me now to indulge you with the relating of my most recent esoteric adventure. It is the last, and of them all, the most humbling.

For you, who with that easy acceptance of yourself, met the censure of the university and the snubbing of our society, and worse, my personal mockery, have been vindi-

cated. I stand corrected of those philosophies of yours that rubbed my shallow propriety as immoderate, earthy, and shamelessly human. As much for this overdue vindication as to renew the friendship that I alone allowed to stray, read on my particulars for not wishing to leave. You have always been the most courteous doubter and listener regarding my occult obsessions. And when it is finished, perhaps you will understand why I believe your forthright and unapologetic soul would be piqued to share the secrets that I have been shown.

It was during the sixth week after my arrival into the village as the new schoolmaster that I stood at the doorway of the newly designated schoolhouse, watching the last of my pupils return home for the day: two sisters, skipping off hand in hand. It had already been a fully frustrating day. Just keeping my thoughts to the subject matter had been a labor. But now the cold bath planned for my return home vanished from thought as my eyes clung to the sight of Maresa's dark braids flying over her shoulders and Laurea's long blond tresses bouncing over her voluptuous hips. They glanced back just before prancing off the lawn for the smooth dirt street. They were giggling, and their eyes were bold. My face flushed smartly, but the awkwardness did not show in my bearing, of course, for I had years of experience in wearing the stern countenance of the schoolmaster. I knew they saw it, too, for a chagrined bloom rose at once in their fair cheeks and their mouths pursed like scolded children.

But children they were not; and what luscious mouths they had—tinged with rose, as smooth as their legs that peeped out beneath the hems of their frocks. My pupils had a distinct fashion to which they adhered: shin-length lacy frocks dyed in various shades of pastels, with white bodices so tightly laced that their breasts heaved vulnerably close to spilling out. On their

feet they wore little white leather boots that came to their ankles. The slender heels of these boots only added to the allure
of their peeping legs. From the youngest to the oldest, they
wore these innocent enticements. My students were all women
grown, daughters and wives, imbued, each and every one, with
a seductive mystique that was utterly distracting.

For the first five years after acceptance into the exclusive
academics guild in Berne, I was assigned to instructing history
at the secondary academy in Brussels. During the subsequent
five, I served as a private tutor to the young sons of military
families in the Netherlands and then England. During these
years, when my brain was not immersed in the routine of edu-
cating the young men under my supervision, my time was consumed by pursuing my personal hobby. While my peers spent
their evenings and holidays relaxing in taverns or romancing
prospective wives, I browsed for occult manuscripts. From
shops of antique dealers and curiosity collectors to private li-
braries and auction houses, I had dedicated every spare moment of the last ten years to building my collection of texts.

My routine had not been complicated once in ten years. I
rarely thought of women other than those fleeting, nameless
images a man creates and utilizes to afford a decent night's sleep.
Marriage was on my agenda, as surely as advancement in the
guild house, but advancement came first. Advancement would
then provide the connections a man of my station needed to find
a woman of acceptable social status and quality for the matri-
monial proposition. Other than this regimented plan, I had no
use for, and certainly little interaction with, women.

This was, until I arrived in the charter village of Urdhels.

I had just spent several months tutoring history and German
to the son of a minor English nobleman and had returned to
Berne for further assignment when the messenger from France
arrived. It was a financially lucrative offer: to teach the women
of the German settlement in history, calligraphy, and poetry. A

decision had been made by the settlers' council that their women would benefit with some acquaintance with contemporary world events, history and poetry, and furthering their comprehension of the French language, which was surprisingly deficient. It was the council that had approached the guild regarding my services and welcomed me en masse upon my entrance into the valley. To say the least, I did not voice my unease with their dialect, which, in actuality, was not the contemporary German I had expected from our correspondence, but rather an obscure dialect of old German, which made for a certain awkwardness between myself and my hosts during those first days in the village.

On the day after my arrival, the councilmen had brought me to the schoolhouse they had prepared. As they introduced me to my waiting class of provocatively frocked and apple-blushed new pupils, I was suddenly and completely aware of how very far I had ventured from the sterile academic halls and chambers. My pupils were their wives, their fiancées, their daughters; and yet, they had no compunction of leaving their fairer sex under my utter and closeted supervision.

Wisdom tempered complaint, of course. These people had paid the guild twice the average salary for my services. I had been given a small cabin in which to dwell. It was clean and furnished, and there was even a servant boy by the name of Weistreim who took care of the small household and brought to me the generous baskets of food sent in the morning and at night from the Burgomeister's own table. The landscape of the valley was wildly enchanting, and the village picturesque with its medieval-style buildings and homes. The half-day hours were certainly less demanding than those of any other position in my career. The councilmen let it be known straightaway they would not pry into the affairs of my classroom, as long as religion and politics entered not into my rhetoric. In fact, they informed me that I was expected to be stern with my pupils. I had to smile at this, for I simply could not imagine grown women giving me the disruption often encountered with the headstrong male children I was used to. I felt welcome, and strangely so, for I detected from discussions with the councilmen that they were none too fond of strangers in general. Before I had set out from Berne, the guild director had provided me what information he personally knew of the charter tribe. They had settled in the valley hundreds of years before.

There was some rumor as to their ties with certain old Teutonic fraternities, but there were a few verified bits of information on record too. An exemption from taxation and the right to keep their own customs was still yielded from the original edicts of the provincial duke who had allotted them the land. In exchange for these grants, the Urdhel men were bound to uphold the hereditary title of their patrons and their descendants, as well as serve in some huntsmen capacity, the exact nature of which the director's documents were unclear. There were some accounts of rifts between several of the dukes and their spiritual and political detractors regarding this tribe. The chronicles I read made repeated references to the pagan Urdhels, and there were accounts from missionaries testifying to their strident refusal to accept Christianity. Chronicler after chronicler commented disparagingly on the Urdhel settlers' godless and unexplainable fortune to have avoided the fate of the Cathars and Knights Templar. The same chronicles alluded that through the generations, the province dukes had suffered censure and scorn—from relatives of their respective wives to their kings, and from uncertain but vocal religious orders for keeping the compact with the settlers.

Not that I was concerned with overly theological disputes. I was wisely adherent to customs of faith as it served propriety, even if personally I was skeptical of institutionalized religion. So it was, upon first entering the valley and setting eyes on the medieval-like village, it occurred to me a marvel, indeed, that these people had held on to their primitive ways for so long without interference. But on this day, it was all I could to do to draw my appreciating eyes from the young women and return inside my classroom. I gave myself some time to tidy up the desk and check the floor for misplaced papers—I had long demanded tidiness from my pupils, as well as their full attention. Of course, I could not imagine myself scolding grown women for something haphazardly fallen to the floor.

As I straightened my papers, I had to ignore their perfume that lingered in the air—the heady scent of pure femininity. I had to force my mind to matters other than all those flowing tresses and pretty flouncing skirts. I left the classroom as quickly as I could, welcoming the sobering outside air as I locked the door.

The village was quiet, and I knew that, officially, this hour was regulated as a time for rest for women and children. I left the school behind and started to stroll down the well-trod clay path that stretched through the village. To the little bridge that spanned over the small brook at the eastern end of town I walked. From there, I crossed the path that skirted a fenced-off field where stood a great spiral of wattle beehives. The bees flew drowsily through the air here, glutting themselves on the nectar of coneflowers and lilac sowed thickly between the shade trees. The path led me around, toward the wilder part of the valley that cupped the eastern rim of the gorge. The grass was high here, green as emerald, and surrounded by the woods blanketing down the slope. I was in the mood for some fresh air and quietude, and to forget the tantalizing, yet discomforting, job I had unwittingly been assigned six weeks before. At least the school's hours were accommodating compared with most of my previous assignments; the town council had determined the classroom hours would commence at nine and end at two in the afternoon. So I had time to research the books I had collected over the years—manuscripts and scrolls on alchemy and the occult—that I had had little time to truly read before, because of the exacting obligations to my former clientele.

As I approached the edge of the eastern woods, I found a small retreat in the soft grass. Alone and calmed of the emotions that had raged in me all day, I took from my vest the small, leather-bound volume. It had cost me a small fortune in Berne, but the translation was challenging, and the cabalistic subject difficult enough to demand my full concentration. The unfamiliar and humbling awkwardness imparted by my new pupils dispelled for a time as I allowed my thoughts to drown in the arcane text.

But in my determination to relax, I had forgotten the monastery; and as the sunlight stretched farther toward the western horizon, a shadow fell over the whole of the meadow. I looked up once to the eastern summit, and the sky was a shade of ill blue behind the religious structure. Of Romanesque design, it was built very close to the lip of land above the steep ravine, standing like a disapproving watcher over the picturesque valley. I studied it now dispassionately. The masonry was somber and dark; the columns and piers thatched with vines. The nave and spires contrasted brightly with the otherwise gloomy ambience of the place. Plated by metal with a sheen much like silver, the nave and spires reflected the sun off the levels below it, so as to further enhance the forbidding ambience of the rest of the edifice. I had been obligated to pass by the borders of the place on the carriage ride that had brought me to the entry path that ventured down to the charter village. The councilman who had been waiting to greet me seemed hesitant to answer my questions regarding the monastery, saying only that the fraternity who dwelt there were members of a privileged religious order.

Civility had prevented me from inquiring further, but I was left with a sense that there were some unspoken ill relations between this mysterious order and my hosts.

Now, I turned my eyes from the monastery and was surprised

to glimpse four young women—two brunettes, a redhead, and one with auburn tresses that swept down to her hips—running across the valley from the path. No more than twenty yards from my retreat they stopped, divested of their school frocks, and hung these across the bottom of a small hazelnut tree. I forgot the book entirely and watched the women run out of the tree's shade. They were laughing as they took hands and formed a circle. A soft melody they began to sing as their feet padded clockwise in the long, velvety grass. Their nubile breasts swung lightly, and their unbound hair waved down their backs. Lovely, all of them, and my loins stirred pleasantly as I stood and walked quietly to the opening of my retreat for a better view.

It was then I could see their faces. The four women were, indeed, all pupils of mine . . . and looking from one to the other I recognized them. But it was only upon seeing the face of the auburn-haired one that my heart surged in my chest. Carina!

My knees weakened even as my cock swelled under my trousers. The daughter of one of the town councilmen, Carina Walpurg was 20 years of age, and one of the most bashful creatures I had ever met. She rarely spoke in class, and her responses to my questions were always answered softly and with courtesy. And yet, of all the women, her presence had especially proved uneasy for me. I am not certain exactly the cause for the inner turmoil she caused, for she was no more lovely than her companions, and certainly not as lively or giddy as most of them. Her large turquoise eyes seemed hard-pressed to address me; but when they did, I lost all sensibility for a moment, and whatever thought was in my head in that moment was swept away by decadent, unabashed desire. Several times that very day I had found myself strolling between the rows of seats while my pupils studied their history books on the chance she might lift her pretty face and give me a smile. And though she hadn't, I had caught my share of glimpses of her cleavage pressing against her snugly bowed bodice. A lavender ribbon looped through the eyelets, the bow of which had lain perfectly between her rose-kissed bosoms.

Giggling merrily, these four pupils fell now as one to the grass. Catya, one of the brunettes, sat up on her knees and threw her hair behind her shoulders. The breeze snatched her voice to me, though her silken words were uttered in the native dialect with which I had trouble. Her tongue lolled lazily over her plump lips, and with a shriek of laughter, she fell upon the redhead, Sascha. The latter was thrown to her back, and the brunette kissed her mouth and throat, drew her mouth over the other's breasts. Sascha sighed wantonly, and her legs parted a little as the brunette's hand massaged the dark patch of hair between her own thighs. Carina and the second brunette, named Dagmar, lay on their bellies side by side, chewing on daisy stems as they watched the other two embrace fervently.

Sascha whispered something soft and urgent. Her pelvis rose pleadingly toward Catya. The brunette smiled and turned toward Sascha's legs and drew them apart. A thatch of red hair glistened between Sascha's thighs. With a husky sigh, Catya forced her legs widely apart. Her face dove over the thatch, eliciting a loud moan from Sascha. Her hips undulated immodestly under her companion's ministrations. Catya's long legs widened and she lowered her pelvis to Sascha's face. Gingerly, Sascha unfolded her sex and licked the crimson labia close to her mouth. The brunette's buttocks clinched ever so tellingly, and as I watched, their naughty tongues flicked hungrily over each other's founts. Soon their heads were bobbing up and down as they feasted in mutual abandon.

An abrupt shriek from Sascha told me she had climaxed first. Catya's frenzied mouth worked almost brutally now upon her, for Sascha's hips began to twist this way and that as she pleaded it was enough, she could bear no more. At this moment, Carina and Dagmar crawled over to them. They pulled Catya off and pressed her onto her back on the ground. Catya struggled, but quickly Carina caught her arms and pinned them on the grass over her head. Dagmar, holding her ankles, pried her knees apart. The blushing Sascha sat up, and now, grinning languidly, crawled up beside Dagmar and draped herself over Catya's left leg. Both of these girls' tempting derrieres danced toward me as Sascha's face dove forward and she began to feast on Catya's exposed nether mouth. Catya's pelvis arched forward, and she moaned wantonly against the sweet flesh that constrained her. Soon the shriek of her orgasm filled the valley.

My mouth watered and I glanced away a moment. When again I looked, the girls were helping each other to their feet. Standing, they gathered hands and began to sing and slowly sway on their feet. As their voices rose, they pranced widder-shins in a circle. The prance escalated into a wild jog; their song a cheery, paganish hymn.

Suddenly, their hands released and off they went spiraling across the grass. Their song was now an angelic chant that ascended into the air and rose from the valley. I soon realized the whole eastern wall of the gorge was vibrating. The four nymphs ran toward the gorge, and facing it, they fell simultaneously to their knees. At once a breeze lifted as if from the very ground itself. My pupils' hair was tousled every which way. Carina's hair caught the rays of the sun, and I was enraptured by her supple, shapely, naked form!

Their faces lifted, and in unison they clasped their hands over their chests. Their song transformed into a commanding chant. The breeze pitched into a violent wind that tossed grass and flower across the landscape. It battered the shrub I hid behind, so that a hard limb thrashed my face. Pushing it aside, I saw the four staring upward as one. I looked to find what their wide, sober eyes contemplated. It was the monastery, and their chant, I sensed, was directed toward it.

They continued to chant steadily. I watched as the scrub and stone of the gorge quivered in root and gulley, and above the desolate monastery, the clouds darkened and gathered together. To my astonishment, these clouds cut over the entire fortress, concealing it almost instantly from sight. The four continued their monotone for perhaps five minutes. A hostile lilt rang in their voices; their faces turned scarlet, enraged. Their pretty hands balled into shaking fists as the sound escalated into a shrill, synchronized scream.

Abruptly, the chant ended. The valley echoed with an unnatural silence, and the wind died just as suddenly as it had come.

My spine tingled, and I crept a little ways back into my retreat. But I could see the women as they returned to the tree and reclaimed their garments. Although instilled morals cautioned this was best and proper, my heart sank with disappointment to see Carina dressed again. With their little frocks back on, the young women took hands and headed toward the village. Not a word was spoken between the four as they returned from whence they had come.

I exited my retreat and looked to the crest of the gorge. The dark clouds still hung low. In a moment or two they had drifted a little, just enough that I made out the silhouette of a dark figure emerging from the structure. Only the slightest breeze wound through the valley, but my skin tightened with apprehension as his tiny eyes narrowed and scaled the valley. Some unfamiliar repulsion urged me to move out of the retreat altogether and run for the bridge. Only as I reached it did I look back. The figure I could not see now, but the clouds were rising with sluggish steadiness from the monastery.

2

I slept fretfully that night. My dreams were intruded upon by a recurring image of my class interrupted by the pounding of a hammer. Time and again, I went to the window of the school, to see a man, in the garb of a cowled monk, crouching on the ground outside. His back was to me, so I saw only the rise of the hammer in his hand before it swung down. I called for him to stop, to wait to finish his work at least until my class was over. He either didn't hear me or simply ignored me. With each new dream, the hammering grew louder, and I grew less patient. It wasn't until I turned from the chalkboard and found that the rhythmic hammering was putting my class to sleep at their desks that I went outside to confront the man. Jogging up behind him, I tapped his shoulder.

"Monsieur," I said politely. When he did not acknowledge me I strode around to face him. And there, I saw the task he had been working on: a short cross of wooden bars, and upon the eye of the cross section he had nailed a mass of gelatinous viscera. The blood that had seeped from it already stained the standing beam. Disgusted, my mouth opened to ask what in the name of hell he was doing. But my eyes raised to the fearsome sight of my own face glowering back at me from under the cowl.

After awaking from this last dream I could not return to sleep. So I sat up until dawn arrived, then dressed and ate some of the rye loaf and butter left over from the dinner Weistreim had brought the evening before. I was not hungry, but it seemed wise to eat and to ground myself, and hopefully, lay to rest the residual disgust imparted by the malignant dreams.

It was only later, when Carina made her timid way into the schoolroom, that I was able to discard it wholly. With the memory of seeing her lovely body dancing over the grass, I was more uneasy than ever. She sat behind two of the other girls who had danced, while the fourth sat behind her. It pained me not to look at her, but I could not dare, lest I found myself unable to fight the urge to order her to my desk and strip her out of the confining little dress. This dilemma strained my focus so that I grew brusque with them all. And when several of the women began to fidget and whisper anxiously between themselves, my constraint snapped. The book I was carrying I slammed on my desk, bringing at once a resounding hush to the room.

"Have you no manners?" I said coldly. "Is this the etiquette your fathers and husbands expect?"

The mass of dismayed eyes and becoming blushes only added to my frustration. I looked squarely at Carina. She sat with her face bowed as usual, and the apples of her cheeks were rosier than ever.

My palms dewed with perspiration as I fought the urge to order her out of her seat and to come forward. I eyed my desk drawer where was kept my old stiff-leather flog. Upon discovery my pupils were women grown instead of children, I had put it away. But now I felt like taking it out. I wanted this innocuous girl—this arousing girl—humbled for disquieting my composure. She deserved chastisement for the frustration she had wrought, a chastisement thorough and sound.

But in that moment, something quite unexpected happened. Carina raised her face and met my eyes without hesitation.

Her composure was distraught, but in a way different from the chagrin of moments before. Her brow was crumpled with the distress of one stunned. I blinked, thoughtless but for the desire to kiss that distress away, and the softest of smiles turned up the corners of her mouth, bashful as a butterfly's caress. My frustration fled, and my blood ran pure and heedless of social expectation.

I excused the class, then watched as Carina's cousins and sister-in-law tried to coax her from her seat. She sent them on with reassurance she would be along soon, and they all gave me a parting look unknown in the society from which I came—a mix of emotions that would have confused polite society beyond this village. I did not think of its source at the moment, I was enraptured. Later, I would have time to consider, to appreciate it. And when the other women were all gone, Carina stood and approached my desk.

"Would you care to accompany me outside, schoolmaster?"

I nodded, and led her outside and locked the schoolhouse door. Indeed, it was an unusual situation; but I did not feel so much under the spell of surrealism as having suddenly awakened from a delusion to the crisp hold of a reality that had eluded me a lifetime. I had known this young woman for only a few weeks, yet in those moments I realized I could not bear the thought of letting her slip from my life. Her fluttering eyes held the beckoning light to eternity; her elusive smile the single link between banal existence and living.

I took her arm in mine and escorted her through the village. We conversed for many hours, forgetting all else save the thirst to drink our fill of one another's experiences. She was fascinated with my travels, though she said she dared not think of leaving the valley. And then I laughed and told her I should just roll her up in a carpet. "As Cleopatra had ordered her servants that she might be presented to her lovers."

She squeezed my arm and laughed. No silvery bell ever rang so precious.

At length we crossed the bridge into the wild part of the valley that spread out to the eastern border of the gorge. I took off my waistcoat and spread it across the grass that she might sit. As I helped her down, I looked up at the monastery and noticed the clouds had departed completely. No figures walked about its estate now, and I perceived the oddest standoffish feeling from the forlorn place. Ridiculous, I knew, and I forgot about it at once and sat down beside Carina. Her hand was small without frailty, the skin and bone delicate in my clasp. She looked up at me, and the kittenish fire that glowed in her demure eyes compelled me to kiss her.

She murmured faintly, pressing her bosom against me. My loins swelled, and I embraced her, kissing her throat and face, and enduring the honeyed torture of her scent and timidly roaming hands. I wanted her fiercely and contemplated taking her to the retreat I had found the day before. But for all her body and desirous sighs, I feared the consequence of such an act.

"You had the most forbidding look in the classroom," she whispered, caressing my stiffening cock as I nibbled the cleft of her throat.

Her fingertips slowly stroked the length of me through my trousers. I drowsed in the sensuous torment of desire and confided against her ear, "I wished to chasten you, Carina. And I am not so certain I have changed my mind!"

She pulled away suddenly, and with her head cocked adorably to one side, she regarded me with much seriousness. "There is none to stop you, monsieur."

I smiled with all the affection she had so guilelessly inspired. "You are impudent, and yes, it would be an honest expression . . . but not wise."

This brought a little frown to her brow. "No? Why do you say that?"

"Would you have me lose all civil restraint, Carina?"

She smiled winsomely. "Yes, that is exactly what I expect, if you intend to court me."

I laughed tenderly. "I do wish to court you, sweet Carina. But with discretion, of course. To do otherwise would lose me the confidence of your father, and all the village councilmen. Then we should lose what opportunity the future offers."

She shook her head. And truly, she seemed perplexed. "This is ridiculous, Marcel Rolant. Are you so educated you have allowed yourself to become dense?"

Her question and tone both seemed bent to goad me. I had to grin. I could not be angry, though her displeasure intrigued me. "I do not know how to answer such a charge."

She blinked and crushed her lips softly against my mouth. "You feign ignorance well, monsieur," she sighed, and parted my lips with her tongue. I accepted her kiss, and lacing my hands about her small waist, pulled her to me. Her bosom heaved hotly against my chest, and with her fingers, she traced my manhood again. It took all my resolve to take her pretty hands away, but I did, and pressed my lips chivalrously over her hand.

"How simple I wish it could be," I sighed at last. "But I am a professional, a man of manners and breeding. I shan't allow my desire to disgrace either of us."

This brought a sharp, vexed sound from her. Suddenly, she cast herself away and got to her feet. She was shaking, and my heart sank to see tears brimming in her eyes.

"You dare condemn my confessions as disgraceful!" She was breathless as she wrapped her arms snugly about herself. "We have enemies, my people—evil and eternal and ancient enemies.

And we are shunned by your proper society. But between the two, I would bow to the forces of the unholy before disgracing myself again with the touch of such a coward as you!"

I was confused, distressed by her evident anger. Before I could summon the words to speak, she turned and sped off. I chased after her, nearly catching the ends of her flying tresses as she rounded the field of beehives. But as she flew over the bridge, I could hear her sobbing and stopped. I watched as she ran up the path and into the village, and cursed myself for what I had done. An image of her father paying a visit to my door and demanding an explanation for her tears complicated my regret.

But no one came that night, and the next day Carina did not attend class. On questioning her cousin, Avelina, I was informed that she had seen Carina come out of her father's house that morning with a breakfast tray for her brothers who worked in the blacksmith's shop. Avelina confided that the two of them had spoken briefly. Yet, the relief for Carina's health was plagued by remorse. I vowed to myself that if she returned, I would mantle myself in a wholly new directness. In retrospect of our last encounter, I felt inarticulate and stupid. I could have tried better to convince Carina of reason. And there was now no honest denial of my feelings toward her. My professional career mattered nothing to the need to have her close to me.

That night, I considered the options thoroughly and came to the decision that if she did not return to school the following day, I would pay a call to her father. I would announce my intention—no, my decision—to court his daughter. He could upbraid me for the audacity of inciting her emotions and for dallying with her beyond the scrutiny of a chaperone. Even if my confession cost me my position as schoolmaster, it was a consequence I was prepared to accept.

My new-found assertion ushered in a sound night's sleep, and I was whistling as I got up the next morning and shaved.

A thunderous knock at my front door so addled the atmosphere that I cut my chin. I had not yet put on my shirt, but the knocking grew frantic. I dropped the razor into the brass dish beside the bowl of water on my dresser and with a linen dabbed the stream of blood inking down my throat. I opened the door to find Weistreim standing there. His arm was around the shoulders of a trembling and weeping Avelina.

Her reddened eyes sought mine, and my heart was touched by a dreadful augury even before the words slipped from her mouth.

"Oh, Monsieur Rolant! Carina is dead!"

I felt faint and had to steady myself against the solid door. My desolate eyes raised to the sky beyond the two young people. It was then I saw the unnatural, mocking hint of blackness that swirled amidst the scattering tangerine clouds of sunrise.

What malady had stricken my precious Carina I was not told that day. I followed her cousin to the household of her father. A crowd had gathered on the lawn. None of this grieving crowd spoke, though some of the women were red-eyed, and all seemed reluctant to answer my inquiries if it were true, indeed, that Carina was dead. One of my pupils noticed me and called over the heads of those clustered through the front door. I did not understand her vocabulary, though it rang of some Germanic dialect. A minute or so later, the crowd there parted and Carina's father appeared. He was at least a foot taller than myself, a hardy tailor I knew, with hands huge and callused. Remembering Carina's flight home, I feared I might have intruded on unwanted ground. But the giant's solemn countenance gave way the next instant. He fell to his knees, sobbing pitifully.

An old woman, with a mane of startling white hair, emerged from the house and went to stand beside him. Her thin arms enfolded his head and drew it to her bosom.

And so I knew the news was true. My head reeled, and I felt sickened at the thought of how I had mocked Carina. Unintentionally, and with the most scrupulous of intentions. Yet, I had, and shut out the first breath of life beyond routine that I had dared to think of inhaling in years. I stared at the old woman as if she might comfort my own disbelief.

"Carina," I whispered.

The woman's small blue-green eyes bore into me, and the intimidation she exuded vied to slam me back into the crowd.

What had befallen Carina, I was allowed only to surmise from the few words secured from some of my pupils. A sudden sickness, some malady that once had been common, but which the village healers supposedly had kept in check for years by the use of certain precautions. When I asked what these precautions were, and the symptoms of the malady, the young women shrugged unconvincingly and excused themselves.

Carina's funeral was two days later. The procession followed her father and the young men who carried her casket to a grove near the western wall of the gorge. It was a casket of impressive craftsmanship, of dark-stained rosewood and silver pall handles. The bedding and pillow were white-laced silk. A great section of the gorge's natural wall was used as catacombs; caskets were slid into deep shelves in the soil, and the shelves, once the dead were placed inside, were covered over by cedar panels. These panels were carved with the name of the respective deceased, as well as images of animals and flowers, tools, and various other icons. A shelf had already been created for Carina's remains by the time the mourners gathered in the grove, and nearby stood a rough oak table. I stood to the sidelines and watched the pallbearers set her casket upon this table. They stood at their positions like wary warriors, and I heard a voice from behind the bier. It droned solemnly in the native language, and peering about the heads in front of me, I saw that the voice came not from a priest of the cloth, but the same old woman with the streaming white hair I had seen before. She wore a shapeless leather dress, so thoroughly beaten that the whole of it retained a tawny sheen.

From her neck hung stringed flowers, beads, freshwater shells, runes, and countless other things. Circlets of gold clasped her forearms; her ankles were cuffed with bands of meshed silver. As she lifted a staff of twisted oak over Carina's body, a reverent and expectant hush fell over the crowd of mourners.

Raising the staff high, the old woman continued. She turned toward the open burial shelf and delivered what seemed to be a blessing upon it. When this was done, she opened a leather pouch hanging by rawhide about her neck. A handful of what appeared to be ground peppercorn she fished out and pitched into the shelf. When at last her litany fell silent, one of the pallbearers raised a guttural hail, and at once all six youths moved away from the casket.

It was the first clear look I had had of Carina's body. She had been divested of all clothing, her long hair brushed out so that it lay shining and even over her white shoulders, and sprinkled with sprigs of wild violets and Sweet Williams from her crown to the ends of this beautiful hair. Like a napping fairy she looked! So still and bereft of bloom were her lovely cheeks; yet, her features bore the illusion of mortal vibrancy. I was compelled to advance closer to the casket, and as I looked down at her, this vibrancy played upon my mind. I half expected, half wished she would simply leap off the bier. I imagined her laughing and dancing again as she had done in the verdant valley grass. I touched her silken hair and admired sadly the magnificent white rose that had been placed over her navel. Her hands had been folded over the long stem. They, too, looked vibrant, as if with my next breath her lovely fingers would quicken and prick one of the thorns.

I could hardly believe this girl was dead. But my disbelief receded in that moment under an unexpected deluge of loss and injustice. Carina was to never enjoy the pleasures that had so elegantly imbued her spirit. This touched me as even more regrettable than her untimely passing. I did not know that I was weeping until a pregnant woman offered me a handkerchief. Thanking her with a nod, I unfolded the cloth and wiped my eyes.

As I looked down on Carina again, I noticed something ugly just beneath a lock of her hair at the side of her neck. Dismayed, I lifted the auburn lock aside and saw two dark, puckered puncture marks upon her throat.

The sound of shock that rose to my lips was lost under a wail that rang through the grove. Carina's father rushed forward on the other side of the table to stand beside the old woman. His face was ravaged by grief, and he held in his left hand a worn battle-axe with a highly polished bronze handle. The crone inhaled deeply and nodded to him, then raised her arms over Carina's body. As she began to chant in their Germanic tongue, Carina's father raised the weapon to his lips. He turned then and gripped the handle firmly in both hands, and raised it high over his head. With the howl of a wounded bear, he slipped to one knee and brought the blade sweeping down. It bore deeply into the earth and the quivering handle sang lightly.

I was too lost in my own self-reproach to ponder the reason for the weapon or his action . . . until the old woman looked over at him and gestured him up. He rose and came to stand beside her, and with the back of his right hand caressed the cheek of his dead daughter. The old woman drew from her pouch a posy of dried valerian and laid this beside Carina's head. She mumbled something and unfolded the dead girl's lips. The grieving father held them apart with the first two fingers of his free hand and gently separated her jaws. I watched, mystified, as the woman lifted the posy and started to crumble the dried valerian into Carina's mouth. When she was satisfied, the crone nodded to the father, who ever so gently re-closed Carina's stiffened lips.

His head fell forward and he sobbed now without reservation. The crone's eyes raised to the mourners. There were family members all about me, yet it was directly at me the woman's eyes descended. Hardened with an emotion beyond my understanding, her gaze punctured my grief. It found my conscience, my cultured propriety. It needled straight through the prim repose that had been cultivated so long now that it sheathed me as securely as secondary flesh. Time bogged down in those moments she examined my soul, so that she and I seemed removed from the grove and the mourners. An intelligence that transcended even the wisdom of her years burned in her absorbing gaze.

Nocturne Liaison.

I heard the term, of this I had no doubt. A graveled whisper, audible only between our mutual consciousnesses.

I could not draw my vision from the crone, not even blink as she disrobed my educated reason and falsehoods with her unseen picks and claws. Her eyes widened into two great mirrors: In one I saw the reflection of my cowardice; whereas in the other, my sophisticated arrogance smirked back at me. Shallow was any excuse I could deign to speak against the stark, revealing images. By becoming a servant to propriety, I had compromised my claim to manliness and rebuffed my humanity.

The crone's consciousness bade me to contemplate the thing I had destroyed. And as my eyes lowered to the casket, the impact of my failures accelerated time again. Carina was dead, and never again would I have chance to speak the words that self-deceit had restrained. My shame and regret transformed into anger, an anger so torrid I felt the skin of provinciality burn away. I saw another man help Carina's father to his feet, and my sympathy for the grieving father released me from the hold of timelessness. The emotion on his face was unreadable as I smoothed my fingertips across the auburn strands over her shoulder.

Ruefully, I admired her fair shoulders, which I had foolishly refrained from touching while she had lived. Her lips were sculpted rosebuds, beseeching me even yet to throw off the shackles of respectability and kiss them with unabashed desire.

The crone touched my hand with her bony fingers. As heated as Carina's skin was cold was her soft, living flesh. I looked up at her again and perceived a flash of the girl she had once been: a bashful, playful kitten just like her granddaughter. Her lips glazed with radiance as she smiled.

"Nocturne Liaison."

The words were only a whisper, yet they sliced through the air as clean as the blade of the battle-axe. I felt a momentary jarring in my chest, and a sharp pain seized both my temples. When these sensations passed I felt much as if I had sobered from the most indignant intoxication. I looked at the crone, and her eyes had taken the mist of the aged again; her narrow, leathery lips puckered so that she looked only tried by my presence.

"Return home, schoolmaster."

My fingers curled mournfully about Carina's hair. But I turned as the crone bade and left them all to their pagan rite. I made my way out of the grove, and as I stepped into the unveiled sunshine, I heard the crone's wail. Never such a flesh-shattering sound had I heard than that scream of unforgiving, savage wrath. It was not directed at me, that much instinct confirmed, and the shocked, soft response it brought from the mourners prompted me to stride quickly for home. Only the lingering sense of intoxication kept all questions mercifully at bay.

Alone in the house and needing something to help forget the funeral, I uncorked a bottle of wine brought along from Berne. I had rarely allowed myself to indulge to the point of inebriation, but this time I quickly guzzled a quarter of the bottle while re-reading the last newspaper I had bought before taking my new position. At last, too blind with drunkenness to read, I stumbled to the bed and fell across it.

As my eyes closed, the funeral shifted back into my mind. I

drifted to sleep mumbling curses upon myself. And in my dreams I stood beside the casket. As I touched Carina's face, a vine fell from the branch above my head. It landed on my hand and twisted around my fingers tightly enough to draw blood. The harder I attempted to remove it, the tighter it squeezed, until at last the fibers broke through my flesh and my blood spurted everywhere.

A scream drew my attention away. Looking down, I saw Carina's body had disappeared. I turned and scanned the grove but saw no one bearing the body away. There was no one at all, except a shadowy serpent slithering toward a great cross in the darkest recesses of the grove.

I awoke with the fingers of my right hand throbbing. It was only the spectral pain of a dream, but as I rubbed them I saw a wisp of something bound about the first two fingers. I got up and went to the hearth where a dwindling fire remained. And as I examined my hand, I found several auburn hairs caught between the fingers. I pulled them off carefully and laid them on the nightstand before finishing off the rest of the bottle.

3

The next day, I awakened with a chill and the gloomy determination to see no one. It was Sunday, and throughout the village some festivity was being prepared. From my windows, I watched as women garlanded the doors, shutters, and lintels of the shops and other buildings with flowers. Young men carried in kindling from the woods and built a great cone for a bonfire in the village square. Elders and children were setting up tables and singing. The cheery lilt of their voices and the occasional whoops of the young men rankled me in an indeterminate way. On arriving with the morning meal, my servant brought two plates of smoked meat, a large wheel of cheese, and an entire loaf of bread. Weistreim explained he would not be back that day as he was attending the celebration planned for that evening.

"And what celebration would this be," I asked politely, but I heard the sourness in my tone. Since awakening, my habited priorities had returned to haunt my demeanor. It reproached the memory of seeing myself through the crone's eyes, arguing with erudite persuasiveness that the ordeal had been nothing more than having allowed my misplaced guilt to be swayed by the pagan funeral.

His answer was bright, but guarded, "In memoriam of certain ancestors. You would not be familiar with them, monsieur."

At the moment, I was not interested to inquire either, and when he left, I pulled the shutters closed and laid the tray he had brought inside the pantry. Although the weather was temperate, I could not shake the feeling of being cold. I threw some kindling onto the low flame in the fireplace, and when there was a good, steady fire, I browsed through my collection of books and manuscripts. At length I found a treatise by Grigori Rastrelli, "The Mathematical Properties and Mystical Symmetry of Musical Notes." I sat down in the overstuffed chair before the fireplace. My grasp of the Russian was sufficient and the text absorbing. Soon the sounds of growing merriment from outside were inaudible to me.

Most the day I sat reading, rising only when necessity called or I wanted to nibble on something from the pantry. The celebration outside was in high order by mid-afternoon; drums began to beat from the square, and their pagan toll grew steadily deeper and more fervent. Eventually, it became so loud I could no longer concentrate. I laid the book down and went over the assignments I had planned for the next day's class. But as I pored over my notated journal, a chorus of shrill voices suddenly pierced the monotonous drumming. Laying the journal aside, I went to the window and peeked out again. The bonfire was burning high above the silhouettes dancing and sitting cross-legged around it, and the smoke that wafted from the flames lazily licked the orange threads of twilight on the horizon.

As I watched the arcane festivity, I saw women amongst the shifting throngs of dancers. They were naked, and the light of the bonfire made their bare flesh gleam like smooth cream. It seemed so indecent to me suddenly; and though propriety tried to convince me it was morality that was offended, my heart knew better.

Carina had been in the grave less than a day.

Later, as I cut some of the bread and cheese for dinner, I was startled by an abrupt silence. The drums had quieted, the voices of merriment hushed completely. I sat, embraced and expectant while I ate, but the festive sounds did not rise again. I returned to the treatise for some time, and when I was too tired to read anymore, I looked out the window one last time. The crowd had emptied from the square, and the bonfire remained burning. A single man paced back and forth before it. I squinted and made out the familiar features of Carina's father. His arms were crossed, and his eyes were buried beneath an iron-hard furrow of brows. With a twinge of sympathy that softened my earlier judgmental indignity, I left him to his privacy and readied for bed.

I did not reach bed, however. The troubling image of Carina's father pacing the ground stirred my remorse again. Before it could compel the illusions I'd surely suffered in the grove, I returned to the chair. Draping a quilt over my legs, I read long into the night until at last I fell asleep.

So deep was my slumber I cannot swear what next my conscious mind knew. Whether it was real or something from a dream, I was startled by a scratching sound, like sand rubbed against glass, somewhat away from my chair. I believe my eyes opened, long enough for me to see or imagine the text in my lap. The next moment, my mind lulled into black numbness.

I dreamed of a viper that slithered over the shingles of the house. It maneuvered over the underlaps of the shingles slowly, so that the splinters snagged its old skin and loosened it from the creature's body. It was a slow process, but I heard the echo of each old scale as it peeled from the body. I flinched with every snap of parched skin, knowing that soon the viper would find its relief, and make its way down the boards and search for some tiny cranny or hidden hole. It would enter the house then and find me, asleep and vulnerable in the chair.

The image dimmed and I started to return to a deep sleep. Then, abruptly, I perceived a low grating sound like the tearing of tin. A distant image of opening fangs glinted at me in the beckoning blackness. My heart rate accelerated as I fought to open my eyes. Ice grazed my cheekbone. The minute hairs froze beneath the chilled touch, and the tissue and bone under my seared skin throbbed with intruding coldness. This coldness at once spread throughout my face, as intense as if I'd dived into artic waters, and my nostrils and throat felt frosted completely.

Rattled to full consciousness, I gasped for air. My eyelids opened and shattered the crystals that seemed to bind the lashes.

It was then I saw it. An obliqueness, too dense to be shadow, crouched between my chair and the hearth. I was struck with an instinctive terror; my limbs were paralyzed with fear. But as I beheld this unnatural blackness, my fear was surpassed by the dawning determination to know what this was. My determination ignored the rational voice that warned to get up and move away.

A flicker from the hearth embers caught a glint of sculpted form. I gasped and jumped, and the sudden acceleration of blood in my system intensified the voice of ration. But as the form began to take substance and definition, my natural inquisitiveness silenced it. The lightless figure slowly rose so that I could make out the silhouette of a head, shoulders, the distinct and rounded outlines of a woman.

It was then my consciousness screamed for me to flee. But her thoughts broached the space between us, and with an unspeaking command, she inflamed my curiosity—goaded it, willed it to a frenzied, single-purposed thing of which she alone held power. Rational fear lay dormant, so that I sat as in a stupor of fascination under her demanding will. It was a maneuver known and taught by unseemly spirits, ancient and potentially lethal to mortals.

But at the moment I could not have cared less.

Her hands rose and she lifted the length of her hair. For the first time I perceived more than a dark outline as she let go of the strands and they cascaded like glowing copper over two slender shoulders. My heart skipped a pace, and her skin began to take color and texture—all pale, satiny cream. As I stared at her rounded, desirable limbs, I felt my curiosity drained forcibly away. I heard common sense beckoning from a remote distance, and I attempted to respond. But as I started up from the chair, the ghostly figure pounced into my lap. I was weighted down by sheer, primitive horror.

Her thighs straddled my legs. I discovered I had lost control of my body. My limbs were utterly immobile, though I could feel with acute clarity the cool hands that laced the back of my neck, the dewed sex that glided lightly over my crotch. Her face was still blackness to me, but her mouth braised my chin and her chilled tongue flicked over my gaping lips. She spoke something to me. The resonance of her voice lulled my fear as if it were hers to control entirely. Even now I do not know what it was exactly she commanded, only that I could not refuse. My jaw moved, and I began to recite some lengthy, mystically imbued alchemic procedure. In the original Arabic, I related this knowledge of which I was acquainted only by chance from a manuscript I had come across during my university days. My brain was raped, slowly and steadily, in the pilfering of this arcane formula.

At the same time, my other senses were aroused by the closeness of this unearthly, nocturnal figure. And as the mechanical recitation echoed against the wall boards, the copper halo dimmed before my eyes and the disguise of darkness fell away.

Carina was as lovely as always. As real as if she had never died. My stomach knotted with dread; my heart pounded with guilt. Tears burned at my eyes, and as they fell, she licked them from my cheeks. I wanted to speak her name and demand explanation, but my speech was entirely under her control.

Her thighs slipped over the armrests of the chair. She began to undulate over my lap, so that her auburn hair whipped my shoulders and her nubile breasts bobbed before my eyes. My face burned with the smoldering urge to lift her up, throw her across my lap, and deal that chastisement I should have dealt her that day in the classroom.

The thought of it honed my passion to an almost painful need. She must have suspected my thoughts, for her eyes lowered a moment. As they raised again, she smiled, that kittenish smile I so adored, and reached between her thighs and unbuttoned my trousers. Drawing my cock out, she rubbed it curiously. It swelled and hardened in her hands, which brought the most delighted purr to her lips.

She tilted forward a little and rubbed her moist slit back and forth across me, tantalizing my anger and need sorely. I longed to suckle her nipples and devour her nubile breasts. Instead, I had to endure her husky coo as she tore the buttons of my shirt and flicked her fingernails across my nipples. She licked them both, sucked them until they panged, then pulled my trousers down over my hips. Her pelvis and pert bottom raised. Holding to my shoulders, she mounted me. Quite timidly, her nether mouth swallowed the length of my cock. Tight was her orifice, and she rode gingerly, pouting ever so softly, leaving me with no doubt that this was a virgin who ravished me.

I no longer heard the words that flowed from my mouth. My muscles were tense, my thoughts focused wholly on her almost cruelly slow strides. My jism shot into her, so that the next word stifled in my throat. She heard and kissed me tenderly, inhaling the word from my throat. With kisses she drank the rest of the procedure as the words spilled forth—every addendum and comment of the text from which I had memorized. And when she had devoured the final remark, my consciousness faded.

"Marcel, Marcel, we are not finished! Marcel . . ."

My eyes opened to her rueful eyes. She kissed me until I was roused to full consciousness. It was then I felt the blood of her maidenhead, cool and thick, seeping over my cock and drizzling down my balls. I still could not move of my own volition, and watched as her pelvis grinded over my spent cock. Her nether muscles clenched it desperately as she weaved up and down, and very soon my passion was coaxed back.

This time she was a little bolder, clasping to my shoulders and throwing her head back so that her hair swept down between my thighs as she rode. I struggled in the fraught aim to cast her to the floor and pummel her so hard that her seductive little backside would spank the floorboards. But it was hopeless, and as my pleasure escalated, she rocked with growing abandon. Suddenly, her little mouth parted wide and her brows raised; her fingernails sank into my shoulders. I felt the orgasm ripple through her nether muscles. The sweet contractions gripped me like the hands of a skilled milkmaid. Almost immediately, my seed surged into her again.

She folded her naked body over me and kissed me. Such a light and ethereal thing was this woman-child who controlled me with invisible bonds. For a time she simply looked at me, and her face grew more rueful with each passing moment. A sharp twinge of my remorse softened my dread, clarified my passion. In that instant, I saw what my guilt, the crone's tricks, and the restless indifference of that day had failed to grasp. If I could just put my arms about her, never again would I let her go! I would discover and banish whatever strange malady had distorted her mind with the delusion of her own death.

A hollow rapping sound from the other side of the room snapped Carina's attention away. Her eyes narrowed hard on something past my shoulder, and so great was her sudden change of focus I could feel my bones and muscles released from her spell. I tried to slide up in the chair a bit, but I had not yet the strength; in fact, my intestines and stomach were wracked with nausea nearly as debilitating as the paralysis. Carina's countenance was wary, incensed, and as my lips and throat vied to speak, I heard the rapping again and knew now it was from the outside window beside the bed. I tried to turn my head, but my neck was like a wilted lily.

Carina pitched herself forward and clasped my face between the fingertips of her cool hands. As weak as I was, there was nothing I could do but look into her eyes. Her lips brushed my mouth and my loins stirred anew.

"Do not venture out at night, my handsome schoolmaster," she said softly, "for I can see to it they obtain what they seek without you meeting my fate."

I frowned, and straining with all my willpower, my fingertips touched her firm, succulent hips. A whisper of a smile touched her mouth, and suddenly she reeled back from my lap into the drape of obliqueness. With my head falling over one shoulder, I saw her dark form billow from hearth to the door. There it changed into a lightless mist that threaded itself through the keyhole and passed out of the house altogether. My chest reeled with horror. I was either mad, or Carina had become the victim of something more abominable than any malady that could create the illusion of death for the sufferer.

What seemed like hours passed before I was able to rise from the chair. But slowly my sluggish limbs, bones, and muscles obeyed my need. I was inspired by the single thought to find Carina and bring her back, and whatever the cost, free her from the evil that had claimed her. Once on my feet, however, I took no more than three or four steps before the darkness of unconsciousness obliterated my vision.

4

I awoke in an unfamiliar room. Dusty beams crossed the ceiling over my face, and the sun shone through a cheesecloth drape from the window above the side of the bed. I sat up and pushed aside a worn quilt that had been spread over me. Kneeling, I pushed aside the drape and looked outside, but the flowering brambles that grew against the glass were too thick to see past.

I didn't know if it was the bedding or the room that was so pungent to my nostrils. Surveying the room, I saw herbs and bulbs of numerous varieties hung to dry from the higher beams in the center of the room. On the wall across from the bed was a small fireplace. Something aromatic that made my mouth water simmered in the brass cauldron that hung there. A table stood against the wall facing the bed's footboard. I rose, thoughtful of my light-headedness, and stepped curiously to it.

There was a wide oil cloth laid atop it, and over this was strewn a hodgepodge of things: glass jars containing more herbs and liquids, mortars and pestles, stuffed leather pouches with securely knotted drawstrings, bowls filled with items such as clay, honey, moss, and the teeth from a variety of animals. There was a small white cabinet, like a child's toy, painted over with delicate flowers and tiny dragons. A slender iron chain hung tautly between the handles of the doors, complete with a miniature iron lock.

Upon a circular wooden stand in the center of the table was a preserved human head. Had I not seen such displays in the homes of acquaintances who collected such morbid paraphernalia, I might have been shocked. It had evidently been meticulously preserved by whatever process had been implemented, so that the skin was imparted with only the slightest of tawny felt texture. The lips and nostrils had been sewn closed before the process, and the ears likewise at the entrance of the canals, but whatever gutting or thread had been used had been tailored from the inside, so that the outside of the orifices retained their basic original contours. What most fascinated me was the care given to the hair, eyebrows, and mustache. Whoever possessed this curiosity had just recently combed out the mustache and brows and the long flaxen head hair, and wound this last neatly around the wooden stand. I reached out to touch the shiny hair when the creak of door hinges sounded from behind me.

My resolve startled, I spun to find it was my servant, Weistreim, who stood at the entrance. But he did not enter until the woman with him crossed the threshold first. It was the white-haired woman in her beaten leather dress. Weistreim cast me a quick congenial smile. He did not speak, however, and I sensed his silence came from an intense and habituated deference toward the elderly woman. As she came to stand before me, an expectant quiet braced the entire room. Her bluish green eyes looked me up and down, the crow's feet tightly drawn in the corners, and her mouth was pursed with an uncertain displeasure. My stomach knotted and the nape of my neck crawled, much like when I was a child about to be interrogated by the nuns who administered the school I had attended.

This sensation turned my next thought to the time. It was surely time for me to be headed to the classroom, if I wasn't overdue already. I wondered if my pupils had arrived at the schoolhouse door and found it locked. Were they fretting over what had happened to me, or had someone already informed them that I was occupied elsewhere?

Then I remembered the one desk that would be absent of its pretty occupant . . . and my chest panged miserably.

"I am Irmhild, Monsieur Rolant. And I know you have seen my daughter's child, Carina."

Understanding now the nature of their relationship, I could not bring myself to speak of the passionate, heartrending incident with her. Instead, I feigned self-interest, "How did I come to be here, madam?"

"This boy found you, of course. He fetched Carina's father to help bring you to me."

I glanced at Weistreim, but he was staring at his feet. "I must thank you, then, for whatever—"

Irmhild cut me off briskly, "He thought you ill to be lying on the floor so pale and almost lifeless. But I have found no fever, no sign of illness. Tell me what quelled your strength, schoolmaster?"

As I rubbed the chafing tenseness from the back of my neck, she sighed and spoke something to the boy in a language I did not understand. At once Weistreim slipped out again and shut the door behind himself. The crone gestured to the bed.

"Sit."

I started to protest that my pupils needed me, when she grasped my arm. She pressed me to comply, and I did not realize how very weak my body was until I relented the burden of standing. My head spun with relief as she walked over to the hearth and took a clay bowl from the stones. From the cauldron she ladled some soup into the bowl and brought this back to me.

Irmhild said nothing as I took it into my hands, but even to me the shaking of my hands was disconcerting. Still, I managed to blow on the soup and take two or three sips of the broth. My stomach spasmed painfully, but in a few moments I felt it settle.

"This might be your last meal, if you insist on keeping your secrets concerning Carina."

I was shocked by her implication, and she went on, "No, it is not I whom you should fear, schoolmaster. But I see that those who have used my Carina have already commenced to thieve on your vitality—though I suspect it is not your body or blood they seek."

I winced and listened as she continued in the same stony voice. "I can help you. I know who directs her, just as I know why she left no marks on you."

I sipped on the broth again and tried to keep my emotions from my voice. "What is it you believe happened to me, madam?"

"My Carina told me of your demonstrated wish to court her—until she acknowledged an acceptance of the desire you feigned."

The very lack of criticism in her tone sharpened my guilt.

"I was thoughtless, I apologize." I felt pressed to give Carina's grandmother some understanding of the cultural conflict that the encounter of which she referred had rattled in me. "You must understand, madam, in the world beyond this valley, such arduous expectations are considered imprudent."

"Your world breeds senseless inhibitions, monsieur." Irmhild paused, then said in a voice as brusquely compelling as that of any schoolmaster, "I feel you regret your decision—Am I correct?"

I flushed hotly. It was not that I would have dared contradict her, not now that I had my own resolutions concerning Carina, but her probing questions were almost as invasive as her mind had proved during the funeral. Thus, to give prelude to my own speculations regarding Carina, as well as sidetrack the old woman's curiosity, I replied frankly, "Before I answer, you must tell me what you believe befell your granddaughter."

The left corner of her mouth turned up to give me a derisive flash of age-darkened, but hardy, teeth. "We of the ancient ways are not the stupid chickens those of your society make of us. Your credentials were well reviewed before our councilmen decided you were the best candidate to teach our women. But it was not a man who made the final decision on your suitability, Marcel Rolant."

Her telling gaze made me feel like a child. In her no-nonsense sage tone, she continued, "You know as well as I what has befallen Carina. She has fallen victim to that race known as the vampire."

I blinked. According to everything I knew, vampires were no more than allegorical archetypes. Whether it was the infant-devouring Lilith or one of the countless legends of the vengeful spirit, erudition preached that these creatures were pure superstitions invented by the minds of the unsophisticated.

"They are real, schoolmaster. And were it not for Carina's melancholy, they never would have dared take her. She was a priestess-guardian of ancient faith, one of the women who serve as living wards to our village against the beckon of the vampires that, in times past, lured our little children into danger. But Carina had never loved before, let alone ever been spurned, schoolmaster. I know how devastated she was. She had come home and told me of your practicality. She could not eat; she could not stop weeping. Thus did she set out to the wilds where she and her priestess sisters perform the old rite. I stopped her father from following after her, thinking she needed time to collect herself. But evidently, her self-doubt drew the vampires from their lofty lair."

As wild as this tale was, self-reproach needled my gut. But it was the echo of the words *lofty lair* that quaked the foundations of my arcane education. For a moment, I could not see the wrinkled face before me, but instead heard the climatic scream uttered by Carina and her friends as they stood naked and shaking before the eastern summit of the gorge.

"These priestesses summoned the clouds over the fortress monastery," I whispered. Startled by understanding, I nearly dropped the bowl. Carina's grandmother righted it in my hands.

"So you watched them," Irmhild sighed, "and still you did not see."

She tut-tutted like a disgruntled mother, and chagrined, I finished the soup as she continued, "My people were avowed to the destruction of the vampire race ages before setting eyes upon this valley. There were six branches of the vampire family, all spawned passionlessly from the wombs of six of the Trickster's seven malevolent daughters."

The word *Trickster* was a pagan term I thought I'd heard somewhere before. My unspoken concern, however, for once outweighed my selfish curiosity, and I listened attentively as she went on, "My forefathers were avowed to eradicate one of these branches entirely, the spawn of Griselda—to slay them, destroy their every lair for the honor of the gods we worship. The bloodless matriarch, Griselda, is mad as are all the Trickster's self-propagated daughters. She is mother to vampires, and yet she is more. Unlike the life-hating chaos from which the Trickster came, Griselda is a being of corrupted mortal desires. This is as the Trickster designed; bringing himself into the flesh of one who is neither male nor female, yet both, that he might self-propagate. The daughters he bore—these six by self-conception, leastwise—are human abominations, corruptions, mockeries of mortal needs and desires. These six were born to his designations; beings of insatiable desires and self-interests that they might be a plague to humankind."

Irmhild paused a moment, and a single fearful furrow crossed her brow. "There was a seventh, sired by an even more abhorrent method. But this one did the Trickster so misuse she evolved into a force so frightful that even her father cowers at her approach. She is not one of the vampire mothers but a dark and brooding leech upon mortal life in another way, and which no man or magic may stop."

I was piqued once again, but before I could ask of this seventh daughter, Irmhild continued, "Griselda was the Trickster's first offspring, his favorite, the testament to his own powers. So proud of this feat of self-perpetuation, the Trickster transmuted into a peacock after her birth and assaulted the first peahen he came across, therefore placing an anathema upon the tragic offspring of that union. Even to this day the doomed peahen's descendants live constrained to lionize Griselda's creation with their morbid call.

"But as the Trickster's other self-conceived daughters, Griselda has no maternal instinct. She did, however, have need of an army of unswayable allegiance. Thus did she conceive her brood through the seed of a dead man. And these undead children she has nurtured to believe themselves unworthy to share in the very delights for which they were sired. Loathing their existence, they remain torn between the perpetual desire to feed on the flesh and the need to serve her in shame of themselves while clutching to the futile desire to gain her maternal love.

"When our ancient seers discovered she had led her vampire brood over the Alps in the quest of finding fresh pillage, they pursued. Griselda and her brood managed to elude them during a blinding snowstorm and came to this province while our forebears were forced to wait out the winter in icy caverns.

"But they are crafty, these descendants of the Trickster, and knew their trackers would pursue them until the end of time if need be. Thus did their matriarch instruct them to act on the political animosity felt at that time toward the familial prince of the province, Duke Boheme. Toward this aim, the vampires sought to gain the favor of the king of this land. The duke was not Christian, you see, his power reliant entirely and vulnerably on his ancient bloodline. The vampires discovered that if they aligned themselves with the Church of Rome and took the vows of the faith, they could more easily gain the king's favor. This they accomplished; and that king, happy to have sympathetic ears and eyes ready to spy upon his rival, had built for them a holy fortress. He recruited masons educated in the antediluvian knowledge of how to build a sanctuary that would serve—unknown to the king—as a sanctuary to the vampires. And so, when my people at last reached the province, it was to the discovery they could not enter the lair of the vampires or even trespass its property without consequence of immediate death.

"We remained, however, safeguarding the province from the vampires' unholy hunger. As well, we are indebted to the descendants of Duke Boheme, for it is he who gave us this valley in which to settle. Throughout the generations, his descendants have braved hostility and censure to defend us from the scourge of the Church. The Dukes protect us, and in exchange, we protect their family and people."

The room was silent except for the distant voices of children from beyond the bramble-covered window. The talk of vampires with unholy hunger echoed brutally against their laughter and blithe chatter.

Irmhild's anger softened her tone, "I knew they had taken Carina when I saw the marks on her throat. But I could not say this until there was undeniable proof. And you, monsieur, are the testament of what she has become. But tell me, did she come to you alone?"

At the hesitant flush in my cheeks, she pressed on, "How do I know Carina came to you? There is no manner of illness that drains the vitality as I see has been drained from your aura. She will kill you, perhaps even unwittingly, monsieur, unless there is intervention. But I would like to know first her manner of draining your vitality."

My lips clamped as one morally shocked. It was not that

which she sought to hear that prevented my vocalizing, but rather the remnants of propriety that still possessed me. How could I admit the carnal truth to this, Carina's granddame?

"You are a fool, schoolmaster," she seethed with a fierceness that startled me. "Did she bite you or not? Do not allow modesty to bar me from possibly saving her!"

I was startled further. But now I had no question that she cared nothing about whether I had had relations with Carina.

"No, madam. She did not bite me."

Her eyes closed a moment, and when they opened again, tears spilled over her cheeks. "Good. Then she is not willingly aiding them. But still, there had to be a bid of welcome on your part for her to have entered your house."

"Bid of welcome?"

She smiled sadly. "The foul creatures cannot enter the valley for the wards of the priestesses. But through a priestess taken can their damned souls interfere with us. Carina had to know she was welcome. There could have been no other way for her to enter. Did you call out her name or have some item that belonged to her?"

I nodded uneasily. "I was speaking aloud to myself shortly before . . ." My voice trailed and I remembered something else. "On the nightstand was a snag of Carina's hair, which I had inadvertently carried back from . . . her funeral."

Irmhild bit her bottom lip. "Alas, had I foreseen Carina's passion for you, I would have sent for another with the potential of breaking through their wards."

My voice sounded distant to my ears, "What are you saying?"

"Their sanctuary can be entered," she explained, "but only by one educated in the very sorceries on which the blueprints their very lair was designed and constructed by the mortal magicians hired by that long-dead king. Secrets from the realm of chaos these sorceries come; magical incantations, devices, and rituals whispered into the minds of men, recorded by foolish, greedy mortal hands. As all her sisters, Griselda had no patience to learn these secrets that could protect her from the interference of humankind. But they are powerful secrets, the implementing of which can either be the bane or succor of the vampires. My folk discarded most of them as the tools of evil and practiced instead the rites of the good gods. Griselda, obligated to bide her time in her cloistered refuge, awaits a mortal versed in the sorceries, a Nocturne Liaison. Through draining the knowledge of such an educated mortal, Griselda can, in this leeching way, obtain the ancient secrets she seeks.

"Doubtlessly, Griselda sensed your potential the moment you were close enough for her to read your thoughts and heart. And she hungers for more than the blood her sons need, and would prefer to have you with her, to adore and worship her as other men have. Whether just by draining your knowledge or by possessing your body and soul, she will stop at nothing to have at her command the secrets that can free her from need of her monastery. But more important than even that, she wishes to obtain the secret by which to become completely invulnerable to mortal interference."

I was speechless at this revelation. I could have been angry as well, to understand I had been unwittingly chosen for this fantastic quest of Irmhild's. This was a story all educated practicality urged to discount. But this was no hysterical peasant sitting beside me, and my prejudices were not so strong as to deny that this woman's decisions were inspired from reason. She had jeopardized my life and future. Yet, it was for a purpose more precious to her than even the granddaughter she had unknowingly sacrificed.

"But my augury has weakened with age," she sighed. "I do not believe I shall live to see Griselda defeated. I can only hope to save Carina. Now that the proof they have taken her has been shown, we must act promptly."

She looked at me calmly. "I am trained in the ancient secret of the only amulet that can save Carina without killing her. You possess the fortitude and passion required for the amulet to work. If you are willing, I will instruct you in what preparations must be carried out for this design. And show you how to construct a weapon of personal protection in case the ravenous predilection of Griselda's sons complicate her purpose to recruit you for her cause.

"But be assured, Carina will visit you again—not only on their command, but for her desire of you—and the increasing wasting of your body that will result from these visits cannot long be kept secret. As a priestess, I am sworn to speak only the truth. And when our men begin to suspect the reason of your illness, they will come to me to deny or confirm their suspicions. For they, monsieur, are bound to hunt her down and destroy her body. More reason than the rest has Carina's own father. Her mother was returning from a visit to a friend out in the province when she was attacked and devoured utterly of both flesh and blood by these vampires. My daughter's widower is a good man and will abide no hesitation to release Carina's soul from the power that murdered his beloved.

"Of course, it would be wrong for me not to explain that you could just leave the valley now and be done with this. It is my failure of vision that has brought this upon Carina. You will know no blame if you choose to depart now and return to the civilized world."

I looked around the cozy room and smelled the comforting aroma of the last of my broth. But as I turned to the worn face beside me, not too far beneath the heavy drapes of wrinkles I saw the resemblance between this woman and her granddaughter. Her eyes were bluer than Carina's, but they implored me now, with a passion alike Carina's ardent confession that day in the grass—a passion to match my love for my auburn-haired pupil.

And I heard again the concern and desperation in Carina's voice as she had warned me to avoid venturing out at night.

I lowered the bowl to the floor and inhaled deeply. I did not know that my body quaked with anger until Irmhild's feather-soft fingertips combed soothingly through my hair.

"Whatever must be done," I told her lowly, "tell me now."

Irmhild rose, and bolted the door and closed the shutters at the window. Within the following few hours, I learned more magic from the old crone than days spent devouring the pages of one of my arcane manuscripts. If there was a price for sharing her people's earthly sorceries, and more so, for unveiling the mysteries of their principles, Irmhild never commented. Out of respect, I vowed that afternoon to bide my tongue forevermore pertaining to these pagan mysteries; though even then, I knew it doubtful that any intellectual and haughty soul beyond these remote borders would consider their value worthy of interest.

5

Before a streak of twilight amber even breathed into the sky, I was home again. Irmhild had sent Weistreim along with the crate she'd filled with the items necessary for making the amulet. I carried a basket of preserved meats she had sent along as well. She had reminded me twice to eat this, all of it, before commencing the project, as I needed my strength for the ordeal and it would be the last meal I could eat until the amulet was made. The invocation that would imbue the amulet with its powers rang as fresh in my mind as when she'd shared it. This runic verse was a magical incantation that she had taught me by singing it over and over while she had tattooed the runic symbol for Carina onto the inner flesh of my left thigh.

So, at Weistreim's departure, I ate, then set the loaded crate beside my desk. Before evening was fully set in, I drew water from the well at the back of the cabin and filled the oaken tub in the house. When it was filled, I bolted the door and undressed. When I was clean, I dried well but did not dress. And starting a fire in the hearth, I fetched a large, clean kettle from the pantry and set this in the center of my desk.

From the crate I took out a pouch of thick muslin. The gold dust that stuffed it was worth a fortune. But this I poured into the kettle, spitting into it to make it mine, as Irmhild had said. Then the kettle I hung from the iron hook in the warming fireplace. Three vials I took from the crate and set these upon the hearth. The last item I fetched was the birch spoon I had cut and whittled to Irmhild's specifications.

One of the items I had brought home was a small wood hammer I had whittled as the old woman had waited outside. It had been christened with my jism, and this impregnated the hammer amulet, as were the ritual hammers that the Urdhel menfolk wielded when they battled vampires. At Irmhild's instruction, I had pricked my palm with a needle. With my blood I had drawn upon the hammer head the runes she specified, and with this accomplished, I went on to whittle the handle to a sharp and useful point. But the practical and magical purposes for this weapon awaited the future. So I left it in the crate for the time being while I turned my attention to the pressing matters.

I laid the spoon upon the stones of the hearth as I opened the first vial. A gelatinous liquid it was, the color of cobalt, and before pouring it, I spit into the vial too. As I upturned the vial, the liquid dribbled slowly over the gold and formed glassy teardrops in the dust. Another vial contained seawater, and as water is free and mother of all life, I refrained from claiming it with my spit. When it was added, I uncorked the final vial. My blood was drawn by Irmhild's leeches, and as such, was already claimed. With it combined, I kneeled, and with my right hand grasped the spoon. And holding this over the mouth of the kettle, I inhaled and uttered the incantation for the first time.

Seventy times I stirred the concoction with my right hand, seventy times I repeated the words. I thought of Carina. Not as the specter as she had come to me the night before; no, but the living girl who had captivated me with that becoming blush, which had so attractively concealed her earthly desires from the world. With the last stir, I laid the spoon atop the kettle again and lay down in my bed.

For some time I reminisced of things I had longed to do with her—and to her—before, that was, bloodless propriety stayed my hand. I envisioned her naked body as it danced on the open grass, and the branding touch of her lips upon my throat as she had pleaded that last day we'd spoken. My desire to take her in living flesh was almost unbearable as my hand sought my manhood. My scrotum was tender from Irmhild's red-hot needles, but my need was thoughtless to this. It was the calculated, slow strokes that were stressful, the necessity to restrain my mounting pleasure. But I succeeded in building my pleasure to the point of ejaculation and stopping before my passion released.

As Irmhild had suggested, I immediately drank a cup of cool water and then relieved myself in the chamber pot. I checked on the kettle before retiring, to find the concoction just beginning to bubble. And throwing on just a small piece of wood to keep the hearth flame alive, I settled back into bed.

I was almost asleep when there sounded a rattling on the shingles. At once I sat up, not daring to let my will slip away into the shadow of dreams where I would be helpless to another attack. Now I recited the second incantation Irmhild had taught me. The command of hindrance, words that would keep Carina from entering the house, without diminishing in the slightest her desire to do so.

The spell of mastery, Irmhild had explained . . . and as I repeated it, my voice grew in boldness and clarity. The rattling turned into an agitated scraping. But as the magical words resounded through the room, the scraping paused a moment or two. Then there came a knock at the door, as clear and familiar as if it were Weistreim come with breakfast. It sounded once, twice, then continuously. A chilly sweat filmed over my flesh and my loins pulsated warmly, yet I ignored these sensations and concentrated on the incantation.

After a time, the knock died away. The words did not falter any less than when Carina had forced the alchemist secret; and this was wise, for soon I heard Carina whimpering from the other side of the door. This sublime note of abandonment and feared rejection in the sound might have at another time swayed my course. Now, instead, I listened raptly only to my own voice and took dispassionate satisfaction in the command projected.

Slowly, her whimper faded away.

6

_____

I opened the classroom the next morning and gave my apologies to the class for my absence. Somehow I managed to take up the recitations in proper feminine and masculine inflections, and resume the lesson on medieval ballads. As they practiced their letter writing, I thought only of what lay ahead that night, and rehearsed the coming incantation in my head until I forgot time itself. Only when the women started to fidget and whisper more than usual was I drawn back into reality. And smiling, I apologized again and sent them home.

The concoction was bubbling steadily in the kettle when I returned to the cabin. I stirred it the appropriate number of times and read until evening set in fully. Then I performed the cleansing rite once more and stirred the concoction again. I went to my bed and performed the heated rite as before. I could almost taste Carina's skin as I worked myself that night, and feel her beautifully molded limbs and every firm curve. My body pleaded for satisfaction, but again I denied it release. When I was finished this time, my mind was clarified of all else but the single purpose of my design. I could not sleep, yet I felt no need. I read for a time in bed ... and when later the scraping commenced on the shingles, I knew no desire but to quiet my beloved until I summoned her. The command of hindrance silenced at once, all but her frustrated whimper.

Then, abruptly, the whimper was silenced by another voice outside the door. Like the chords of an iron-strung mandolin it uttered, dismantling my composure and puncturing my focus. The words were alien to me, but the tone of their meaning held undeniable malevolence. At the sound of Carina's fearful cry, I sat up tensely. The subsequent heavy impact against the house prompted me from the bed. I took the hammer from the crate, and hoisting it over my heart, I opened the front door.

I saw nothing from the threshold, yet the soul-pricking voice grew ever more scathing. Following it to the eastern corner of the house with all the stealth at my disposal, I advanced on. At once my searching eyes found Carina. She wore a flimsy white silk gown, but her lovely knees had fallen to the ground and her arms crossed over her head defensively.

In the shade, beside my Carina, stood her assailant. A towering woman in a clinging gown of purple velvet. Even with the moonlight to her back, her complexion glowed pale and flawless. Her voluptuous ruby lips were drawn back angrily, her dark eyes gleamed like the choker of black diamonds at her throat. Her hands were graceful, her fingernails sensuously long and sharply manicured. Upon one thumb she wore a wide ring with a large carnelian orb. As she continued to browbeat Carina, her voluptuous body shook so hard the moonlight sparkled in her flowing waves of dark hair.

Her tirade stopped with a frightful silence, and as her face turned to me, her hazel eyes shone like two beacons pulling me toward some sensuous realm. Despite the lust that surged spontaneously in my loins, instinct avowed this creature was much more than a drinker of blood and life.

She was an enemy of the living, birthed in chaos far older than tale or legend.

Yet, this enemy possessed a flawless, tempting body, and a face so exquisite, it surely humbled the goddess Aphrodite. She drew herself to her full height, and her confident smile attested that already she had enslaved a legion of mortal men with the faith that evil design was inconsequential beside such beauty.

But my heart was already mastered by my submissive Carina. With a growl, I ran forward and thrust the hammer between her fair head and the vampire.

"Let her be!"

The vampire's eyes flared. For a moment, I saw the shock and terror in her eyes; the next moment, a force impacted my chest and sent me reeling back against the boards of the house. As I charged a second time, her lips pursed tightly into a crimson bow. With an exhale, she sent me reeling back again, this time so hard my skull thudded against the logs. As she clutched Carina by the roots of her hair, I raised the hammer high with my left fist.

"Let her go, I say!"

I rushed forth and grabbed Carina's arm with my free hand. Her arm could not have been colder had she been carved of ice, and her tears—like globules of rose glass—confirmed that she was no longer human. But the melancholy and terror in her eyes melted suddenly into the canvas of night. A whirlwind spun me about, knocking me back against the house. I tried to run back to the spot where I had been assaulted, but the whirlwind was as impassable as limestone. My ears perceived no sound but its violent scream. I felt an intelligence from the unnatural zephyr, one that mocked the wrath that pulsed in my veins. The next instant it tore straight through the nearby wood, leveling the copse and cleaving branches as it plunged through.

My sense of impotence was as encompassing as the moments of stoic power known only minutes before. Slowly, the powerlessness bled away, and I grew curious over what I had witnessed. The vampire woman had not attacked me, and with a stunning, but unshakable certainty, I knew that the temptation had not even passed her dark thoughts.

I went back into the house and returned to bed, but wrenching visions of the vampire woman hurting Carina allowed for shallow rest. The she-demon had been furious with my Carina; why, I neither knew nor cared, but my uncertainty as to what she could be doing compelled me to throw off the covers a couple of hours before dawn. I jumped out of the bed and quickly dressed. The hammer I placed under my trousers, with the head hung over the waistband at my hip. I took a lantern and set out of the house once more. The villagers were peaceful as I'd suspected; the only person I met was a constable who patrolled the street. He pulled me aside and asked, in the mildest of tones, where I was off to so early in the morning. I explained that I had forgotten some papers to read over at the schoolhouse and that, without my diligent attention, my pupils would find their expected lesson in romantic ballads unprepared. With a nod, he let me pass and continued on his way. I plodded on in the direction of the schoolhouse but deviated at the crossroads in front of the long lodge house where the councilmen held their meetings. The new path I took led out of the village main and through the woods that ascended up the southern valley side. The path grew very steep within these primitive shades, but it was well cleared by use, so it did not take me long to ascend to the top.

The path ended, or began here, depending on one's perspective. The fertile countryside lay silent under the heavens before me. With the lantern's light guiding the way, I strode eastward across the rim of the valley. It was a lengthy walk, and I was panting by the time the lamplight found the fence of blocks I sought.

On the day of my arrival, a fellow passenger aboard my carriage had explained to me what these blocks bordered. As high as my hips and separated each by good yard, these black objects encircled the whole of the monastery parameters. They were uncluttered edifices, without a strand of the dead overgrowth that so heavily carpeted the grounds beyond them.

I placed a hand on the block standing to my left. Smooth as satin was this uncertain stone, and although the morning sun poured down on its surface, the block was colder than steel. With the pads of my fingers, I caressed the sharply hewn edges of the top. After a moment, a leaden vibration began to resonate from within the block. I drew my hand back and heard a crow cackle angrily behind me. Another bird chirped worriedly, and another squawked in warning. In moments, it seemed every tree I had passed on my way resounded with avian discontent.

A banshee-like shriek jarred the pre-dawn air. It was a peafowl's call, and its foreboding sound silenced the other birds.

I set the lamp on the ground long enough to draw the hammer from my waistband. It looked so unthreatening, this toyishly made tool, but I brandished it in front of me as I picked the lantern back up and started across the property. It was only seconds before the lantern light revealed the dour masonry of the monastery. It was the southern transept, with a single portal hewn at the crux. As I contemplated which direction to take, a sulky, fretful cry trailed toward me from the right. Padding quietly, I came upon a passageway of black tile laid between two limestone archways. This passage, I knew, led to the eastern crux of the monastery, and as I drew closer, I saw that the limestone was covered by vines with thorns as large as daggers. The cry sounded again from down the long vista. I breathed deeply and turned the lantern's oil down to only a hair of a flame. I whispered another charm learned from Irmhild and proceeded between the archways.

It was darker than I had imagined within this intimidating

corridor, and the thorns shivered as I passed through. My ears picked up the distinct sound of vines rustling across the stones, but I did not walk into any of them, and to the relief of my suspicion, they did not offer to touch me. Another, more agonized cry hastened my gait, and soon I exited the dreadful passage and stepped onto a courtyard of the same black tile.

I stood silently, allowing my vision to adjust to the open night air again. A peafowl screeched close to my left, but when the ungodly sound faded, I heard the cry again. My eyes moved to the direction it issued from and alit upon a large object in the center of the courtyard. After a moment or two, my scrutiny clarified so that I knew what I looked upon was a very deep rectangular stone sarcophagus. Its flat, unornamented lid, however, had been edged away slightly. I saw movement suddenly behind it, and raising my eyes, I made out two or three shadowy silhouettes.

Lowering the lantern silently, I took a few steps until I could make out their dimensions clearly: two lean, robed and cowled monks, and between them they held Carina by her wrists. She struggled to release herself from their impassive hold; her flimsy gown was torn, and her hair smudged with mud. The monks ignored her struggle, and when one of them peered suddenly over his shoulder, I saw another monk advance out of the shadows from the far side of the courtyard. The cowl of his robe was pulled back so I had a good look at his sickly white face and pious sneer. He walked up behind Carina and snatched the ends of her hair with one hand. With her head forced back on her neck, she had no choice but to endure his scrutiny. Chiseled, porcelain scorn was the glare that bore down on my Carina.

He tapped her brow with a bony forefinger, making not only Carina jump, but my heart as well. My breath was anxious, but I dared not move, at least not until there was an undeniable indication of violence from the vampire monks.

I listened as the one gripping Carina's hair spoke (and if disease had a voice, its resonance could have been no unhealthier than the one I heard at that moment): "Your continued effrontery to our mother is unforgivable, Urdhel fräulein. It is time you learn to serve properly, with that simplicity and humility that is our condition and duty. Just as we, you shall not insult the laws of the universe by assuming the passions that our gracious mother has sole prerogative to indulge and the wisdom alone to utilize."

Carina's mouth quivered. "Please," she sobbed, "just let me die!"

"You will be grateful for the state we have offered you, after you have learned to serve properly."

Carina shook her head. Her tender eyes glistened with contempt. "No, I will not nurse Marcel's thoughts again—not as a passionless leech as you, or even as a glutton of flesh and blood like your vain and greedy mother! I would rather die than serve her!"

A sharp hiss cut through the night air from beyond them. Before Carina could turn her head, Griselda emerged. As graceful as a gazelle she moved, but she strode up to Carina so quickly that the uncowled vampire jumped timidly and backed away from the other side of the sarcophagus. Griselda grasped Carina's face between her trembling hands. The other two held on to Carina all the firmer, but their mother's luminous scowl cowered them visibly.

"You will die, human sow, when I am ready for you to die," Griselda said. She had spoken in Carina's own language, but now that I was unaffected by her startling physical allure, I perceived a distinctly coarse but undefined Anglo timbre in her accent.

One of the vampires holding on to Carina made a low and uncertain murmur. At once Griselda snarled at him so savagely that his knees buckled slightly as he cringed.

"She is unworthy, you fool. How dare you voice sympathy for a vile creature, one who would assume those privileges only I can appreciate!"

The vampire's head shook vigorously. With an indignant grunt, Griselda turned her imperious attention back to Carina.

"You are an ugly insect compared with me! The only reason you have not met death yet is that we need you to guide us past the trifling wards placed in the valley by you and your damnable priestess sisters. Death will come, justly and soon, you ugly, brazen thief!"

Griselda released her and wrapped her arms about herself. She spat on Carina, then glared at her for a time with the pout of a spoiled child. But her next direction came in the voice of the practiced self-victim, "Place her in the sarcophagus. There she may plead with the spiders and other insects until she is persuaded to serve me willingly."

The uncowled son moved about the sarcophagus eagerly. He untied the hemp cord from his robe, and with a nod to his brothers, the three of them wrested Carina's struggling arms behind her. While his cowled brothers secured her elbows, the berating vampire tied Carina's wrists together with the hemp. But when he bowed over and grabbed for Carina's knees, she shrieked and flailed her legs violently. Pinned by the other two, however, she was no match for his determination, and at last his ashen hands vised about her ankles. Together, the three conveyed her over the rectangular opening of the sarcophagus. As they raised her high over the portal, I caught a glimpse of something dark and hairy scurry down from one corner and into the murky recesses. Carina shrieked again as they dropped her inside, and the thud of her impact upon the cold interior surface stilled the next beat of my heart.

I squeezed the hammer's handle in frustration as they worked to push the lid back into place. Carina's screams echoed within the stone confines. My chest was heavy with the impulse to run forward and challenge them right then and there. Only Griselda's last heartless words reassured there was still time. They were not planning to leave her in the stone coffin forever, and so would not yet harm her in any way that might damage her priestess's ability to avail them safe passage into the valley. No, Griselda's aim at the moment was merely to condition through terror.

When they had sealed Carina inside, Griselda's sons began to utter some heavy, woebegone chant. The words were not Latin but some unknown language, though its cadence was reminiscent to somber Christian chants I had heard in other parts of the world. Griselda's lips turned up in a self-assured grin. She spun and paraded over the courtyard toward the shade from whence she had come. Her monstrously blithe laughter wafted through the air as her sons turned and filed after her.

I despaired to leave Carina alone in the sarcophagus. But the rite was not finished, and I knew she would suffer more if I acted rashly. I waited a while, until her panicky screams deteriorated to thin sobbing. I let the sound of this imprint itself on my memory and welcomed the vision of what vile creatures must have that moment surrounded Carina in the blackness. These things were branded upon my purpose, and clarified the ration of my hatred.

My grip crushed around the hammer's handle so that some of the splinters gave way under my hand. Drawing a long, calming breath of air, I turned away and headed back through the archways.

7

I did not sleep the rest of the night. I was miserable to think of Carina shut up in the sarcophagus, yet I knew my feelings were unproductive. Compelled to search through my collection, I found the hemp-paged copy of *The Breath of Life.* A manuscript I had only skimmed through before, I spent the remainder of hours until dawn digesting it.

The book was only one of five known existing copies of the personal and quite priceless diary of the sorcerer-priest Catullus of Aricia, written before his death by assassins of Constantine the First. Those historians who were acquainted with the rare manuscript discounted it as the delusional testimony of a half-mad pagan fanatic, but the few educated minds who had actually read it without religious bias considered Catullus's notes some of the most practical and easily understandable manuals of demonology ever recorded. In the past, my personal infatuation with ostentatious ritual had allowed little credence for the importance of such an unelaborated work. Something within me had changed; for once, I had no consideration for what aesthetic ambience I came away with. All that mattered was finding the information that I sensed was to be found within the diary's pages.

Later, after morning had come, I at last put the diary away. I went to the schoolhouse and opened class. My thoughts were on the ritual that awaited me to finish and of all my eyes had drank in the night before. My teaching duties did not interfere with the fidelity to my cause; I performed with mechanical, yet flawless, self-possession. This worked, so that even when the whispering little discussion between two of my pupils escalated into impertinent disruption, I reacted but was undaunted.

The familiar, comfortable strictness that I had feared to exert over the past few weeks came back to me. In my most implacable voice, I ordered the women—Rosemar, and her daughter, Gildemar—to their feet. They obeyed with giggling apologies that only confirmed my suspicion that unless the situation was handled with a firm hand, I would soon lose all respect in my own classroom.

Without a second thought, I ordered them to lift the hems of their frocks to their hips. The daughter's mouth fell open, and her mother crossed her arms and raised an eyebrow to deliver me a most disproving look. It was this matronly haughtiness that had to be humbled first. Snatching up my crop, I strode toward Rosemar so swiftly that she jumped.

"Dare you, sir!"

"Madam, you will remain silent or I shall send for your good husband straightaway."

Her pretty mouth puckered angrily, but there was a frightful blush in her cheeks.

"There shall be no more impertinence demonstrated in this classroom, madam. Now, you two shall lift your frocks, bend over your chairs, and hold firmly to the seats."

I caught the terrified glance exchanged between mother and daughter, but solemnly they complied, lifting their frocks ever so fastidiously. Each wore a pair of white silk underpants with scalloped lace hems. Sublime complement of sensuality and innocence were these delicate garments. As they turned and bent over their seats, a couple of gasps elicited from the rest of the class. I ignored it, poised myself behind Rosemar, and laid a steadying hand over the small of her back. As I raised the crop over her backside she let out a low, agitated groan and her shapely buttocks clenched in expectation beneath the silk undergarment. At the first thrash of my crop she shrieked loudly, but the following strokes I dealt so rapidly she hardly had time to gasp between them. Fifteen sound strokes I dealt her, and warning her not to move from her properly humbled position, I proceeded to the daughter. Gildemar received the same number of thrashes, but I allowed her to lower her frock when the punishment ended. Only Rosemar, I deemed, needed further chastening, not only for her challenging behavior of before, but to set an example to the rest of the class. Thus was the daughter allowed to sit back in her seat with a discomforted pout to keep her company while her mother remained bowed over her chair. I returned to the lesson they had interrupted, at ease for the first time within my sphere. And though I spied an occasional teardrop fall from Rosemar's face to her seat, not a single peep or whisper did I hear from any of my pupils for the remainder of the day.

8

Irmhild was standing under one of the apple trees outside as I left the schoolhouse that afternoon. A small wicker basket lay at her feet, and the green cloth inside prevented me from seeing whatever she carried in it. Her hands were behind her back as I greeted her, and the staunch timbre of her voice was a little more subdued than I recalled.

"You have the look of the famished," she said.

I smiled humorlessly, though it was a comfort to see her.

"The hunger has passed. And though my perceptions are clearer than ever in my life, it seems I do not think, but rather functionally go about my routine."

Her eyes glinted. "And never have you been more assured in your actions, yes?"

"Yes."

"I hope you have slept, at least a little."

I nodded. It was an embroidered gesture, but it seemed kinder than offering a comment that could inadvertently bring up the wrenching scene I had come across the night before. Irmhild smiled blandly. She had the faraway look of one contemplating some old inner turmoil as she peered about the lush violet-sprinkled grass.

"The gods seed paradise by men's actions," she spoke absently, "and harvest it through the desires of women."

At my silence, Irmhild sighed, and brought her arms forward and took my hand. Turning it over, she laid in my palm a wide band of cast iron. It was pliable, but only enough for the task for which Irmhild had brought it. The very feel of it made me eager to return home and finish the rite before nightfall.

"This is the last thing I may provide you. It will bring Carina out of darkness, but only your knowledge can keep her out of the shadows and exorcize the evil from whence it comes."

I stared at the metal in my palm: a fragile piece of simple iron, yet it seemed at the moment weightier than gold.

She touched my chin with her warm fingertips, and again I was struck by the resemblance between her and Carina.

"I have kept Carina's fate secret thus far. But if you fail, or if you fall into their hands, I must speak to the council. Carina must not suffer any longer. And if Griselda possesses you, likewise she possesses your knowledge. Then shall she be empowered with the means to leave her haven and resume her pillage of mortality, and worst, be immune from our wards and rites that have thus far limited her power."

The breeze tousled her long white hair, and her wrinkles seemed more pronounced as I regarded her. "I have wronged Carina by my zeal to see the vampires destroyed once and for all. Do not insult her injury by jeopardizing yourself, Marcel. Save her if you can, but do not confront Griselda. Promise me this."

I felt her mind touch my thoughts. These thoughts, bastioned by keen and sobered intent, allowed only the reassurance she sought. Smiling, I took her hand and kissed it. A wilted touch of rose shaded her cheeks.

"It is my mistake that led Carina to resign hope, not yours,"

I said. "And I intend to do nothing more now than to recapture and protect her."

She seemed content with this, and stooping, handed me the basket.

"After your work is finished, eat," she instructed. "Weistreim is the baker's apprentice and made this himself from the old recipe."

Without waiting for a reply, Irmhild turned and started up the street toward her home. Her shoulders were rounded and her gait wearily patient. My gut twisted with outrage to know the cause of her weariness. But smartly, I subdued the emotion, useless for the time, and tucked the items she had brought beside whatever was covered in the basket. Then I tidied up the classroom and hurried off.

I did not return immediately to my cabin. Carina's unexpected entombment obliged certain extra measures on my part than for which I was willing to admit to her grandmother. I made a trip to the blacksmith's shop and asked to see the sturdiest iron rod available. The man showed me an assortment of simple rods that could be used as base material for other tools. Nothing, however, sturdy enough to pry open the sarcophagus. Then I noticed a rusted poker standing by the fireplace. A weighty-looking object, it stood at least to my shoulders—too large an item for an ordinary household. Interested, I inquired of it.

"Came by it from one of the duke's donation fairs," the man explained, "or as they are known here, his housecleaning fairs." The blacksmith's eyes widened as he regarded the thing. "I would not wish to have to maintain the hearth for which that thing is required, would you?"

I went and examined it carefully. The rust flaked away easily, and I saw that the poker was only iron plated. The core was steel.

"How much would you take for it?"

He looked flustered and thoughtful at once. At last he replied with an earnest nod, "Promise to come to the wedding when I marry little Gretchen next month and it is yours, schoolmaster."

The name brought the image of one my pupils to mind.

"Gretchen, the carpenter's daughter?"

He nodded, and the corners of his mouth turned up proudly. "The very one. And I promise, once we are married, she will be on time to class every morning."

I laughed gently, and a few minutes later I left the shop with the poker posed over my shoulder. It was cumbersome, but I managed to carry it and the basket back home. Inside, I stood the poker against the frame of the door, which I then locked. I placed the basket on my nightstand, then undressed and performed the ritual bath anew.

Clean and still naked, I approached the cauldron over its steady flame, repeated the incantation, and performed the proper number of stirs. A deep bowl of water I set upon the hearth, and with tongs from the pantry shelf, I lowered the iron band into the bubbling gold ooze. Releasing it for several moments to swirl in the mixture, I closed my eyes and imagined the culmination of my desires. Then with the tongs I lifted the band out and submerged it into the water. The water hissed for a couple of minutes, and when I was satisfied, I again grasped the band with the tongs. This fashioned collar I laid over a clean linen on the desk.

While it dried, I fetched a tiny wooden container from amongst the items brought from Irmhild's abode. This I set beside the wisps of Carina's hair on the nightstand by the bed. When the collar was dry and satisfactorily cooled, I took it to the bed and sat down cross-legged on the mattress. I turned it in my hands and admired for a time the gleam the gold retained despite the other ingredients that had gone into its mixture. The entire collar tingled against my flesh, like honey when held in one's mouth. Laying it beside me on the mattress, I glanced at the poker beside the door once again. Then I lay down with my head upon the pillow. It wasn't even close to evening as I closed my eyes. I thought of Carina, of course, but the time to indulge fantasies was over. Yet, I knew that the realization of them was not an egg I could wisely count yet. I smiled at my own growing superstitions. My focus and resolve were primed to an almost hypnotic sharpness and cleansed entirely of interfering mortal doubt or hesitation. I envisioned what was to come later that night, a thing unfamiliar, yet my mind had rehearsed it so well that my envisioned steps touched me as familiar. I recited to myself the incantations learned throughout the years that would make me invisible to the vampire's eyes when I returned to the monastery. I repeated the words Irmhild had taught, words of power that would bless my wielding of the magical hammer. And I rehearsed the banishments she had shared, those that would break any spell Griselda had placed upon Carina to compel her to fight against salvation.

But as I allowed myself to drift off into a half sleep, it was a rite from the Catullus writings that illuminated before my mind's eye. A certain exorcism that had fascinated me the night before, one fashioned not of ceremony and detached determination, but of primordial emotion. A process as uncivilized as the demonic spirits that it was intended to eliminate. I was not certain of why my mind needed reiteration on this rite, but soon I lost all sense of everything but for the sound of my unspoken voice repeating it.

A dozen times, fifty times, maybe a hundred I recited it. The words resonated through every visceral particle and spiritual vestige of my being. I was swept away into the invocation, so utterly was I aware of nothing afoot in the house until an iced blade touched my forehead.

I gasped at once and opened my eyes to find what I had felt was not metal or ice, but the nails of fingers caressing me.

It was Carina. She wore a coarse blue-dyed gown with heavy,

bell sleeves. Only a peep of white cleavage could I see, but her skin was aglow with the radiance of health and life. She gifted me with that smile I had so missed as she bent down and imparted a kiss to my mouth. A freshly plucked rosebud, still cool from the morning frost, were her lips. They trembled with the promise of delights fulfilled.

My drowsy mind was rapidly becoming inebriated. My loins inflamed and stiffened. She drew down the coverlet and sheet with one graceful hand, and shyly stroked my stomach and chest.

"Schoolmaster," she whispered, "I need you. . . ."

She sat down on the bedside and traced her fingertips down to my left thigh. With a rustle of a giggle she cupped my balls. My mouth watered under her caress and the very sight of her. So alive she was, or so my eyes told me. With a bashful tilt of her head, her fingers glided up and down my shaft. How warm, alive she felt, and the light sensation she impelled was maddening, defying all the logical warnings that shouted in my brain. She bent over me, and my skin was set aflame. My nipples hardened beneath the weight of her pressing breasts.

Carina's tongue lapped playfully over my chin. "Will you not kiss me of your own accord, schoolmaster?"

I could only look at her. I was a man sinking under clashing waves of desire and patient caution. She kissed me again, moaning softly into my mouth. Grasping the root of my cock, she began to stroke me. I was plunged deeper beneath the waves, and the contrasting currents were vying to blind me now to everything except the physical need to claim her.

Her mouth released me, her hand too. She inclined over me carefully, and her weight was as inconsiderable as straw. Her eyes held mine; but though they glinted with passion, there was a mechanical steadiness to all her movements, even in the somber pout that came to her mouth. My desire slackened and rational thought buoyed me up to crest the waves.

"I know your wishes now, Marcel."

I felt a power emanate through her, an intelligence alien and separate from the true sweetness of her character. It was not even similar to the passionate vampire who had ravished me before. This power sought to captivate me with ardor, confuse and bind me with my own affections. My cock was squeezed gently between her thighs. I released a deliberate moan. I felt the power try to scour through my mind, and it was faux desire alone that now shielded my reason.

"Yes, you still desire the beauty you've always denied yourself. . . ."

I granted her a convincingly entranced nod.

With an approving purr, she bunched the hem of the gown up to her thighs and straddled my waist. Sublime confidence sparkled in her eyes as she regarded me. She toyed with my nipples, pinching them slightly, and trailed a fingertip from my chest to my collarbone. Her hips undulated a moment, and I realized how very dry her nether mouth was, nothing like the lathering, ardent little portal I had known before. She gathered her hair atop her head and peered at me with the look of a triumphant Amazon. She expected me to be spellbound by her gaze, lost of will utterly, as if I had been born and destined to lose myself to the unholy pillage she planned. And so, I feigned just that.

She pressed my wrists into the mattress over my head and leaned forward to kiss me roughly. Her lips skimmed over my ear, then down to the cleft of my throat. She released my arms and pinched my nipples, harshly enough I had to suppress a protest. But it brought a careless laugh to her, and as her lips buried into my throat, the fingertips of my right hand sought out the smooth metal of the collar on the coverlet beside me.

Her mouthed roved over my jugular vein. Her tongue flicked over the area, pumping my circulation with the brisk movement.

She arched her back and pressed me deeper into the mattress, and with a wanton sigh, her lips drew back. I felt the sharp tips of teeth press into my flesh.

I snatched the collar firmly, clasped my arms about Carina's shoulders, and took hold of both ends of the collar with my hands. The iron frame lengthened easily. Carina grunted, but unaware of the reason for my sudden movement, only pressed harder on my shoulders. I clamped the collar down hard against the back of her neck. She hissed uneasily, and at the moment her head raised, I noosed the thing about her throat.

With a squeal, she leaped back on her heels. My force held staunchly as she thrashed and tore at my hands and the collar both. I sat up and she was trapped, straddled over my thighs as I held on to the collar. Her hair was snatched between the thing and her neck. The more she struggled, the more disheveled her hair became, and served as a barrier against her scraping nails and my hands while I spoke the last incantation of the rite.

When the last Germanic word was uttered, Carina stopped struggling. But she began to growl angrily, and through her tousled auburn locks I saw her eyes had lost the sweet light of life. Black they looked, devoid of even the memory of humanity. The radiance seeped from her skin, the semblance of heat as well.

"Pull your hair out," I commanded.

She shivered in fury, and when she did not comply, I said, "Do it now or receive punishment."

Carina howled with malicious laughter. The next moment, she gasped and shook her head violently. In utter frustration, she screamed and beat the crown of her head with her fists. At length she slumped and began to sob. I raised to my knees and allowed her to fall back on the bed.

"Marcel?" She sounded honestly bewildered, and I felt Griselda's possession slip away.

"Oh, no," she said faintly, shaking her head. "No, Marcel, let me go! What you have done is dangerous, foolish!"

I retained my hold on the collar with my right hand, and with the other, brushed the hair from her face. Her tears were running down her cheeks so that her face looked like that of a rain-misted alabaster statue. Slowly, carefully, I pulled her long hair free of the collar and pressed the ends to my lips. The corners of her pallid lips turned up sadly; her tears spilled heavier.

"I am dead to all the world, poor Marcel! I have wronged you and insult your household to be here. I am a failure to my very people."

"No," I murmured, "that is not true, none of it."

"Yes, it is. Allow me only the mercy to die now!"

My heart sank to hear her anguished words. But the time to finish the rite completely had come. I straddled her chest now, keeping the collar cinched steadfastly. She winced shamefully and turned her eyes, weeping desolately. With my thumb I caressed her bottom lip.

"Look at me, Carina."

When she closed her eyes tightly and shook her head, I spoke with unwavering firmness, "You will look at me, Carina, as I say."

At her hesitant compliance, I grasped my cock. I admired her beautiful face, those eyes that haunted me always. I remembered her sitting astride my lap, and the taut, virginal orifice that had swallowed my manhood. All the fantasies I had avoided while she was living surged with unbridled zeal into my conscious mind. My cock swelled, and I outlined her lips with the head. How sorely I wished to see her feed upon me this way.

Later, sweet later, I told myself.

She stared as I stroked off. When I felt my climax approach, I raised a little on my haunches and released over her chest. The orgasm was painfully, thoroughly rapturous for the delay of the ritual. And when my mind was sober, I stretched over and snatched the wooden container from the nightstand. This I showed to Carina.

"Open this."

Her hands trembled as she removed the lid. I dipped my fingers into the red resin within and gathered a gob. I clenched the ends of the collar firmly again and carefully smeared the resin on the touching ends. Then, reaching to her chest, I dipped my forefinger into my jism, and this I dabbed over the resin. Carina made a startled whimper, but I did not meet her eyes then; rather, I watched as a soft, faint yellow glow burnished the magical glue. The glow spread about the entire length of the collar, then intensified to a sunlit radiance a moment or two before fading away.

When it had dissipated, I looked at Carina. She was sobbing still, quietly now, unaware in her shock of what I beheld: the pallidness fading quickly from her skin, replaced by the bloom and suppleness of real life. The blue-green of her eyes shone forth brilliantly once more. So joyous I was to feel the genuine warmth in her body again that tears sprang to my own eyes.

"You are no longer theirs, Carina. You are free to live under the sun's gaze once more, to see your own reflection and know you are warded securely from the touch or compulsion of Griselda and her brood."

Her eyes widened, blinked, and as she nursed her bottom lip, it was apparent she felt it too.

"Oh, Marcel," she whispered. "It is true, it is true!"

I got off of her at last and sat down on the mattress. The container of resin I pitched to the pillows, then draped over and kissed her. The touch of her mouth sent a wave of relief and possessiveness through me.

"I will never let you go again, Carina," I declared. "The collar cannot be removed except by magic as ritualized and resolute as that which created it. And that is a secret I will share with no one, not even you. While a single vampire roams this earth, you are vulnerable without it. And even were I to discover they had all suddenly vanished from the world, I would still keep it there, as reminder of what you mean to me."

I touched the enchanted band about her throat. "Here it is, and here forever it remains."

I felt her heartbeat pitch as she searched my eyes. "Truly, Marcel?"

"Yes, Carina. Why else would I have gone through all this?"

She was silent, frowning hesitantly, as if still she could not quite believe. I kissed the salted tears from her face, and laid down beside her and pulled her close. Taking her hands, I started to kiss her palms when I noticed how dirty her hands were. A nameless suspicion roused the hair on the nape of my neck.

"Sit up and remove that gown," I said.

At her shocked tremble, I repeated the order. She obeyed slowly, and I saw with bitterness that numerous angry scrapes and raised, dark bruises were appearing over her arms and legs. The injuries, I knew, were doubtless from her struggle to escape the sarcophagus, and probably from initially unearthing herself from the grave as well. My wild and wanton woman-child had been so sorely misused! I threw the ugly gown to the floor and lay her down. I looked upon, with human clarity, the breadth of all she had suffered. Her breath was fatigued, yet her gaze had lost none of the adoring ardor since that day we had spoken in the valley. I embraced her fiercely. I rued for the secret of turning time back, to stifle those proper, cowardly words with which I had spurned her. At least fate had been merciful to have directed the vampires to let her free, instead of forcing her to remain in the sarcophagus until I could free her!

"Marcel, I could not stop myself. I was torn between following her orders and protecting you as best I could, or at least in the only way I could fathom."

"I know," I said, "and you will not reproach yourself on this, not ever again. But I hope you can forgive me."

"What is there to forgive?"

I smiled sadly. "For that shameful propriety that I allowed to hinder me from claiming that which you offered so earnestly. I was a fool, Carina."

"Oh, Marcel," she sighed. "It is only that I love you."

"Yes, and never again will you reproach yourself regarding this that befell you? If you do, you shall regret it . . . most sorely."

Her eyes shone with unshed tears. Her whispered answer was ripe with passion, "As you wish, Marcel."

"As I command," I corrected, and her cheeks flooded scarlet.

I could not help but smile and kiss her palms fervently. I reflected again on the delicious chastisements I should have given to her before, and vowed they would be administered soon enough.

I stroked her hair and patted her raised hip. I was just about to rise and get her something to eat when I heard an ungodly sound from outside the house. It brought an immediate image of a nest of angry snakes to my mind. Gooseflesh sheeted over me, and I realized my task was not yet complete, nor would it be as long as Griselda's brats existed to carry out her desires.

Carina raised her own head and whimpered. "They have followed me."

For several moments, we listened as the hissing of the vampires grew angrier, louder. The sound seemed to blanket the entire frame of the house. The windows clattered against their sills, the interior walls jarred. From the kitchen we heard the cups and plates fall off the shelves and break over the floor. After a time, the sound began to recede, and the house stood again quiet.

"They dare not enter or make trouble," I assured her. "The

rites are complete, and you wear the collar. Without you, they must return to the monastery. They cannot venture out without your power to guide them past the wards."

She did not seem any less troubled by my words. Although I wished more than anything to stay with her all night, I sat up.

"Listen to me," I instructed. "You are safe. You will not leave this house until I can return to explain your presence to your father and the others."

I stood up from the bed to find my clothing. Carina got to her knees and grabbed my hand desperately.

Anxiety broke her voice, "Marcel, what is this? I know I am safe now; I feel it. There is no need for you to go . . . out there!"

I took a clearing breath and closed my eyes against the provocative vision she was on both knees upon my own bed.

"Obey me, my kitten," I said. "Your collar may not bind you to my will, but bound you are nevertheless. Another word, and I will demonstrate here and now how well I have divorced my hesitations regarding you."

She let go my hands, but as I dressed I saw she had not moved, and her face was crumpled with conflicting dread and the desire to obey. When my boots were laced, I came back, kissed the crown of her head, and gestured for her to lie down.

"I expect to find you in this bed when I return."

She did lay down but started crying again. "You will not return! And I will live a lifetime in the sun, yes, but without you!"

For a moment, I thought to toss her over, punish her at last, soundly, thoroughly. It would silence her and would consummate all that heaven had brought between us.

It was not cowardice this time that stayed my hand, but the niggling apprehension that she could be right. As well as she needed my stern discipline, and as potently as I wished to deliver it, at that moment I needed more to kiss her mouth.

And so I did, relishing the taste as a condemned man carries the smells of his last meal to the gallows. I went and got the poker, and though I knew she was perfectly safe, I deemed the steel of which it was made might give her some comfort and laid it beside her on the bed. Then, taking the hammer, I left the house. Her sobbing grew forlorn as I closed the door behind me. But neither of us could afford my regard for it now.

I raised the hammer and pushed out all thought. On Griselda's brood alone I focused, honing in on the malignant feel of them imparted to the landscape. I smelled their lingering corruption in the air. My eyes skirted here and there as I proceeded, suspiciously scanning every obstacle I approached or passed along my way. My head jerked toward every uncertain sound, and my hands clenched firmer and firmer about the hammer's handle.

It was not until I had climbed the path out of the valley and stepped onto the dewy pastureland that I spotted the first ones: two lingerers, draped on their knees under the moonlight with their backs to me. Their cowls were thrown back, and they were devouring the entrails of the dog brought down on the ground before them. The animal's face was turned toward me, but by the cloudy, unfocused look of its eyes I knew it was dead. A low, bestial growl emanated from the vampires as they gulped the entrails and slurped the blood.

I did not breathe as I came up behind them. The first swoop of the hammer met the skull of the one to my left. He let out a shrill scream, and instantly the second literally flew up to his feet. As his immaculate white hands tore at me, I pivoted and struck. The hammer struck him in the shoulder. He screamed and tumbled away. Leaping back, I raised the hammer again and turned on the first, who was slithering toward me on the ground. For a second, I saw that the indention in his skull was minimal, but what appeared as a liquid smoke tendril trailed out of the flesh and bone of his tonsured head. Just as I was about to deliver my blow, the second grasped his arms about my own. The impact was halted, and I wrestled with him until my arms lowered. I thrust both back hard, and my elbows thudded into the creature's robed solar plexus. He hissed balefully at my ear; his fingers gouged through my shirt into my flesh. With a roar I drove the hammer backward and felt the staked handle pierce his torso.

At once I heard something like a heavy sigh. The first vampire let out a desolate wail. The next moment, I felt the weight on the handle dissipate and the soft rustle of a robe falling to the ground. I had no time to see what had happened; the first was clawing at my legs. Whether he was trying to raise himself or draw me down I did not know or care. I was blind to thought as I cast the hammer high. Aiming the staked end, I bore it down, straight between the vampire's eyes. The same gasping sigh I had heard before issued from the punctured brow. Blackness veined rapidly over his features; smoke steamed out of the pores of his skin. His now dusk-lipped mouth gaped in disbelief, but no other sound did I hear. His form seeped into itself before my eyes. His robe sank over the earth. A silhouette haze winked where he had been. Then this, too, vanished.

I stood panting and studied the robes lying on the grass. They had been Griselda's real children, not vampires sired by other vampires, and the question as to whether they had souls crossed my mind. But only for a moment. I headed on in the direction of the monastery. As I neared the hedge of black blocks, the skin at the nape of my neck raised. I was urged by instinct to turn around, and just as I did, an oblique shadow swooped silently from the nearest tree. I dodged left, in time to see a figure in waving, voluminous cloth alight on the earth beside me.

My arms raised with the hammer as he threw back his cowl. I looked up at the face of the vampire who had reproached Carina with the diseased voice the night before. The surprise in his face entailed nothing of what I expected; rather, he regarded me with only mild disgust.

"You come now? After taking what does not belong to you! What demonstration of vain human fealty is this to our mother?"

His question baffled me, but more so the conflict that rang in his tone. My ears detected others slithering closer through the brambles, but I also felt their hesitance as I did from the speaker. They encircled me, and as I spun in preparation to assail them all with the hammer, I saw they had no intention of attacking. An aura of discontent emanated from them. It stagnated the air with an uncertain madness, and yet, it seemed to stay the aggression I had fully expected. The condemnations of the others rifled sourly through the air.

"Make him humble for pardon," called another, "before presenting him!"

"See, brother, how he struts even now with his precious human toy!"

The one with the hideous voice gestured for silence, and their ranting subdued to only hoarse grumbling.

Whatever it was I had done to displease them, I sensed it would work more readily to my advantage at the moment than wielding the hammer. I faced the disease-voiced one who was obviously the leader.

"I will leave the hammer at the entrance to your home. It is not hers until I have inspected her to my satisfaction and am certain she is all that I traveled to this land to find, and certainly before giving my life for the cause."

This brought a round of seething contempt from the pack. But their leader summoned them to peace.

His shoulders slumped as he pulled the cowl back over his skull.

"Be prepared, Nocturne Liaison, to give your apology for your high-handedness. Our mother has spurned sorcerer kings of your race! I should think a simple schoolteacher would demonstrate at least humble gratitude."

The air congested with silence then. He approached me and

gestured ahead. "But I see no reason she should wait any longer to at least welcome the one she has chosen."

The others stood back as I followed him through the brushed land to the passageway between the limestone archways. The vines that had touched me as unnatural before seemed nothing more than harmless flora as we passed through. As we entered the courtyard, two peahens flew before the vampire guide, and a peacock, standing near the shadowy thickets, raised his magnificent show of tail feathers. The hateful sarcophagus had been left with its lid moved partially aside, and a large, hairy spider skirted across the open frame. My chest tightened, but it was the only remnant of emotion that touched me. We continued into the dark grove on the other side of the courtyard, only a short distance this, and came out into a slender clearing.

The eastern portal of the monastery was here, and torches lined the clearing. Their light illuminated a statue of a leonine angel that stood on a marble pedestal. His magnificent wings were caught in graceful flight, and his robes had been fashioned in such a way that the sculpted fabric appeared to cascade in ripples down his body. His face was beautiful, and his fine features were rendered with the severest of countenances. I was astonished to see the depicted fabric had been sculpted in such a method as to lend the impression of an immoderate phallus bulging beneath the robe. The angel's right hand grasped at his hip the head of a female carven figure by its hair. The angel's left hand wielded a sword. Its stylized rippling blade was aimed at heaven. The head's mouth was frozen into a disfigured circle; its eyes sunken and open in shock.

More surprising than this, however, was the door at the eastern facade. This was an unusual element, as most Christian buildings of cruciform design were absent of eastern portals. The door itself was made of the same stone as the black blocks that bordered the monastery property. The vampire monk pressed it in easily enough, and light from within the monastery seeped out as he stepped inside. This light glazed the clearing grass in luminous silver.

"The pagan toy," he spoke, "leave it at the doorway. I will present it to mother . . . after she has voiced satisfaction in you."

His evident fear of the thing tempted me to bring the hammer inside just to torment him. But I put aside the selfish notion and leaned the weapon upside down against the frieze casing before crossing the threshold.

I blinked against the brilliant light, then saw that we had entered the eastern apse. The walls of the semicircular room were fashioned of pale wood, and the floor was tiled with ivory. Little ebony sconces set with wax candles protruded in at least a dozen places from the walls, producing the illumination that bounced off the walls and floor. A brazier sat in the center of the room. Some dried vegetation had recently been thrown over the flame. It gave off a rich, calming aroma along with its milky smoke. My eyes flashed to the ceiling only long enough to glimpse the mural of a strutting peacock gazing down on us. As I followed the vampire monk toward the ambulatory, I detected a sour, putrid smell to the air that the incense could not completely mask.

My guide was silent as we proceeded past the crowded cedar walls of the ambulatory. His shoulders slumped ever more with each passing step. At length we reached a wall of black stone. It was a curious obstacle; I would have thought this way led to the high altar, though I kept my musing to myself. A rounded marble lintel thrust out, and beneath this was a door of the pale wood as found in the apse. The vampire raised the knuckles of his right hand. With a flash of a repulsed glimpse to me, he knocked.

Within a moment, the door opened, and he gestured me before him with an exaggerated bow. As I stepped into the room beyond, my nostrils were overcome with the invisible waves of a smell much like refined ambergris. The circular room was large, paneled in the costliest mahogany, and carpeted with thick indigo rugs. Black lace curtains sparkling with jewels hung haphazardly from ruby pegs on the ceiling, which, I noticed briefly, was muraled, too, with the titanic image of a masculine face. This face was beautiful, exotic, haloed by waves of black hair, and dominated by a pair of languid Aegean-blue eyes. It took only seconds to realize it was the same face from which the statue outside had been depicted.

I only regarded it a second, maybe two; but as my attention returned to the room, I saw a lithe figure moving toward us from out of the curtains of black lace. The vampire guide bowed low as a pair of gold-sandaled feet glided into view.

She was more statuesque than I remembered, an inch or so taller than myself. The perfume of her body was so potent that my brain was momentarily addled. Her high-throated gown was of peacock blue silk, and her hair was piled in soft waves atop her head, and pinned with pearled and silver-leafed combs.

The moment I looked into her face, my chest panged with desire. The lashes of her long hazel eyes were naturally thick and dark. I noticed for the first time the beauty mark at the left corner of her wide, sensual mouth, and how perfectly sculpted were her subtly arched eyebrows. She regarded me with a strange pout as she laid one hand upon a hip and tapped the fabric of her gown there with her long, ruby-hued nails.

My every masculine sensibility felt lulled, tempted, drugged, aroused. It was not only her incomparable beauty and flawless physique, but the smell of her, and the unseen and confident aura that clung to her as uniquely and surely as her own skin. I knew she had every right to be so proud. Perfect in every physical detail, highlight, curve, and abstraction.

Not like Carina, with her short-lived mortal beauty and limited human potentials.

If this thought had come from my own mind, or was offered by Griselda herself, I did not want to know.

All my desire for Carina was welcomingly cast away. I spoke with the voice of the intoxicated lover, the impassioned challenger, the constant worshipper.

I fell to one knee and lowered my head before Griselda. "I have been mistaken," I said humbly. "In your presence, I have found all that I have sought. I am yours, Griselda—and willingly surrender the secrets that will free you."

She stepped toward me and placed a sandaled foot upon my thrust knee. My eyes swept up her ankle and to the hem of her gown. I relished the image of well-proportioned legs that were inevitably veiled beneath the fabric.

"You come without weapon. Do you truly believe it so simple to make amends for the insult of chasing after that female?" Even with the underlying displeasure, her husky voice was sweeter than the best tuned harp. "I should take you now, reap the fruits of thy knowledge, and be done with you!"

I looked up and saw the tight purse of her mouth. She was as insulted as she was needy for my knowledge.

"I am a fool," I declared. "Take my knowledge now—quickly—for what I have done! I do not deserve a moment to worship you."

"Yes," spoke up the son dryly, "even unto tonight has he proved his faithlessness."

Griselda's eyes narrowed and she lowered her foot again. I expected her to question him on what he meant; there was no denial I could give to excuse my actions. But to my surprise, she turned on her son.

"It was your duty to curb the beast," she said. "I told you of the poison she was capable of plying into his heart. If there is any to be held accountable here, it is you."

The vampire flinched. His head lowered humbly, though I caught the dimmest glint of exasperation in his voice as he said slowly, "Yes, my lady. But you were not there; you did not feel what we felt at his windows when—"

His words were cut off abruptly by a release in her snug aura. It spilled over us both, a half-visible vapor that in its fury vied to snatch my breath away. It turned on the son and knocked him backward from where he stood. As I struggled to inhale the thin oxygen, her unspoken wrath reverberated through the room. "We have had this discussion before! You will not accuse me, ever! It was insulting enough to have to follow the bitch mortal once. It is not for me to roam these lands unless I choose to roam! You would have me go into mortal land without proper procession like some unrefined peasant? Perhaps it is time I turn you over to these pagan peasants and let them deal with you to the full measure of their boorish delight!"

The son regarded her inanimate body dispassionately. His eyes were two hollow, wounded black orbs. "No, mother, that is not what I wish. All I meant—"

A gust of unseen energy knocked him back again, this time so rudely he was pushed to his backside on the floor.

"I decide what is of consequence. Leave now—inform your brothers I am not to be disturbed. And then you, my presumptuous son, are to wander the province until the approach of sunrise."

He looked as crestfallen as a deserted child as he got to his feet.

At his silence, her voice thundered again, "Go, now!"

He bowed deeply, then turned and fled out the door. It shut heavily behind him, and looking up at her stony hands, I saw the fingers quicken and felt her contained aura draw itself back into her body.

But as I dared to meet her eyes, the white-heat anger that had marked her face disappeared. A smile came to her lips, so elegantly severe that my mouth watered to kiss them.

"Remember this, Marcel Rolant," she said, "it is I alone who determines what is of consequence. And I alone who determines how my requirements are carried out, and when."

Her fine chin raised and she regarded me indifferently. "There will be no easy amends for you. Now, onto your knees, Nocturne Liaison."

I went to all fours and languidly kissed her feet. The feel of her toes against my mouth sent a pleasurable ripple down my spine. I readily welcomed it, and envisioned the calves above my brow, the portal of her womanhood between her legs. My desire plummeted and centered into my loins, taking my willed conscious thoughts with it to color my aura. I felt her vampire eyes pore over my pulsing aura, so boldly presented that her narcissistic regard was silently pacified.

Griselda displayed no reaction as she scrutinized me, but at length she turned and snapped her fingers. I crawled after her clicking soles past half a dozen more black lace hangings, through a door that opened into a smaller compartment. There was a great fireplace here, burning low with scented herbs, and upon a marble dais, a huge bed covered with a rich blue coverlet and quilted over with peacock feathers.

She sat primly on the edge of the bed and crossed her legs. My eyes lowered as I waited for her to speak or act. And when she reached to my head and stroked my hair, my manhood grew erect and inflamed.

Griselda leaned close to my face. Her mouth was the scent of roses and ambergris. "Why did it take so long for you to present yourself to me, handsome Marcel?"

I did not answer at first. At last I thought the truth was sufficient, "I did not understand at first that it was for this moment that destiny led me to this valley."

She laughed softly. "And I am not so anxious as to allow myself approached easily. Unlike your mortal slut, schoolmaster."

The words were meant to barb me, test me. But there was no taunt that could dismantle my aspired lust.

I replied in words she could appreciate, "You cannot deny there is a sublime satisfaction in the claiming of another."

Her smile turned languorous, and the flick of her tongue across her bottom lip heightened my passion to an uncomfortable level. "My forgiveness for the fleeting indulgence of vanity will be my gift to you. But you belong to me now, Nocturne Liaison—body, soul, and mind."

"Yes." I bowed my head to kiss her feet again, but her fingers clutched the roots of my hair and held me back.

"Do you know that Solomon himself could not approach me so close?"

I shook my head, and her mouth swept over my face. Her cool, poised lips scorched my flesh. I trembled with heat and hindered desire.

"Up to your knees," she breathed. I raised humbly to my knees, and she fell back on her elbows to the mattress and lifted a foot to my shoulder. She drew up the hem of her gown just enough that she could caress my cheek with one of those calves I had so earnestly imagined. Silken alabaster was her skin. I did not grasp it as I suffered to do so, but turned my face and kissed her leg. She gave a throaty note of approval.

"Worship me," she commanded. "Demonstrate your fidelity is to me, and not only to the cause of my father."

"You are my only cause," I sighed.

She fell back completely, raised her feet to the edge of the bed, and pulled her gown back over her knees. Her milky thighs parted and I looked greedily upon her brunette pelted sex. As my knees padded closer, she coddled the front of her gown, pulling her breasts over the bodice and groping her large areolae. Reverently, I parted her thighs and kissed the inner flesh. My face lowered to her fount. The ivory lips were swollen and dewed, perfumed with a musk more tantalizing than a cabalist passage, more potent than any pagan incantation. Her damp pubic curls tickled my face, luring the passion into a torment. A proud temple of unsurpassable promises was this portal my lips touched.

With my fingers, I gingerly unfolded her labia. My tongue darted between the fine, inner lips. Ice and fire was her pulsating flesh. I slid my arms gently over her thighs and licked her cunt. I heard her sigh, and glancing up, saw that her lovely eyes had closed. She was massaging her breasts still as I gave her portal an adoring kiss. She moaned, and I drew my tongue lightly over her clit's satiny hood. Hard as a diamond, and like a diamond, it drew the very heat from my mortal tongue. For a moment, I tantalized it by licking the hood back and sucking gently on the organ. Griselda moaned deeper, and I saw her fingers rake through the coverlet.

She was abandoned now in her passion, and satisfied, I clutched her thighs firmly. She made a lush, curious sound, but with the gentle kiss I gave her clit, her hips buckled urgently and she closed her eyes.

With a final, deliberate kiss to her clit, I inhaled deeply. I envisioned the lust congested in my loins. I exhaled steadily, forcing the physical lust from my body. It seeped from the pores of my skin, and my will thrust it along with the shielding aura from my body. I shoved her thighs widely apart now and positioned my lips at her fount. Again, I inhaled, and drew to the forefront of my thoughts the bided intention of my goal.

As I exhaled, my breath must have tickled her, for her muscles flinched and she made a surprised little murmur.

But my senses were focused for a single purpose now. The words of the Catullus exorcism departed from my lips and penetrated her vagina. The echo, as I spoke the incantation, pealed softly through her sex, and I felt the resonance shatter her nether muscles and pour into the blood vessels and arteries.

Griselda cried out painfully and tried to rise.

"Release me!"

Her knees pitched against my arms, and she tried to wrestle loose from my grip. Fighting her immortal strength, I had to dig my fingernails into her thighs to retain my grasp of her. Her hips bucked back and she struggled fiercely to kick me off. As the incantation continued to pour into her sex, she clawed at my head. Her long fingernails scraped savagely over my forehead and into my brows. Her back arched forward, and digging her heels into the mattress, her thighs strained up. I was brought off my knees, and as her hips tossed this way and that, I pulled her legs toward me and buried my face as deeply as possible into her bleeding sex.

"Faithless bastard—what have you done?"

Her thighs vised against my face. Just as I felt her twist at the waist and my own balance give, the last syllable of the exorcism passed into her. She screamed, and the next moment her labia quickened violently. Her sticky flesh curled away from my mouth.

I nearly fainted. My hold released and I fell to my knees. Her sandals beat wildly against my head. With a roar, she crawled on her back away from me, the peacock feathers waving under her weight as she retreated to the other side of the bed. I half swooned to the floor, and for several moments lay in a lightless fog with only her screams to keep me company.

When I recovered enough to get to my knees again, Griselda's furious wails resounded upon the walls. But I did not see her. Staggering around the bed, I found her on the floor. Her long, beautiful fingernails scraped over the tiles of the floor as she stared up at me. Her mouth was agape, her shocked eyes bore into me like two rusty flames.

My eyes moved down and saw that her hips had already imploded into her pelvis; her vagina, nothing more than a tangled mass of tissue now, was sinking into the crushed pelvis. Her belly and spine were pulling together, and looking down at her, I saw that the toes of her feet were nothing now but cavities where the digits had sunk into the sandaled feet. I heard the bones of her legs snap methodically, loudly; and before my unsympathetic eyes, her feet started to recede into her ankles.

"Help me!"

Her plea did not stir compassion. The shock of her humbled vanity gave me only delight. The only regret I had was that Carina could not see the vampire queen's fitting demise.

I watched a few minutes longer, until her legs had vanished into what gore remained of her torso and her breasts bowled into craters on her chest. I wanted her to suffer the last alone, sans any admirers, without the tears of her devoted, unloved sons to comfort her ego. But I did not depart with uncivilized silence.

"I go now to make love to my own queen—whose beauty of heart and spirit will be stamped upon my memory more surely than even the secrets you strove to pillage."

She tried to scream, but the sound was faint and raspy, desolate like the peafowl she kept for pets. It did not haunt me, though, and I turned then and left her. Past the drapes of black lace I walked, and through the door I had entered. I ignored the mural face with its glowering hedonist eyes, made my way through the ambulatory, and reentered the apse. My heart beat with confidence as I opened the door and reclaimed the hammer. Two of Griselda's sons stood talking in the clearing as I walked out. They regarded me reluctantly; obviously, Griselda's earlier warning had reached them. I smiled benignly. And hoisting the hammer baton-fashion, I ran upon them.

With the hammer's head I bludgeoned the one to the left. He staggered back, screaming as I then swung to the right and rammed the stake through the chest of his brother. I pulled the hammer out just in time to pivot upon the first who was lumbering toward me with his lower jaw extended like a snake. The sheen of two barbed canines and a flicker of a long tongue were my last impressions before lancing the stake through his midriff. I broke through the grove and entered the courtyard, pumped and heedless of everything except the desire to punish those who had harmed Carina. Three more of Griselda's sons I encountered in the courtyard, and two assailed me from the air upon exiting the archway. They seethed reproaches as I battled them, something about their mother, charges of treachery. But I was like a berserker out of a fairy tale, at one with my impetus and blind to fear, hesitance, mercy, even that sympathy the pitiful creatures deserved.

I slaughtered the ones that pursued, and there were at least a dozen of them. But at length I knew Griselda's vindicators were all dead. I walked freely toward the path that led down into the valley. It was in the distance across the pasture I saw the son that Griselda had dismissed lurking behind the trailing ground mist. He alone I challenged before advancing.

I charged forward then, ready to destroy him as his brothers. But by the time I reached the spot where he had stood, he had vanished, leaving no trace or even sense of his presence behind. I caught the single melancholy note of a peacock. A moment later, I heard the awkward rustle of its wings. I ran over the landscape in the effort to catch sight of it. I searched until dawn, until the cocks were crowing from the farmyards and my throat was parched and constricted from the night's exertion. He had eluded me, and to which direction I had no guess. My only consolation was that I knew somehow he was the only one who had.

The cabin had never felt more welcoming as I walked in that morning. I laid the hammer on my desk and stepped to the bed. Carina lay there with the sheet pulled over her head like a shroud. I turned it down gently and found her asleep on her stomach with her head cradled against her folded arms. It must not have been too long since she had cried herself to sleep, for her eyelids were swollen and red, her long auburn lashes damp.

The poker I removed from beside her and laid it on the floor under the bed. I was fatigued, but upon lying down, I could not help but look at her for a time. I drew back the heavy lock of hair that shielded her face. She was perfect to my eyes: radiant complexion and supple skin. Her hips were wide but firm, and it was all I could do to refrain from stroking her back or massaging her taut buttocks. At length I closed my eyes and let her enticing smell lull me asleep.

Later that morning, I awakened while she busied herself in the kitchen. I rose and came upon her as she stood peeking into the pantry. She gasped when she realized I was beside her. The blush that suffused her cheeks was adorable.

"You are hungry, Carina?"

"Yes."

I told her to sit on the bed while I filled a plate with what I could scrounge together—bread and honey, a lovely quince from one of my pupils, a smoked sausage that I cut into slivers. I could see how delicately she tried to eat in front of me, but her hunger was ravenous, and it was no time before every bit of food had disappeared.

"Are you not going to eat, monsieur?"

I smiled but said nothing, and brought her a cup of water from the pitcher. She blushed again as I sat down beside her, and began to weep softly.

"Hush, sweet, I will have you home soon enough."

She smiled brightly, but the tears still flowed. And handing me back the cup, she suddenly gathered the sheet up around her.

"I—I apologize," she whispered. "Please find me a suitable garment."

"Is that it?" I laughed, not meaning to, and she blushed even harder and turned her face away. "Now, you are again the timid little teaser?"

Her eyes widened as if wounded, and I cupped her chin. "I would have you no other way," I admitted. "But the time has arrived for me to right a great wrong I have done you."

I leaned close into her and kissed her mouth. Sweeter than

Egyptian honey was her trembling mouth! I peeled the sheet away, took her by both wrists, and raised her to her knees.

"Monsieur—"

With a swift but gentle tug, I pulled her across my lap. I let go of her wrists, but cautioned her at once, "You will not struggle, Carina."

She whimpered loudly, but I ignored it and laid my right hand upon her smooth back. Her dangling legs had clasped tightly together, but now I parted them and stroked the soft flesh between her thighs. I felt her body tense, and as I drew the fingertips of my roving hand over her buttocks, she whimpered again. Without another word, I raised my palm and dealt her one smart spank.

"Oh!" She tried to get up off my lap, and when my hold proved more determined than she expected, she looked back and cast me a most impertinent frown. Her mouth opened, but before she could speak I clamped my right hand over her mouth.

"You will not speak and you will keep your eyes straight ahead, young lady," I instructed. "If you dare try to wrestle away again, it will be much worse for you, I promise."

I released her mouth and grasped the bundle of her hair firmly by the roots. My left hand raised again, and this time I punished her thoroughly. She cried out in stunned little gasps, and her hips twisted fitfully, but she did not protest. And when at length I deemed she had had enough, her buttocks glowed a pleasing shade of pink.

Letting go of her hair, I helped her to her feet. Her face was aglow with proper humiliation, and when she dared to stomp her feet, I flung her over my lap again. I spanked her much harder this time, so that her buttocks moved this way and that, and she was sobbing loudly. This time when it was finished, I did not let her up, but raised her chin with my hand and addressed her firmly.

"You will obey me, Carina, and be well-behaved from this day on," I said, "or know the swiftest reprimand."

I felt her heart pound wildly as I raised her to her feet. This time she stood before me unquestioningly. Her humbled eyes lowered, and she shielded the triangle of soft curls between her thighs with her clasped hands. My need for her was wild, consuming. But for some several moments, I just savored the chastened, absolutely frustrated look on her face that came with her full realization that, indeed, I had changed. Under my stern regard, her tears began to spill again. They rolled down her chin and splattered softly to her breasts.

Satisfied at last, I stood and scooped her up into my arms.

My mouth draped over her lips. They were heated, welcoming, and as I lowered her to the bed, her eyes shone with the same bashful wantonness that had first enamored me. I disrobed, and grasped her legs and drew her toward me so that her buttocks dangled over the edge of the bed. She moaned as I spread her thighs and lifted her hips. Her sex was fiery against my urgent cock. I looked down at her lithe and rosy body, adoring the way she sucked on one finger and undulated her hips in such a way that told me she fretted if I approved of her demonstrating her passion.

I touched her pussy and found it drenched. I rubbed her little clit until it was hard as a pearl. Her hips arched against her will as I incited her and she moaned helplessly. She was a sublime image of the abandoned love slave, against which I could no longer hold my own passion. I plunged into her and stroked hard. She was as taut as I remembered, and sweeter now was the feel of her—for I was the possessor and not the possessed.

She climaxed with a squeal, and my own orgasm burst into her, so powerful that the strength almost abandoned my legs. I crawled atop her then and swathed her face with kisses. She cupped my face in turn and kissed me deeply.

"My dearest, Marcel," she whispered.

I kissed her hardened nipples and lay my head against her chest. For a time, we rested, until finally I knew I had to get her home. Into one of my shirts I dressed her, and covered her head and shoulders with a large linen towel. And thus with her safely concealed so as not to frighten those we met, I walked her to Irmhild's house. Carina fell into new tears in her grandmother's arms. Irmhild beamed at me silently as she comforted her. Soon Weistreim was summoned, and he went with me to the house of Carina's father.

The man's reaction to my news was almost violent joy. He embraced me so fiercely I nearly lost consciousness. I bided my time the rest of the day before giving him any more startling news. I accompanied him to see his daughter, and watched in the background as he gathered her up in his bear arms and smothered her with kisses.

A great feast of celebration was given at Irmhild's house that night. I must have been toasted by every man at the table, and kissed by all their women folk and children. Carina, bathed and sitting dressed in a pretty green dress at her father's side, endured the questions of these relatives with soft-spoken grace and her friends ogling over the shining collar at her throat. And when it became apparent she had had enough of relating the details of her ordeal, her father thoughtfully, but firmly, changed the topic of discussion.

When the feast was over and most everyone had left the house, Carina's friends drew her away to the parlor. Irmhild drove the younger cousins into the kitchen to wash the dishes, while she persuaded the aunts and uncles onto the lawn to open a keg of ale.

I was alone with Carina's father at last. He wanted to compensate me for what I had done. I was offered my choice of any of the family heirlooms, several of which he said were priceless relics dating back many centuries.

"Manuscripts too," he smiled knowingly, "these, too, I possess. I can understand the language of only a handful, but of those with which I am acquainted, I know a few were written by sorcerers many, many years ago."

As touched as I was by his generosity, there was only one thing I sought, and that with or without his consent.

To my relief, he proved more than consenting when he heard my words. He jumped up and summoned the entire family to the table. Carina came back amidst her cluster of friends and listened attentively as her father announced to her my intentions. The whole house waited in silence for her to respond. Her mouth formed a startled circle, and her face smoldered pink. But as her eyes sought out mine, I knew her answer. And with a demure smile, she rose to her tiptoes and delivered a tender kiss to her father's cheek.

"Yes, certainly. I will marry our brave schoolmaster."

Cheers resounded through the house. They congratulated us heartily and broke open a fresh keg of ale. Carina's friends pressed her toward me, and I rose and embraced her, kissing her with all the shameless pagan passion my love for her had inspired. Her family and friends only cheered louder. One of Carina's uncles brought out his fiddle, and the little children sang while the others danced the whole night long.

Before morning came, I took Carina's hand and led her outdoors to the lawn. We talked until dawn emerged of future and sweet promises yet to be fulfilled. And as the sun gilded the eastern horizon, I watched Carina as she silently welcomed it. Its light splayed against her face, bringing out all the subtle hues of her eyes and the healthy tones of her skin. I had never been so content as I laid my head in her lap. She twisted my hair between her fingers, soliciting a lusty warning if she dared pull too hard. I took pride in the blush that crept into her face, and daydreamed about all the ways I could compel these blushes when and where she least expected.

My revelry was intruded upon by a faraway wail. My chest

panged warily, but Carina's amorous smile attested she had not heard the bird's melancholy cry. And so, I pulled her down beside me on the dewed grass and pushed concern for it aside for a time in the pure, shameless enjoyment of her.

So now I see all those things you so long understood, Alain. I have found the truth that transcends the written word, even the words of the most elucidated alchemist. My beloved's eager submission is more precious than gold, more addictive than the pursuit of the philosopher's stone. My pupil, my love, my captive . . . she has wielded a magic more akin to divine purpose than all the words of Solomon. The Urdhels call me the Liaison. But love, with its many reciprocal delights, is the master here, and I am the bound.

Alas, vain propriety, it is a confession I yield with no regret!

Your friend in good faith,
Marcel Rolant

Turn the page for a preview
of Sharon Page's BLOOD DEEP!

Coming soon from Aphrodisia!

London, April 1807

Lord Sebastien de Wynter was bound to the bed, his arms and legs spread wide. A white sheet lay over the ridge of his erection. Four dark-haired courtesans smothered him with kisses— one hungrily mashed her lips to his, one licked circles around the root of his cock, and a third leaned over his chest and sucked his nipples. The last flicked her tongue around the toes of Sebastien's right foot.

Zayan smiled at his friend's long, fierce moans. He saw Sebastien thrash in pleasure against the ropes binding him. Good. It was what Zayan needed tonight. It let him forget . . .

"Master?" The woman's soft, questioning voice floated to him. She was tied up as Sebastien was, but her ropes held her up against a wall. Weights of beaten gold dangled from clamps at her nipples. He had hung small globes of black iron from hooks he threaded through piercings in her labia. She waited, submissively, for him to take her to the next step.

"I wish to learn, Master. I wish to be trained to serve ye."

Soft, throaty—hers was an exquisite voice marred only by her country accent.

She expected to be whipped, but he did not want to do that. He had waited two thousand years for this night.

Slowly, everything in the room—every being, living and undead—took on a red glow. The red shadow crept around them all, perfectly matching each form in the act of writhing, jiggling, and driving toward sexual ecstasy. No one else saw the caressing mantel of red. He did. Brilliant crimson, it was the exotic, vivid color of blood.

It began faintly at first. A light outline. On his courtesan, the glow traced the full curve of her bare breasts, the flare of her wide hips. It burned brighter at the points of her nipples, partly hidden by the metal clamps. It glowed fiercely at the junction of her thighs, where the weights dragged at her nether lips.

Zayan dropped his head back and let his hands rest on his thighs, palms up. He lay on a mound of silk cushions, surrounded by courtesans waiting to attend him.

The spoils of war . . .

This had once been his life, two thousand years ago, when he had been a mortal man. To return from battle and be treated like a god. To feast on the most delectable treats—plump grapes, luscious figs, roast meats. And the orgies. Women to feed him succulent food and pour his wine and pleasure him with their tongues and their scented bodies.

He closed his eyes.

Blood. In his mind, sightless eyes stared at him from pale faces surrounded by a halo of blood. He had seen thousands of blank, lifeless eyes. He had joined in the games his men played with skulls, artfully kicking them back and forth.

He had never thought he would see blind, unseeing eyes on the people he loved.

Do you remember their faces?

A woman's voice. It came from the haze of red that now

filled the room and gave him the peace and serenity that other men sought from opiates.

This had been the voice that had sung to him as he had surveyed his battlefield and saw his army mowed down as though smote by the gods. Lush and alluring, it had called to him. It had promised him everything he needed to be victorious and its price had not seemed like a price at the time . . .

His soul. Immortality. To become undead.

Do you remember the sound of their laughter? Do you even remember their smells as you held them close?

No. He fought every day to remember, but the faces of his children drifted farther away.

Embrace me and I can return them to you. Embrace me and I can give you what you truly need.

A woman waggled her bare bottom in his face. She had a thick ivory wand pushed up inside and long, luxurious peacock feathers flowed from its base like an exotic tail. Another approached and presented her derriere for him to view. She had two candles in her bottom, tied with a white satin ribbon. Another series of ribbons were wound around that one and affixed her candles to her thighs and her waist. The wicks were lit and the molten wax dripped. Some droplets hit her stockings and she squealed. The last whispered, "I have nothing inside, master. Won't you fill me?"

The woman with the peacock's tail was toying with her own swollen clit, lazily teasing and playing, obviously highly aroused. But her strokes quickly became more deliberate.

"Patience," he barked. "No climax yet."

"I wish to be stuffed with your magnificent cock," simpered the courtesan who had begged to be filled.

"No, slave. Candles for you."

He grabbed one thick one and slathered it with molten oil. At his command the other girls gentled eased it into the moaning tart's quim.

"Light her candle from yours, my sweet."

And they amused him by trying to transfer the light from one of the two wicks to the thick, long one on the thick white candle, without using their hands. They cheered their success, their faces flushed and strained from prolonging their arousal.

But he would not free them.

He needed them like this.

The red power fed on this heightened sexual need—and it gave him blissful freedom from the agony that now racked his body, the shrieking pain that ripped through his head. Opium hadn't worked for him, but feeding this mystical power did.

"Pleasure me," he commanded the bevy of women. Panting, they kneeled before him. The red mist swirled around him. But before the first prostitute could touch him, her eyes turned red. Red fluid poured from her eye and she screamed in horror.

She clawed at her face. The others tried to pull her arms away. Zayan jolted up, grasped her wrists and dragged her to him. He sent rushes of healing magic through her but she still screamed and thrashed.

She slumped in his arms. Spittle bubbled at the corner of her mouth.

The red fluid no longer poured from her eyes and it slowly vanished as though it had never existed.

By the gods, what had happened? He was supposed to take the power into him tonight. It had been promised. For two thousand years he had waited to take the full magnitude of the power the red mist could bestow.

Thank you, a voice mocked him from somewhere inside his mind, and blissfully, the pounding, searing pain lightened in his head.

He felt a sigh rush through his body—when the mist came, it seemed to possess him. It spoke inside him in the way he was able to do with mortals. *Her soul is too scarred to satisfy me long.*

The power had never taken a soul before, but it did not surprise him. He took the blood—and through him the red power consumed the victim's life and soul.

But he felt an odd tightening of his heart and he laid the limp girl gently to the floor. The other girls were whimpering and a crowd was beginning to surround them.

"She just collapsed."

A woman sobbed.

"Was she sick?"

Sebastien pushed his way through the crowd, his face stricken. He was wild, sensual, but softhearted—he had almost torn one abusive customer limb from limb. Pain touched his silvery-green reflective eyes—eyes that fiercely snapped up. "What in blazes happened to her? Did you kill her?"

"He didn't touch her!" one of the courtesans cried.

"She just collapsed."

She had been a favorite of Sebastien's and he lifted her in his arms.

No one spoke of the red fluid.

"Take her to one of the bedchambers," he demanded, and servants rushed to do his bidding, but Sebastien was the one to carry her away.

Zayan straightened. Why this ache around his heart?

Remorse, Zayan, whispered the voice. *If you help me, I can give you what your desire most. You cannot have my power—I cannot give that to you. You did not understand. But I will give you your children and your soul. I will return them both to you as though two thousand years never passed. I can give you heaven on Earth. I can give you both peace and love, and you remember, I know, how sweet they were. But you must serve me. The price is your service—for a few more years, until you find the ultimate prize.*

Of course she could not give him the power—he'd been betrayed again by a woman. *I have served you, damn it, when I vowed to serve no one,* he roared in his head. *For that, return my children to me.*

He had been the most feared Roman general. He had carved a brutal swath through the Gauls. He had been legendary—struck a hundred times by killing blows, only to rise again. Then his emperor, his closest friend, his *wife* had all betrayed him. He had vowed never to serve again—but for the chance at immortality he had broken that vow.

In answer, pain sliced through his skull. Excruciating. He sank to his knees, pain slashing at his body. By the gods, he would drive a stake in his own heart to be free of this.

But he would never be.

He knew it meant the answer was no. The red power would not give him his children back unless he continued to serve. To see his children again, to give them another chance at life, he would have to be a slave.